Cover Art by Victoria Cooper
Copyright © 2019 Bree Wolf

Print ISBN: 978-3-96482-055-6

www.breewolf.com

Also by Bree Wolf

Love's Second Chance Series

A collection of marriage-of-convenience stories with a touch of mystery and swoon worthy kisses that will tug at your heartstrings and keep you up till the wee hours of the morning. Set in Regency England or in the Scottish Highlands!

Love's Second Chance Series: Tales of Lords & Ladies

Ignored & Treasured - The Duke's Bookish Bride (*Prequel*)

#1 Forgotten & Remembered - The Duke's Late Wife

#2 Cursed & Cherished - The Duke's Wilful Wife

#3 Abandoned & Protected - The Marquis' Tenacious Wife

#4 Betrayed & Blessed - The Viscount's Shrewd Wife

#5 Deceived & Honoured - The Baron's Vexing Wife

#6 Sacrificed & Reclaimed - The Soldier's Daring Widow

#7 Destroyed & Restored - The Baron's Courageous Wife

Love's Second Chance Series: Tales of Damsels & Knights

#1 Despised & Desired - The Marquess' Passionate Wife

#2 Ruined & Redeemed - The Earl's Fallen Wife

#3 Condemned & Admired - The Earl's Cunning Wife

#4 Trapped & Liberated - The Privateer's Bold Beloved

#5 Oppressed & Empowered - The Viscount's Capable Wife

Love's Second Chance Series: Highland Tales

#1 Tamed & Unleashed - The Highlander's Vivacious Wife

#2 Dared & Kissed - The Scotsman's Yuletide Bride

#3 Banished & Welcomed - The Laird's Reckless Wife

#4 Haunted & Revered - The Scotsman's Destined Love

#5 Fooled & Enlightened - The Englishman's Scottish Wife

Ladies of Miss Bell's Finishing School *(multi-author series)*

The Spinster - *Prequel to the Forbidden Love Novella Series*

A Forbidden Love Novella Series

A collection of forbidden love stories filled with intense relationships, vibrant chemistry and strong characters that will captivate your heart.

#1 The Wrong Brother

#2 A Brilliant Rose

#3 The Forgotten Wife

#4 An Unwelcome Proposal

#5 Rules to Be Broken

#6 Hearts to Be Mended

#7 Winning her Hand

#8 Conquering her Heart

Happy Ever Regency Series

A new Regency Series of Fairy Tale re-tellings filled with endless and undying love.

#1 How To Wake A Sleeping Lady

#2 How To Tame A Beastly Lord

#3 How To Climb A Lady's Tower

#4 How To Steal A Thief's Heart

To my son
Conquer the world
and make it yours

Acknowledgments

A great, big thank-you to my dedicated beta readers and proofreaders, Eris Hydras, Michelle Chenoweth, Monique Takens and Kim Bougher, who read the rough draft and help me make it better.

Also a heartfelt thank-you to all my wonderful readers who pick up book after book and follow me on these exciting adventures of love and family. I love your company and savor every word of your amazing reviews! Thank you so much! There are no words!

TAMED
AND *Unleashed*

THE HIGHLANDER'S VIVACIOUS WIFE

Prologue

Gretna Green, Scotland, Summer 1808 (or a variation thereof)

U pon waking, Claudia Davenport, sister to Viscount Ashwood, found her head throbbing with such intensity that she feared it would split in two. Groaning, she rolled onto her side, her hands reaching up to cover her face in a futile attempt to shield her from the blinding sun penetrating even her closed lids. Had the world gone mad?

Never in her life had Claudia awoken to such pain. Never had the sun been her enemy. Never had she felt sick to her stomach.

Not quite like this.

Pinching her eyes shut, Claudia buried her face in the pillow, slowly forcing one deep breath after another down her throat and into her lungs. To her relief, she found that holding her head still eased the pain somewhat, and so she simply lay there for a long while, breathing in and out.

After a small eternity, her ears began to pick up on various sounds drifting in through the closed windows as well as the door to her room. The sounds of people going about their business. And yet, the sounds were not quite as she remembered them.

As they ought to be.

Something was different, and a frown emerged on her face.

Slowly, she cracked open an eye and peered at her surroundings.

A moment later, Claudia bolted upright in bed.

Instantly, her head rebelled at such treatment, sending jolts of pain through her being that would have brought her to her knees had she been standing. Her hands flew up, pressing hard onto her temples in the hopes of easing the pain. Still, it took a long while before she dared open her eyes again.

Squinting, Claudia took in the small chamber, the simple and sparse furnishings, the lack of luxury. "What happened?" she whispered to herself. "Where am I?"

For this was definitely not her bedchamber back at Farnworth Manor.

This was a room she had never seen before.

Swallowing the panic that began to rise, Claudia closed her eyes once more, trying to remember how on earth she had ended up in this place. The last thing she could recall was attending Lord Campton's ball.

Once more, she heard the soft notes of the music drifting through the large rooms. Again, she found herself standing with the other young debutantes, eyes gliding over the gentlemen in attendance until-

"William," Claudia gasped as his face took form before her inner eye. "We danced. We laughed. We-" Again, a gasp tore from her throat, and one hand fell from her temple covering her mouth in shock. "We ran off."

Trying to swallow the lump in her throat, Claudia once more glanced about the room as though William might have been hiding somewhere in plain sight all along. But he was not. She was alone.

Careful not to move too much, Claudia inhaled a few deep breaths, allowing her mind to wander back to the night before. Slowly, images returned of her taking William's hand and following him outside into the dark night. She remembered him helping her into his carriage, the way he had held her in his arms as the horses had pulled them toward their destination, his assurances that all would be well.

"We eloped," Claudia mumbled, her eyes drifting around the room.

"This is...this is an inn...in Gretna Green. It must be." The breath caught in her throat, and she slowly turned her head to the left, her eyes focusing on the other side of the bed.

It was empty, and yet, someone had lain there. There was an unmistakable indentation, and...a warmth lingered that sent a shiver down her back. "What have I done?" Slowly, she pulled back the thin blanket and her heart slammed to a momentary halt.

In the bright morning sun, a few droplets of blood shone on the white linen like rubies.

The air rushed from Claudia's lungs, and the nausea in her stomach sent her flying from the bed. Her body tensed, revolted, and she sank to her knees, one arm reaching for the chamber pot. Then her insides contracted expelling last night's dinner-and drink! -into the small bowl.

When it was over, she sank down, head resting against the side of the bed, her mind momentarily focused on drawing fresh air into her body. Her hand pushed the chamber pot away as the stench of its contents threatened to overwhelm her delicate hold on her body once more.

In her weakened state, Claudia felt numb and strangely detached. Her mind moved slowly as though it did not have the strength to provide her with what she sought: answers.

Still, despite an almost desperate desire to curl up into a ball and hide in a corner, Claudia knew that she could not pretend this had not happened - whatever *this* was!

Had she married William? Had they arrived in Gretna Green, sought out an anvil priest and-?

Claudia froze as an image drifted to the front of her mind, an image of William hanging his head in defeat, his eyes downcast and apologetic...as he had stepped away from her...and followed his elder brother, Viscount Crowemore, to their waiting carriage.

Again, panic welled up as her memories cleared.

Yes, they had come to Gretna Green, but they had not gotten married. William's brother had found them first, ending their adventure by ordering his brother to return with him.

And William had complied.

He had bowed his head.

He had left her.

Shocked beyond words, Claudia stared across the room at the plain wall, reliving the moment disillusionment had set in. She remembered her feeling of betrayal when William had abandoned her, complying with his family's wishes and a long-standing contract. He was to marry a duke's daughter.

Not her.

Despite his promises, he had abandoned her.

Left her behind in Gretna Green.

Alone.

A distant part of Claudia's mind tried to remind her that she had refused to accompany them back to England, cursing and yelling at the top of her voice. However, that part was soon shushed by the sense of betrayal and disappointment that washed over her.

Closing her eyes, Claudia wept for a dream ruined, for a life that was not to be, for the harshness of the world. Still, her emotional turmoil only managed to keep her mind silenced for a short while. Before long, it piped up once more, asking questions Claudia now feared to know the answer to.

If William had indeed returned to England with his brother, then who had slept beside her? Who had spent the night in her room? In her bed? Who had she been intimate with? A complete stranger?

It had to be, for what other answer could there be?

Gritting her teeth, Claudia pushed to her feet, doing her best to ignore the throbbing pain behind her temples as well as the slight swaying of the room. She glimpsed her clothes hanging over the back of a chair and slowly hobbled toward them.

Dressing proved to be quite a challenge in her state, and yet, it provided a momentary relief from the panic that threatened to consume her. Once that was taken care of though, her thoughts immediately refocused on that which she did not know.

And panic returned.

"No!" Claudia snapped, forcing herself not to succumb to this line of thinking for it would lead her nowhere.

What was to be done? Now *that* was a productive question. A question that needed an answer. Here and now.

"I need to get home," Claudia said, feeling her mind clearing as she spoke. "I need to get back." For no matter how angry her brother would be once he learnt what she had done, he would never turn from her. He could be a cold-hearted and unfeeling bastard, but he would not forget his obligation to her, his duty to see to his family.

Of that she was certain.

How to get home, on the other hand, was a different matter. After all, they had come here in William's carriage, and as far as Claudia was aware, she did not have any money on her.

A frown drew down her brows, sending fresh pain through her head. How had she paid for the room? Or had-?

Loud footsteps echoed up the stairs outside her chamber, and Claudia froze. Her eyes were fixed on the door, and her mind was reeling with the thought that she was about to come face to face with whomever she had shared her bed with last night. Would she remember him? Or would he still be a stranger?

The echo grew louder as the man stormed down the corridor...and stopped outside her door.

Inhaling a deep breath, Claudia braced herself for what was to come when the door finally swung open...and her brother stormed in.

Seeing his face, Claudia almost sank to the floor as the air rushed from her lungs. Utter relief filled her, but only at first for the dark look on her brother's face would have sent anyone running for the hills.

For a long moment, they merely looked at one another, speechless. Claudia could see the tension holding him rigid, the way his chest rose and fell as he tried his best to contain his anger, his outrage...his disappointment.

Her brother was not prone to losing his temper-never had been-but the quiet darkness that rested in his eyes sent chills down her back.

"What have you done?" he finally asked, his voice low and menacing as his silver eyes took in the room, the bed, her dishevelled state, the implications that hung in the air. "What were you thinking?"

Claudia felt her chin begin to quiver and tears sting the back of her eyes, and yet, she would not give him the satisfaction of seeing her defeated. Raising her chin, she met his eyes. "It was my choice, not yours. You have no right-"

"That it was," he interrupted, raking a hand through his hair. In two large strides, he was in front of her, his hands gripping her by the upper arms. "This is without a doubt the most foolish thing you've ever done, and whether you like it or not, this time you'll have to pay for it."

Claudia gritted her teeth against the pain thudding behind her temples. "What did you expect when you all but locked me away? I am not free to do anything I want. I-"

"Don't blame me for your mistakes!" he hissed before he stepped back and held the door open for her. "We shall discuss everything further at home."

"If you insist," Claudia snapped, relieved to at least have an answer delivered to her with regard to how she was to get home. Glaring at her brother, she stomped past him, along the corridor and down the stairs, all the while berating him, doing her best to ignore the pounding in her head.

"Be quiet!" he hissed once they'd reached the taproom. His eyes took in the many travellers coming and going before he took her by the arm and all but dragged her outside.

Despite digging in her heels, Claudia had no hope of delaying him. "You're the most awful brother in all of England," she retorted, wondering why on earth she was blaming him. And yet, she could not stop. She was not yet ready to face the mess she had made, and at present, he was the only one she could blame.

It was a distraction-nothing more-and one day she would have to face reality.

But tomorrow was soon enough.

Never would she have expected for the one adventure she had ever dared to embark upon to end in this way.

Never.

Chapter One

A HIGHLANDER IN LONDON

London, January 1809 (or a variation thereof)

Six months later

Garrett MacDrummond of Clan MacDrummond, who rarely travelled far from his home in the Scottish Highlands, stood in a corner of a London ballroom. His eyes swept over the throng of people dancing, chatting, laughing-enjoying themselves. If only he could join them, he thought with a snort.

"Anything?" Lord Tynham asked beside him, his kind brown eyes turning to look at Garrett. An Englishman himself, Lord Tynham had familial ties to Clan MacDrummond and had graciously invited Garrett to be his guest for the duration of his search.

Garrett shook his head. "I dunno understand this," he said, unable to look away. "From what people say she's always here at the beginning of the Season."

"Perhaps they were delayed," Lord Tynham suggested, and yet, the look in his eyes told Garrett that he doubted his own words.

From what Garrett had been able to gather since his arrival in town, his wife was a well-known member of English society. There were few who did not know her or know of her, and he had been able to learn a great deal about her love for dancing and mingling, her desire for adventure and unconventionality. Indeed, what he had learnt through discreet and well-placed questions had only confirmed Garrett's own impression of the wayward Lass he had stumbled upon one night almost six months ago in Gretna Green.

"Perhaps you should seek out her brother," Lord Tynham suggested, "and ask about her."

Garrett sighed, "But he isna here either, is he?"

"That, however, is nothing unusual," Lord Tynham stated. "The man is known for his reticent nature. He and his sister are like night and day. As much as she longs for company, he seems to prefer to keep to his own."

Garrett nodded, his gaze still searching.

"Have you considered making the journey to Farnworth Manor?" Lord Tynham suggested next. "Perhaps the family has decided to skip town this season as they prefer to stay in the country."

Garrett snorted, "I doubt she would've agreed to such a plan," he said. "In any case, I did stop there before coming to London, but I was told the family wasna home."

Lord Tynham frowned. "Over the holidays? That is quite unusual."

Garrett nodded. It had struck him as odd as well. Still, short of breaking into the house and searching the premises for his wife, there had been very little he could have done. Instead, he had gone to London hoping to meet her here once the season began.

Now, that notion seemed to be a futile hope.

All he had found in London were whispers.

Rumours circulated about her eloping to Gretna Green with a man named William Montgomery, second son to the Earl of Mowbrey. Still, unlike Garrett's wife, Mr. Montgomery had not failed to attend the first ball of the season-nor the ones following-and he had been decidedly unattached.

In fact, another rumour whispered of his upcoming nuptials to a duke's daughter. Nothing was certain as of yet. However, that was how people preferred it as it gave them the opportunity to create their own versions of the truth.

When Garrett had first heard the rumour about his wife and Mr. Montgomery, he had been overcome with red-hot jealously, imagining his wife in that man's arms. However, as time had passed, it had become clear that the whispers that saw them as young lovebirds were made of nothing but stale air.

Inhaling a deep breath, Garrett allowed his gaze to momentarily follow Mr. Montgomery as the man swept across the dance floor with a blond-haired beauty in his arms. His fiancée? Garrett did not know, but he knew that tongues were wagging without doubt.

Still, if his wife had been with Mr. Montgomery, at least that would have presented an explanation with regard to her whereabouts. At present, it seemed as though she had dropped off the face of the earth. What had happened?

Garrett was at a loss.

The following morning when he had returned to their room at the inn, his wife had been gone. No note. No explanation. Nothing. Only the innkeeper had informed him upon questioning that a young man-presumably English-had come to take her away. Apparently, she had yelled at him quite a bit, calling him *the most awful brother in all of England*.

Although disappointed, Garrett had been relieved to know that she was with her family and, therefore, safe. As much as he had wanted to follow her right away, his duty to his clan had prevented him from doing so.

So, reluctantly, he and the two clansmen who had accompanied him had returned to their laird, bringing with them the runaway couple they had been after. The lass had been a MacDrummond while the lad had been from a neighbouring clan. While that alone would have been far from an easy situation, the fact that the lass had been promised to another had complicated matters further.

As he was well acquainted with the promised lad's family, there had been no way for Garrett to delay returning home. The ensuing talks had taken weeks before all had been resolved, and the two lovebirds had been allowed to wed. For them, everything had ended well.

Garrett sighed as he continued to search the crowd, always hoping that the next face he'd see would be hers. Would he ever find her? How hard could it be to find an English lass? And one as spirited and striking as his wife?

A part of him could not help but worry that she had changed her mind. That she had come to regret their hasty decision. That she did not care for him after all. And yet, Garrett could not pretend that nothing had happened. If she wished to be rid of him, she would have to tell him so to his face.

In all his life, Garrett had never done anything so rash, but she had caught him off guard and swept him off his feet. There had been something about her that had touched his soul and stirred his blood. Even after all these months apart, he still longed for her, knowing beyond the shadow of a doubt that even though they barely knew each other, she was the one for him.

Setting his jaw, Garrett vowed that he would find her no matter what or how long it would take. He would find her, and then he would never let her go again.

Chapter Two

A MOMENT IN TIME

Three months later

Crestwood House was utterly silent, except for the tormented grunts and cries from the labouring woman in the large bed.

"You're doing fine, sweetheart," her mother whispered soothingly as she brushed a wet cloth over Claudia's forehead. "Everything shall be all right. Do not worry."

Sinking back into the pillows, Claudia closed her eyes, desperate to rest at least for a short moment before the next contraction would grip her body and turn it inside out once more. Her breath came in short pants and sweat ran down her temple before her mother could wipe it away.

Again, silence fell over the house-if only for a fleeting moment-and Claudia felt reminded of the past three months she had spent in this tomb far away from everything she held dear.

Far out in the country, Crestwood House was a small manor house with nothing around it as far as the eye could see. There were no small villages or even an occasional neighbour. Nothing.

Only silence.

In order to keep her condition a secret, her brother had insisted she-and her mother-retreat to this place in the middle of nowhere until the child was born. Therefore, the staff had been reduced to an utter minimum, leaving them with only a trusted maid, a cook and someone to tend to the general upkeep of the house. They worked like ghosts, never quite there, doing their chores without being seen.

The silence had nearly driven Claudia mad.

For months, she had wandered the halls, the grounds, any place her feet would carry her with a heavy heart. Certainly, her mother had been there, constantly trying to cheer her up, to distract her, to keep her mind focused on all kinds of trivial things. Still, all her efforts had not been able to lift the fear and dread from Claudia's heart.

While her rational mind had concluded that there was no way she could keep her child, her heart refused to abandon hope so easily. Again, and again, Claudia whispered to herself in the dark of night that she was doing the right thing. That her child would grow up in a loving family, safe and sound. It would want for nothing. Her brother had promised to make sure of that, and he never broke his word.

And yet, the ache never left her.

In her dreams, Claudia often saw her son's smiling face as she rocked him in her arms until his eyes closed and he fell asleep. She could smell his hair and feel the soft smoothness of his skin. She saw the brilliant blue of his eyes and felt the quiet strength in the way he held on to her finger. These dreams brought her peace, at least for a short while; for upon waking, all the pain and dread would return, threatening to crush her.

Then she would curl into a ball, arms wrapped tightly around her rounded belly, and weep into her pillows until the sun rose the next day.

Once a month, her brother and his new wife, Evelyn, would come to visit, which was a welcome diversion from the dreariness of everyday life. Evelyn was a strong and competent woman, a doctor in her own right, who had come to Farnworth Manor to see to Claudia when she had collapsed after an argument with her brother.

Claudia liked to think that if she had not made the mistake of following William to Scotland, if she had not stayed behind and slept with a stranger, if she had not gotten with child, then Evelyn would not have come to Farnworth Manor...and her brother would have missed out on the love of his life. Sometimes fate worked in unusual ways, and sometimes Claudia wondered why everything had happened the way it had. What would come of it? It had led to something wonderful for her brother while at the same time guiding her down a path full of heartbreak. Was this it?

Ever since Evelyn had joined their family, thawing Richard's heart, Claudia and her brother had been much closer. Although she still could not understand the way his mind worked, the way he saw the world, she could see now how hard he tried to be a good brother, how much he wanted to protect her, how much he loved her.

All of them had come closer as a family.

If only she could keep her son.

Why, Claudia could not say, but in her heart she always pictured a little boy, and she had to force herself to ignore the names that rose in her mind. No, she would not name him. She would not be his mother, and so she would not name him. If she chose his name, would she be able to say goodbye?

Her days were filled with dread as she awaited the day that life would rip them apart and send them down different paths.

And now that day had come.

Another contraction gripped Claudia and the pain held her in its iron fist. And yet, it was not her body that suffered the most, but her heart, for she knew that each contraction brought her closer to the moment she would have to give up her child. *Do not look at him!* Something deep inside her whispered. *Not even for a moment. Do not look at him!*

When the contraction released her, Claudia sank back into the pillows, her mind closed to everything around her. She barely heard her mother's voice or noticed the doctor-whoever he was-tend to her. Was it day or night? She could not tell. All her heart had to cling to were the last final moments with her son. Still, there was no joy in it, no happiness.

Only dread.

And sorrow.

And then something changed.

The next contraction had Claudia reaching for her knees as instinct took over. Bearing down, she gritted her teeth, trying with all her strength to bring her son into the world.

This was it. The moment she had been dreading for months was upon her.

Tears streamed down Claudia's face as she forced herself to close off her heart. She pinched her eyes shut, feeling the pain tear through her, and then...he was gone.

Panting, Claudia lay back, exhausted in every way. A new emptiness filled her heart as she kept her gaze fixed on the ceiling. *Do not look at him!*

For a moment, silence fell over the room before soft wails echoed to Claudia's ears. "It's a boy," the doctor exclaimed, lifting up the child.

Claudia pressed her lips together tightly against the quiver in her jaw, her hands curling into the mattress, holding on as though for dear life.

"Would you like to hold him?" the doctor asked, immediately stepping forward, holding the child up for her to see.

In that moment, two instincts collided. Self-preservation urged her to turn her head, to close her eyes, to not see while her mother's heart pushed her to look upon her child, to hold him, to nurse him.

"Mary, will you take him?" Claudia's mother said beside her, her voice filled with sorrow and regret, but also with understanding as her hand continued to hold her daughter's. "You know what to do."

With her gaze still fixed onto the ceiling, Claudia heard the maid's quiet footsteps approach. She heard the soft rustling of clothes as the doctor lay the child into her arms. She heard Mary's gentle voice as she whispered to the softly-wailing child.

In a moment, he would be gone. Mary would take him away, and he would be given to a good family. Claudia would never see him again, but he would be safe. She was doing the right thing. *Do not look at him!*

And then her head moved, and before Claudia knew what was happening, her eyes came to rest on her son's little face.

He was perfect.

Heartbreakingly perfect.

His small round face was scrunched up in complaint as he waved his little fists. His mouth stood slightly open while his eyes were pinched shut. His skin shone warm and soft as the early morning sun reached in through the windows and touched him. For a split second, he opened his eyes as though looking for her, and Claudia could see that they shone in the same brilliant blue she had seen in her dreams.

And then Mary turned and walked away.

He was gone.

Only his soft wails still echoed to her ears, and Claudia turned away, burying her head in the pillows as her heart broke into a thousand pieces.

Aiden!

As her mind screamed his name, loud sobs tore from her throat, and she knew in that moment that she would forever grieve his loss. That her heart would never recover from this. That she would never feel whole again.

Aiden!

A fortnight later, Claudia found herself arriving in London.

Seated in their carriage, she glanced at the vibrant city, the Season in full swing and everyone noteworthy in town. Her eyes slid over the familiar streets and townhouses as they drew closer to their own, promising a moment of rest after this arduous journey.

Aware of her mother's watchful eyes, Claudia schooled her features into an expression of mild interest and excitement. "It is truly wonderful to see other people again," she remarked, her hands tense as they dug almost painfully into the strap of her reticule. "Not to insult your company, Mother, but I'm utterly relieved to be returned to civilisation." A short chuckle escaped her throat as though she were truly amused.

"I still do not approve," her mother objected, shaking her head as her hawk-like eyes continued to drill a hole into Claudia's head as though she could unearth the truth if she only stared at her long enough. "You've only just given birth," she whispered, her eyes darting sideways as though she feared to be overheard. "You need rest."

Claudia swallowed, willing the ache in her heart to subside. However, it would not. "I'm not the kind of woman who enjoys solitude," she said, forcing the corners of her mouth to remain up. "To be shut away in the country while all of London is full of excitement is torture. Quite frankly, I was and am bored out of my mind. But no longer!"

"But-"

"I've lost more than enough time this year," Claudia interrupted, knowing that if she allowed her mother to speak, her kind words would eventually break her, turning her into a sobbing mess. "Half the Season is over, and I have yet to find any amusement. I want to shop and dance and-"

The carriage pulled to a halt, and Claudia's eyes went to the tall, elegant townhouse where she had spent many happy moments. Would she ever be happy here again? Here or anywhere else?

As tears began to prick the back of her eyes, Claudia blinked her lids rapidly a few times before quickly stepping from the carriage. Movement helped, Claudia had come to realise. As long as she kept moving, as long as her mind was occupied, the pain was manageable. What she needed was a diversion...preferably for the rest of her life!

And so, Claudia had come to London, hoping to escape the pain she had waded through at Crestwood House. Every day after the loss of her son, she had spent crying, close to succumbing to despair. Never had she been the mothering type, and yet, this was her son. It felt as though a part of herself was missing. A part she would never get back.

Certain that she would lose her mind or die of a broken heart, Claudia had then decided to leave everything behind and return to the life she had had before.

The moment they stepped across the threshold, Claudia found her brother Richard and his new wife hastening toward them. Greetings and hugs were exchanged, and they soon found themselves seated in the drawing room, a cup of tea in their hands.

"I would never have expected to see you so soon," her brother observed, his voice collected, almost cold. His eyes, however, searched hers with an almost desperate need to know that she was all right.

Once more willing the corners of her mouth up, Claudia smiled at him. "I'm fine," she said, probably for the thousandth time since voicing her decision to return to town. "You know who I am. I was not made to be on my own. I need company."

Holding her gaze, her brother nodded. His eyes softened, and the expression on his face seemed less tense.

Claudia breathed a sigh of relief when she saw that he believed her, reassured by her usual frankness and forthright manner. His wife, on the other hand, was a different matter.

As a doctor, Evelyn had a sixth sense for the truth, her keen eyes now gliding over Claudia in frank perusal and judging from the expression of concern that still showed on her face, she was all but convinced. And yet, she did not say a word.

Not now.

Not with Claudia's mother and brother present.

But she would.

Later.

After tea, they rose to retire to their rooms for a short respite before supper. Claudia was relieved to be able to escape her family's watchful eyes for a short while as their constant concern was exhausting. She smiled at her brother and Evelyn as she turned to the door, and it was then that, out of the corner of her eye, she glimpsed a small, seemingly insignificant gesture that almost crushed her heart on the spot.

Speaking to her husband, Evelyn had absentmindedly brushed her hand over her midsection. It had been only a moment. Fleeting at best. And yet, it was something utterly familiar to Claudia.

To any woman who had carried a child.

Evelyn was expecting!

With her hands balled into fists, Claudia held on to her composure until the door to her bedchamber closed behind her. Then she all but fell onto her bed, burying her face in the pillows and allowed the pain to spill from her lips. Her body screamed in agony as her heart bled with the loss of her son the same as it had a fortnight ago.

Aiden!

If only she had died in childbirth.

Chapter Three

A CHANGED WOMAN

After four months in London, Garrett was close to admitting defeat and returning home to Scotland.

And yet, he stayed. He attended every event he could, always hoping against hope to spot her in the crowd. But he never did.

When her brother and his wife returned to London three months after his own arrival, his heart almost leapt from his chest. He could barely keep himself restrained and would have stormed across the dance floor to confront them if it had not been for Lord Tynham.

"This is not the way," his friend had whispered. "If she never spoke to them of you, this will lead to nothing good. Let me speak to him."

Gritting his teeth, Garrett had nodded his consent, his eyes glued to his wife's brother as Lord Tynham addressed him. In the end, his friend had returned with little news. All her brother had said was that she was visiting relatives in the country, recovering from a mild illness that had befallen her over the holidays.

Fear had gripped Garrett's heart at the thought of her in danger, but Lord Tynham had assured him that neither her brother nor his wife had seemed the least bit concerned. So, whatever it was that ailed her, it was nothing serious.

And so, Garrett kept wondering what on earth had happened, why she had left without a word, why she had not spoken of him to her family. Anger grew in his heart, and more than once, he was tempted to reveal the truth about their connection to her brother.

However, he never did.

Honour held him back. After all, she was his wife, and he owed her his trust and consideration. If she had not spoken to her family about him, then there had to be a good reason. He had to trust in that. He needed to speak to her, but he had to find her first.

Unfortunately, with every day that passed, it seemed less and less likely that he ever would.

The evening progressed as it usually did, and feeling defeated, Garrett soon turned to his friend, wishing to take his leave and then head outside for some air. Perhaps clearing his head would help him to come up with a new strategy.

That was when he saw her.

It was only a moment. Only out of the corner of his eye, but his heart stopped, and the breath caught in his throat as his head spun around.

Accompanied by her brother and his wife, Lord and Lady Ashwood, as well as-presumably-her mother, the dowager viscountess, his wife slowly made her way through the crowd, returning greetings left and right, here and there stopping to exchange a word.

London-or at least those attending tonight's ball-was abuzz with her sudden and unexpected return. Rumours had run wild, and everyone clamoured to speak to her and be the first to know more.

Suddenly rooted to the spot, Garrett stood and stared at his wife, his eyes gliding over her altered appearance in shock.

When he had met her in Gretna Green, her hair had been a mess, her wild mahogany curls escaping the loosening knot in the back of her head. Her gown while exquisite had been stained with dust and sweat and the occasional spilled drink. Her face had been flushed, and her eyes vibrant despite the scowl he had seen on her face when he had first laid eyes on her. She had laughed with vigour, loud and unaffected, and her mouth had rarely stood still, words flying from her lips without pausing for breath. She had been a force of nature, untamed and wild.

And he had loved her for it.

Now, the woman he saw merely resembled the wife he remembered.

While Garrett could ignore the fact that her hair and gown were of the latest fashion, clean and immaculate, he could not ignore the paleness of her cheeks, the way her eyes failed to sparkle, the tension that clung to her features as though she hated every moment she was forced to be here. Sadness and regret hung about her like a dark cloud, and he could see the willpower it took for her to keep smiling.

Immediately, his anger evaporated as his heart went out to her. What on earth had happened to her?

In that moment, her gaze swept over the crowd and then for a heart-stopping moment met his. To Garrett's utter shock, no recognition lit up her eyes, and her gaze moved from his without a moment's hesitation as though they had never met before.

Instantly, his anger returned. Was she truly pretending she did not know him? That they had never met?

Stunned, Garrett stared at her. "We're married," he whispered without breath, his heart beating as fast as it last had the night he had met her. Had he been wrong? Had their night meant nothing to her? Nothing but a meaningless tryst? Had she truly forgotten him?

A hand clasped his shoulder. "This seems to be your lucky night after all, my friend," Lord Tynham said, a large smile on his face as his gaze travelled back from tonight's unexpected attendee to Garrett. "Here is your chance to find out what happened." When he saw the scowl on Garrett's face, his own darkened. "You don't *know* what happened," he advised in a stern voice. "Do not jump to conclusions! Speak to her! Find out the truth! I implore you."

Inhaling a deep breath, Garrett nodded, knowing that his friend was right. Still, he could feel the blood boiling in his veins, urging him to cross to her side, drag her out of the crowded ballroom into a quiet corner and...

...kiss her as he had kissed her that night.

Growling under his breath, Garrett gritted his teeth as his mind and heart jerked him in two different directions. He could still feel his anger stirring his blood, and yet, his heart revelled in the sight of her.

After a little while, the crowd that had gathered around his wife slowly began to disperse, and people returned to their usual evening's activities. The orchestra began to play a lively tune, and soon the dance floor was packed with couples. Laughter filled the air, and yet, the look on his wife's face remained stoic and forced.

Garrett frowned. Did no one else notice?

Still, a closer look at Lady Ashwood told him that the young viscount's new wife was very much aware of her sister-in-law's true feelings. She stayed close by her side, often touching a gentle hand to Claudia's, assuring her that she was there. Although less obvious, even her brother and mother showed their concern in subtle ways, never venturing far and doing their best to discourage others who seemed hell-bent on extracting scandalous titbits from the young lady who had been the focus of gossip ever since the previous summer.

Garrett sighed. Theirs was a close-knit family, and he was relieved to see that his wife was not alone. Still, her family's concern made it even clearer that something had happened. Something that was of great concern to them. Something that clearly should have prevented Claudia from attending tonight's ball.

And yet, she had.

However, judging from the determined set of her jaw, it had been her own doing. *She* had insisted as Garrett knew her to be capable of. In his mind's eye, he saw her stomping her feet and crossing her arms, simply refusing to listen much less change her mind.

And yet, the look on her face was one of defeat. What had happened? Garrett wondered for the thousandth time. And why had she insisted to come here tonight?

"You are aware that the evening won't last forever, aren't you?" Lord Tynham asked the moment a young gentleman approached Claudia.

Instantly, Garrett tensed, watching as the man asked her for the next dance. Although her brother tried to intervene, she squared her shoulders, lifted her chin and then slowly, almost hesitantly offered him her hand.

Spinning to look at his friend, Garrett asked, "Would you mind if I asked your wife for the next dance?"

Lord Tynham's gaze narrowed in suspicion. "You won't cause a scene, will you?"

"I assure you I will not," Garrett forced out through gritted teeth, his gaze darting back to where his wife was about to stand up with the young gentleman. His feet itched to be off.

"Then you may ask her."

Nodding to his friend, Garrett addressed Lady Tynham, finding her shy, green eyes and pale blond curls a striking contrast to the woman who held his heart. At first, surprise showed on her face before understanding came to her eyes.

"It'd be my pleasure," she said graciously and then followed him onto the dance floor, her eyes venturing back to her husband as they exchanged a meaningful look.

Garrett wished his own wife would look at him the same way.

She had once.

A long time ago.

Would they ever get back what they had lost?

All throughout the dance, Garrett's eyes were glued to his wife. He watched her smile and move and exchange the occasional word with her dance partner. And yet, nothing seemed to touch her, her heart, her spirit, her soul. Her eyes remained dim, guarded, almost haunted.

"Will you not speak to her?" Lady Tynham asked, a gentle smile on her lips as she looked at him as one would look at a half-drowned puppy: full of pity.

Garrett grumbled something unintelligible under his breath, which to his consternation only served to deepen the look in Lady Tynham's eyes. Was he such a miserable sight? Were his friends pitying him now?

Deep down, Garrett knew that he feared the answers he sought. Yes, he wanted to speak to his wife. He wanted to know the truth. And yet, he feared to learn that her heart had never belonged to him, that she had all but forgotten about him, that she did not want him.

Still, he could not go on like this. He had barely slept in weeks, his nights restless and filled with outlandish nightmares. Perhaps knowing the truth would finally set his mind at ease, even if it broke his heart.

When the steps of the dance finally led them together, Garrett inhaled a deep breath, steeling himself for what lay ahead. When her hand touched his, even through the glove, a jolt went through his body and he felt that same connection he had all those many months ago.

As though they had been meant to find each other.

As though they were two halves of a whole.

As though they belonged in each other's arms.

Unfortunately, his wife did not seem to feel shaken in the least. Her eyes barely rose to meet his, and the look on her face told him that she was scarcely aware of his presence.

"'Tis a wonderful evening, aye?" Garrett asked, all but holding his breath.

A practised smile appeared on her face, and she lifted her head. Her eyes met his, and for a second, he thought to see a hint of confusion. "It is indeed," she agreed, her voice almost timid and without strength. What on earth had happened to change her so?

"I've never been to London before," he continued, not knowing what to say at her lack of reaction, "as I rarely leave Scotland."

Her hand tensed, and for the length of a heartbeat, her brilliantly blue eyes widened ever so slightly, and she looked at him with a mixture of shock and bewilderment. However, the moment passed as quickly as it had come, and Garrett could not help but wonder if he might have been mistaken, if his eyes had deceived him.

Gathering his wits, he meant to say more but the dance drew them apart in that moment, and he watched her leave his side, the distance between them growing painfully.

"She did not recognise you, did she?" Lady Tynham asked, utter confusion on her pretty face. Then she shook her head. "How can she not recognise her own husband? Do you suppose she's had some sort of an accident?"

Garrett inhaled a sharp breath, then closed his eyes, praying that fate had not truly erased him from his wife's mind. And yet, he had to admit that he had not seen even a spark of recognition in her eyes. Confusion, perhaps. But nothing that would suggest she remembered him at all. How was this possible?

For the rest of the evening, Garrett watched her, torn between anger and confusion, between thinking her heartless and fearing that she truly did not remember him. More than once, he took a step into her direction, only to hold himself back in the last moment. No, his friend was right, this was neither the time nor the place for a confrontation. It would serve no one if he lost his temper in the middle of a crowded ballroom.

Patience, he counselled himself. Patience!

After all, she was finally here, here in London. Her whereabouts were no longer unknown. He could seek her out, and he would. There was no way he would return to Scotland without answers.

She was his wife, and he would be damned before he allowed her to slip through his fingers.

Chapter Four

A HAND DEALT

When they arrived home after the ball, Claudia barely made it up the stairs to her bedchamber. Her whole body felt like lead, heavy and uncoordinated. Lifting her feet was trying, her muscles quivering with exhaustion. Her mind, too, felt numb, and her ears rang after being subjected to the deafening sounds of a crowded ballroom.

Not too long ago, she had revelled in nights like these, but not tonight.

Tonight, she had felt overwhelmed by all those people rushing to her side, asking intrusive questions about her, about her absence, about William and their disappearance from Lord Campton's ball almost a year ago.

All their questions had only served to remind her of Gretna Green, of her indiscretion, of her child.

Closing the door behind her, Claudia leaned the back of her head against the smooth wood and closed her eyes, feeling tears sting, wanting nothing more but to run free.

Then her knees buckled, and she sank to the floor in a sea of billowing fabric. Covering her mouth with her hands, she did her best to muffle the sobs that tore from her throat. At least the tears that moistened her cheeks were quiet. They would not draw her family's attention. They would not call to them for comfort.

Comfort they could not give.

As much as they tried, as much as they felt for her, there was nothing they could do. There was no comfort. Nothing they could say that would ease the pain in her heart.

Every moment of every day, Claudia could see their concern for her in their eyes. She knew that despite her efforts she had changed, grown quiet. She was no longer the cheerful and carefree young woman she had once been, the woman they had known.

And it worried them.

Claudia loved them for it, and yet, she hated the way they looked at her for it only served to remind her of her past.

Of the night she had conceived her son.

A night she could not remember.

And a child she could not help but long for.

Would this pain ever cease?

When the sobs quieted, Claudia allowed her hands to drop from her mouth, her arms no longer strong enough to hold them up. And there she sat on the floor, in her ball gown, her back against the door, in a dimly-lit room and stared at the gentle flames dancing in the hearth across from her.

Her lids began to droop as a soft voice echoed in her mind. It sounded different, and yet, so familiar.

I've never been to London before as I rarely leave Scotland.

Claudia's head snapped up, and she half-expected to see...

Shaking her head, she rubbed a hand over her eyes, feeling fatigue pull on her. She struggled to her feet, leaving her shoes by the door, and then crossed to her vanity, sinking onto the padded stool. Claudia knew she ought to ring for her maid, but the thought of another invading her privacy was too overwhelming.

Blinking her lids, she tried her best to stay focused, to undo the laces and free herself of her gown.

Her costume.

She had hoped for a diversion but had found nothing but reminders of that which she had hoped to forget. If she could not remember the night she had conceived her son, then why was she doomed to remember everything that had followed?

After a small eternity, the dress finally fell away, and she proceeded to rid herself of her stays and stockings as well. Only dressed in her shift, Claudia slipped under the covers, feeling the cool sheets against her heated skin.

Would she dream of him again tonight? Claudia wondered as her eyes closed and she rolled onto her side, hugging a pillow to her chest.

The man she could not remember? Would he speak to her again in her dreams as he had so often in the past few months?

Whenever he would come to her in her dreams, his voice would be warm and throaty, and it would brush over her skin like a caress. He only ever spoke words she could not make sense of, words she did not know. And yet, they sounded like endearments, words whispered to someone who held his heart.

In those dreams, Claudia felt safe and loved. She felt strong arms wrap around her, lifting her up and bedding her down gently. She could feel his fingers trailing over her skin causing goose bumps. And yet, her eyes remained blind.

Upon waking, she could never remember the look of his face or the colour of his eyes. All she ever remembered was the feel of him and the whispered words that spoke to her soul as though they had been made for her and her alone.

If only she could remember him.

Two days after the ball, Claudia was wandering rather aimlessly through the garden when she heard footsteps hastening toward her. Inhaling a deep breath, she blinked her eyes to discourage the tears that seemed to linger day and night before turning to face whoever had stumbled upon her in this remote area of the garden.

To her surprise, it seemed that the disturbance of her solitude was no accident at all. Not only her brother, but also his wife and their mother were all but rushing toward her, their faces tense and their eyes filled with compassion and concern.

The sight sent cold shivers down Claudia's back. What on earth had happened now? Was there any way fate could deal her an even harsher card than the one she already held?

"My dear," her mother addressed her, gently pulling Claudia's hands into her own, "we've been looking all over for you."

"And now you've found me," Claudia replied with the pretend cheerfulness she had worked so hard to attain. Judging from the looks on her family's faces though, it fell far short.

All of a sudden, silence descended over them as the other three glanced from her to one another, each one of them dreading to speak the first word. While Richard and her mother looked distraught to the point of painful, Evelyn had her hands resting protectively on the small bump under her dress as though she feared her child might disappear. For a moment, neither one of them dared meet her eyes.

Claudia swallowed. "What happened?"

Inhaling a slow breath, her brother glanced at his wife who reached out and gently squeezed his hand. He nodded in acknowledgement and then stepped forward. "Come with me, please," he said as his eyes finally found Claudia's.

Nodding her agreement, she followed him to the small stone bench by the fountain and sat down at his behest while he remained standing. Looking up at her brother, Claudia sighed, "Please, say it. Whatever it is, simply say it."

"All right," Richard nodded as his wife came to stand beside him while their mother took a seat next to Claudia on the bench, her hands folded in her lap and her head bowed. "This morning," her brother began, "I received a letter." He paused. "From Mr. Lambert."

Claudia could not prevent the jerk that went through her body at the mention of her second cousin, knowing only too well that he had been the one entrusted with delivering her son to his new family. What could her brother possibly have to tell her that she needed to know? If she was to have any chance of moving on, then she needed to cut all ties? Could he not see the pain his words caused her? Could he not simply leave this alone?

And yet, Claudia felt the almost uncontrollable need to ask after her son, bringing with it fresh pain. "No!" Claudia exclaimed, suddenly shooting to her feet. "I do not wish to hear it!"

"But you must, my dear," her mother whispered, reaching out and taking Claudia's hand. "You may not wish to, but you need to."

"You have a right to know," Evelyn stated before she turned her face to hide the tears that rolled down her cheeks.

Richard took a step toward his sister. "You need to hear this. Please."

Swallowing, Claudia nodded. Then she sat back down, her teeth digging into her bottom lip as she tried her best not to break into a thousand pieces.

"The carriage that was to deliver him...," her brother paused, omitting *to his new family*, "was...was set upon by highwaymen."

Claudia's eyes closed as her teeth cut her flesh and she tasted blood. Her hands grew ice cold, and her heart slowed until it seemed it was barely beating. Fear gripped her, blind panic, and yet, her body froze, unable to move.

"Mr. Lambert took a blow to the head," her brother continued, his voice calm and collected, and yet, Claudia knew that he felt for her, "and lost consciousness. He is fine, but...they took the child." He heaved a deep sigh full of regret. "At present, we don't know where the boy is."

Claudia felt as though time had come to a standstill as the shock of this news slowly seeped into her bones. Fear rose up louder and clawed at her heart, and she felt like sinking to the ground and crying her eyes out.

"I will go and speak to Mr. Lambert," Richard continued in his calm voice, "and discuss with him how to proceed in order to retrieve the child. I assure you that we will find him. You are not to worry."

As her brother's voice faded away, Claudia felt her mother's hand squeeze hers and dimly wondered when her mother had placed her hand on hers. She could not recall. It was indeed the strangest thing to wonder about in that moment.

"I'll be off then."

At her brother's words, Claudia's eyes flew open and she shot to her feet yet again. "I will accompany you!" The words flew from her lips before she'd had a chance to think them through.

Doubt came to her brother's eyes and he glanced at his wife before taking a step toward his sister. "I think it would be better if you stayed with Mother and Evelyn. You-"

"He's my son!" Squaring her shoulders, Claudia raised her chin and met her brother's eyes, barely aware of the tears that now freely flowed down her cheeks. "He's my son," she repeated with less strength but equal determination, feeling her chin quiver with the power of that proclamation. Never had she said those words out loud.

Not like this.

Not as his mother.

For a long moment, her brother looked at her, torn by indecision until his wife said, "She needs to go, Richard. He is her child." Then he nodded and held out his hand to her.

Brushing the tears from her face, Claudia stepped forward and slipped her hand into her brother's, feeling his fingers close over hers tightly. His silver eyes met hers, and she could read a solemn promise in the way he nodded to her. "Ready?"

"I am," Claudia whispered, wondering if she had spoken the truth. After all, any outcome this could lead to would see her heartbroken all over again. Either her son would come to harm or if they indeed managed to recover him, she would have to say goodbye to him once more.

Claudia doubted she had the strength to live with either.

Chapter Five

AN ADDLED MIND

Half an hour later, they sat in Mr. Lambert's office.

As Claudia's second cousin had only expected her brother, a look of surprise came to his face upon seeing her there as well. Surprise was quickly followed by an apology, his green eyes holding deep sorrow as he no doubt thought of his own two little girls, Mildred and Theresa.

His concern for her and her son felt even more genuine as he never mentioned the rather large bruise on his left temple from where he had been struck during the ambush. All his thoughts were for her.

Claudia felt close to suffocating. Her emotions were so raw and painful that she did not dare dwell on them. Fortunately, for once, her brother seemed to know exactly how she felt, swiftly coming to her aid and diverting Mr. Lambert's attention.

"Can you tell us what happened?" Richard asked as they had settled into the armchairs positioned opposite Mr. Lambert's desk.

Clearing his throat, Mr. Lambert took his seat, folding his hands on the table top. "As I wrote in my letter, there were at least two assailants." He glanced at Claudia and dropped his voice a little. "They were armed, lying in wait."

Claudia felt her fingernails dig painfully into her palms as she listened, doing her best to ignore the fear in her heart and listen with her head alone.

"They had dragged large branches onto the road," Mr. Lambert continued, "to ensure that the carriage would stop. Then they approached, first incapacitating the driver," he sighed, "and then me."

"Did you see them?" Richard asked, his eyes focused as his mind worked. "Can you tell me what they looked like?"

"They wore hoods over their heads," Mr. Lambert replied, regret heavy in his voice. "Everything happened so fast that it is all a blur." His gaze drifted to Claudia. "I'm deeply sorry, Miss Davenport."

Swallowing, Claudia nodded. It was all she could do.

"What happened then?" Richard asked, once again redirecting Mr. Lambert's attention.

"When I came to," their cousin sighed, "the nurse sat in a corner of the carriage crying, unable to speak, and the boy was gone." Again, Mr. Lambert's gaze drifted to Claudia but blessedly only for a moment. "I've gone over everything a thousand times in my mind," he told her brother, "and I must say that the fact that they did not kill us gives me hope. I believe it means that there is some restraint in them. I believe they would not harm the child."

Claudia inhaled a slow breath, clinging with all her might to her cousin's words.

"Do you believe they will ask for ransom?" Richard enquired.

Mr. Lambert shrugged. "I have no way of knowing that. However, it does appear the most reasonable explanation. Why else would they steal the child?"

Richard frowned. "Did they say anything that would suggest they knew who he was?"

"I did not hear them speak at all," Mr. Lambert admitted. "I heard their yelling and then they were upon us. I cannot say I heard them say anything." He shrugged. "They might have known or might have not. Perhaps they were lying in wait for anyone they would deem profitable. Perhaps this is nothing personal."

"What about the nurse? Did she take a blow to the head as well?"

"No, but the ordeal has addled her mind," Mr. Lambert said in a low voice. "I returned her home, but she's not said a word since it happened. She only sits and stares at nothing."

Claudia felt as though in a dream. She could hear them speaking, and yet her mind was numb. Nothing seemed real, and yet, her heart still ached as acutely as ever before.

"I would suggest hiring a few trusted men," Mr. Lambert went on, his gaze focused on her brother, "to aid us in the search for the child." He cleared his throat. "Quietly so as not to cause a scandal."

Richard nodded. "Thank you. Yes, I suppose that would be the best way to proceed." He rose to his feet. "Please keep us informed."

"Of course," Mr. Lambert assured them as Richard helped Claudia to her feet.

An addled mind, Claudia thought, knowing exactly how that felt. As she followed her brother out the door and back out onto the street, nothing felt real, and yet, utterly terrifying.

What was she to do now?

When Claudia woke the next morning, for one small, blessed moment the world seemed all right.

Then her memory returned like a blow to her heart, and she rolled over in bed, hugging her knees as pain radiated through her chest. Fresh tears streamed down her face, and she gritted her teeth against the sobs that threatened to rise from her throat.

Another memory drifted before her eyes. A memory of her son in the one small moment when she had laid eyes on him. She could still hear his soft, little wails as though he were calling for her. For his mother.

But she had never come to him.

Anger rose in Claudia's chest, anger at herself. How could she have abandoned her child? He had needed her. He still needed her, and she would not fail him. Not again.

Clenching her jaw, Claudia pushed herself up, determinedly wiping the tears off her face. They would not serve her. Nor her son. She needed to keep her wits about her if she were to find her child.

With a new purpose in mind, Claudia rose and dressed quickly, her mind as clear and focused as it had not been in a long while.

The nurse!

While Mr. Lambert no doubt had men searching the road where the ambush had happened, trying to find witnesses who might have seen something, Claudia knew that he had already disregarded the young woman who had been conscious throughout the ordeal. He had said that she could not say a word, her mind trapped in a world no one could reach.

But was that true?

Claudia herself had spent the past months distancing herself from the world for fear of the pain that would await her. And yet, she was still here. Would she be able to reach the young woman who had shut off her mind in order to protect herself?

Claudia knew she had to try.

A distant part of her mind whispered, *What if the nurse does not remember? You, too, cannot recall a significant night of your life.*

Pushing that thought away, Claudia headed downstairs, almost cringing at the voices that echoed to her ears as she stepped down into the hall. Her family was already up, concern tinging their voices as they talked about her, about what to do, about how to help.

Claudia glanced toward the drawing room and then tiptoed forward, determined to do this on her own.

"Good morning, miss."

Cursing under her breath, Claudia stopped in her tracks. Then she reluctantly turned around and greeted their butler, wishing for once the man was not quite so diligent. "Please bring me my jacket and bonnet."

Bowing, Harmon did as he was bid.

"Claudia, my dear," her mother exclaimed, all but bursting through the door. "You're up already? We thought you would need a little more rest. Perhaps you should lie down and-"

"No!" Seeing her mother cringe at the vehemence in her voice, Claudia forced herself to remain calm, trying her best to smile at her mother and sister-in-law, who had followed the dowager viscountess out of the drawing room. "I need some fresh air," she said politely, holding herself upright in the hopes they would deem her fit to undertake such an activity.

"Shall we accompany you?" Evelyn asked, her right hand absentmindedly resting on her midsection.

Swallowing, Claudia forced her eyes up. "Thank you, but no." Once more attempting a smile, she held her sister-in-law's gaze, knowing that if anyone were to see to the root of her soul, it would be Evelyn. "I need to be alone for a bit."

For a long moment, Evelyn simply looked at her, her dark blue eyes lingering on Claudia's face. Then she nodded in understanding, and Claudia could have hugged her.

"But my dear, I-?" her mother began, but Evelyn silenced her with a hand on her arm. "She'll be fine," she said, her voice strong and knowing.

After mumbling a quick thank-you to her new sister-in-law, Claudia stepped outside into the early morning sun. Perhaps Evelyn could tell that Claudia could no longer bear to have their concerned eyes follow her every step. Perhaps she understood that it crippled her and made her want to curl up into a ball and cry. Perhaps Evelyn could truly see all that and more.

Tying her bonnet under her chin, Claudia took a step back out into the world. And then another. And for the first time in almost a year, she felt as though she had any control over her life.

"I will find you," she whispered to the soft breeze brushing over her cheeks, "if it's the last thing I'll do. I will find you."

Chapter Six

RETRIEVING A MEMORY

Retreating into the shadows of a large oak, Garrett watched as his wife left her brother's townhouse, her steps carrying her forward with vigour and determination-something that had been absent that night at the ball. Had something changed? He wondered as he followed her slowly, wishing he could see her face.

His heart thudded in his chest as he walked on, leading his horse by the reins, his eyes fixed on his wife as she turned corners and crossed streets. From the way she moved, Garrett knew that she had a specific destination in mind and wondered who on earth she would call on so early in the morning.

Leaving behind London's imposing townhouses, Claudia entered an area mostly harbouring stores and offices. A little down the street, she climbed the three steps leading up to a door bearing a sign with large letters, STEVEN LAMBERT, SOLICITOR.

Garrett frowned. The day before he had followed her and her brother as they had come to this office in their carriage. After entering, they had stayed inside for what had seemed like an eternity to him as he had contemplated why on earth they were talking to a solicitor.

His heart had nearly stopped when his mind had drawn the conclusion that she might be getting legal advice on how to rid herself of him. Was she trying to get an annulment? Or a divorce? But why now? Why not months ago? And why had she pretended not to know him at the ball?

Shaking his head, Garrett watched as the door opened and a young man appeared in its frame. The same young man Garrett had seen the day before, undoubtedly Steven Lambert. The solicitor's eyes widened when he saw Claudia, and Garrett could not help but wonder about the nature of their relationship. Who would seek out their solicitor so early in the morning? What solicitor would be surprised in such a way to see one of his clients?

A nagging suspicion gripped Garrett's heart, and he felt his hands curl into fists.

After a brief moment of hesitation, Mr. Lambert invited her inside, but Claudia shook her head. Her hands gestured wildly as words flew from her lips, and Garrett could not help but smile as it reminded him of their night together.

Never had she been tight-lipped. On the contrary, in order to get a word in, he had pulled her into his arms more than once that night and kissed her breathless...and speechless.

At least for a moment.

Enough for him to speak his mind.

After Mr. Lambert stepped into his office and returned a moment later with his coat, Garrett retreated a few paces so as not to be seen, half-hiding behind his mount. The two began walking side by side down the street, each step carrying them farther away from the viscount's townhouse.

Forcing himself to pace his steps, Garrett followed once more, frowning when they entered a part of town that harboured the less fortunate in life. Here, people were up and about, their voices ringing through the air. The streets held dirt and garbage, and the smells were far from pleasing. For the thousandth time, Garrett wondered where they were headed.

Finally, they came to stand in front of a simple structure in desperate need of repairs. Mr. Lambert knocked on the door, and after a while, a young woman opened. Garrett squinted his eyes, however, from such a distance, he could not make out her face.

After a few words were exchanged, the young woman stepped aside and allowed the pair to enter. Then the door closed behind them, and Garrett was left behind in the dark. His jaw clenched painfully, and he cursed loudly, wishing he could simply follow and demand an explanation.

But he did not. Deep down, a part of him knew that it would not be that simple.

There was more to his wife than meets the eye, he thought, and no matter how many nights and days he needed to spend outside her home, he would find out what it was.

As Mr. Lambert waited out in the hall, Claudia stepped into the woman's small dwelling. Her face was pale, and her eyes downcast and red-rimmed as she bid Claudia take a seat on one of the spindly chairs by the table. There was something about her that seemed familiar, and Claudia wondered if she had met this woman before. Had she come to Crestwood House to collect her son? Had she seen her then? Unable to recall, Claudia shook her head, then sat down in the proffered seat. "Thank you, Miss...?"

"Call me Sophie," the nurse replied as she sank onto the other chair, her hands coming to rest on the table, her fingernails scratching across the weathered wood. Her eyes followed her fingers' movements as though she had lost all hold on reality, barely aware where she was and who was with her.

Inhaling a slow breath, Claudia felt her heart go out to the young woman. Still, she could not leave without asking her questions. "Sophie, may I speak to you?" she asked gently, trying to look into the young woman's eyes. "I need..." Her voice hitched, and for a brief moment, she had to close her eyes. "I need...to find my son, and you're the only one who can help me."

Slowly, Sophie's gaze rose from the table and met Claudia's. "I'm so sorry," she whispered, deep sorrow in her eyes. "I'm so sorry."

Ignoring the tears that spilled down her face, Claudia nodded. "I know you are, and I want you to know that it wasn't your fault. You couldn't have stopped them." She inhaled a deep breath. "But you can tell me what you remember."

The young woman's lips pressed into a thin line as she shook her head. "But I don't remember. I don't..." Her head moved from side to side more vehemently as she crossed her arms in front of her chest. "I don't!"

The remnants of shock clung to Sophie's face, and Claudia felt a stab of guilt for putting the young woman through this. "Is it truly all gone?" Claudia whispered. "Or are there bits and pieces you remember? Please!"

Again, Sophie's gaze rose to meet hers. Only this time, Claudia could see the young woman's desperate wish to help, to remember something that would be of value.

"Anything," Claudia pleaded. "Please."

Inhaling a deep breath, Sophie nodded. Then she closed her eyes, her fingernails digging into the table top. "They came out of nowhere," she whispered, her eyes pinched shut as though she did not dare look. "The driver fell to the ground...and did not get back up. Mr. Lambert told me to stay in the carriage, but when he opened the door, he was struck on the head."

Seeing the woman all but cower on her chair, Claudia wished she did not have to ask. "What happened then?"

Sophie's eyes opened, and tears spilled forth. "One of them came forward, and before I knew it, the babe was snatched from my arms. Then they were gone."

Claudia swallowed, momentarily overwhelmed by the woman's recount of her son's kidnapping. Would she ever see him again? So far no ransom notice had arrived. Why had they taken him if not to ransom him? What did they want?

Fresh panic gripped Claudia's heart, and in order to keep her wits, she gritted her teeth until her jaw hurt. "What did they look like?"

Sophie shook her head. "They wore masks."

Claudia sighed, feeling resignation encroach upon her heart. So far she had learnt nothing new. "Did they...did they say anything to you?"

"They told me to give them the boy."

Rubbing a hand over her eyes, Claudia blinked, trying her best to focus. "What about to each other? Did they talk to each other?"

Sophie stilled, and her eyes shifted sideways, her mind at work.

Hope surged into Claudia's heart. "What was it? What did they say?"

A frown came to Sophie's face as she tried to remember. "One of them was talking the whole time," she whispered as though afraid to lose the memory if she spoke too loudly. "He wouldn't stop even though the other one shouted at him to be quiet."

"What did he say?" Claudia asked, sitting on the edge of her seat.

"He was...boasting," Sophie whispered, a frown drawing down her brows, "about how well they'd planned this. He said it had all worked so much better than he had expected. He laughed, saying that he ought to think about changing his profession and that the other owed him a drink once they got to the *Prancing Pony*."

The air caught in Claudia's throat. "The *Prancing Pony*?" she whispered to herself. "Have you heard of that place?"

Sophie shook her head, her eyes still closed as she tried her best to relive what had happened. "They headed north," she whispered then. "They headed north."

When Sophie opened her eyes, a soft smile played on her lips, and Claudia could see that despite the ordeal of remembering what had happened, the young woman was pleased that she had been able to help. "Thank you," Claudia said, squeezing Sophie's hand. "Thank you so much."

The young woman nodded, wiping a tear from her cheek. "I hope you'll find your boy. A child belongs with his mother after all."

Feeling tears sting her eyes, Claudia rapidly blinked her eyes. Then she rose from the spindly chair and reached into her reticule, leaving the young woman a little compensation. Still, from personal experience, Claudia knew full well that no amount of money would be able to right the wrong she had witnessed. Then she silently stepped from the room. Instantly, Mr. Lambert stopped his pacing and crossed to her side, his face expectant as he looked at her.

"Have you ever heard of the *Prancing Pony*?" Claudia asked, refusing to feel disheartened when Mr. Lambert frowned. "I'm thinking it might be an inn."

"That's possible," Mr. Lambert agreed, a hint of caution on his face. "We can ask around; however, there are countless inns in all directions. It will probably take a while to-"

"They headed north," Claudia interrupted. "She saw them head north."

Mr. Lambert blinked, and for a short moment his gaze travelled to the closed door behind Claudia in confusion. "Why did she not tell us so before?"

"She couldn't remember," Claudia said, heading toward the door, knowing only too well how that felt. A part of her wondered if she would ever get her own memories back. Would she ever remember the night at Gretna Green? Would she ever remember her child's father? Or would that forever remain a mystery?

Pushing that thought aside, Claudia knew that there were more important matters to take care of now. She needed to find her son, and thanks to Sophie, she was now one step closer than she had been the day before.

How many more steps would it take her to find him?

Chapter Seven

IN THE DARK OF NIGHT

Pacing up and down the carpet in the drawing room, Claudia did her best to ignore Evelyn's and her mother's concerned glances. She was well aware that she was wearing a hole in the rug, but in that moment, she simply could not help it. Her family's attempts at distracting her drove her insane. Did they truly think that anything could take her mind off her son?

Trying to calm her nerves, Claudia cursed her brother for the thousandth time that afternoon for not allowing her to go along to visit the inn. Accompanied by a handful of Mr. Lambert's hired men, he had set off two hours ago to search out the *Prancing Pony* and find witnesses that might have seen two men and an infant passing through.

Ever since they had left, time seemed to have slowed down.

While her mother worked on her embroidery, Evelyn sat on the settee, an open book in her lap. Still, Claudia had not noticed her turning a single page, her sister-in-law's gaze directed out the window, her thoughts directed inward.

At least they had finally stopped trying to draw her into a conversation.

Spinning to stare at the large clock on the mantle, Claudia wondered if that blasted thing had always chimed so loudly!

Inhaling a deep breath, she avoided looking at her mother who had looked up from her embroidery at her daughter's unusual reaction to such an ordinary thing as a clock's chime. Her arms crossed in front of her chest, and Claudia guided her steps to the window and glanced out at the quiet street. Nothing as far as the eye could see.

At least nothing worth seeing.

Only moments later, her legs began to twitch, unable to stand in one spot, and Claudia continued pacing up and down the length of the drawing room.

More time passed.

Unfortunately, it did so excruciatingly slowly.

When her brother's voice finally drifted over from the hall, Claudia almost fainted on the spot, her nerves wrung too tight. While her mother set aside her embroidery, Evelyn's book clattered to the floor when she rose in a hurry, her feet carrying her to Claudia's side. The women exchanged a tense look and then turned toward the door the moment it opened, and Richard strode in.

The look on his face dashed Claudia's hopes in an instant.

Evelyn's hand grasped hers. "Did you learn anything?" she asked her husband, her voice tense as her other hand came to rest on her midsection.

Claudia felt as though someone had struck her.

Richard's face was collected as always, and yet, the look in his eyes held compassion as well as a hint of defeat. "No one saw them," he said without preamble. "We questioned everyone we saw, but nothing." He sighed, his gaze drifting to Claudia. "I'm sorry. I paid the innkeeper to continue asking around and inform me if anything should arise, but I doubt it."

"Then why did they speak of that inn," their mother asked, annoyance in her voice, "if they had no intention of heading there?"

"Perhaps it was a ruse," Evelyn suggested, glancing at her husband.

Richard nodded in agreement. "Perhaps it was meant to disguise their true intentions. After all, they knocked the two men unconscious and then conversed freely in front of the female witness. After all their planning to ensure they could obtain the child, it seems unlikely that they would have made such a mistake."

Claudia's heart sank at her brother's words. "Thank you nonetheless," she whispered, taking a step back when her mother reached for her. "I'll need a moment alone," she whispered, keeping her eyes down, and all but ran from the room.

Closing the door to her bedchamber with much more vehemence than necessary, Claudia stalked around her room. A part of her felt like breaking down, but that thought felt so much like giving up that Claudia forced herself to stay on her feet. Annoyed with herself, she wiped the tears from her eyes, unwilling to accept that all was lost. Certainly, her brother would keep searching, but would that do any good?

After all, despite the dead-end, it had been she who had managed to obtain the name of the inn. Mr. Lambert had told them that the nurse did not remember anything, and Richard had accepted the man's word. If Claudia had not gone to seek the woman out, they would never have known about the *Prancing Pony*. She had found something the men had overlooked. Perhaps they had overlooked something at the *Prancing Pony* as well. Although Claudia had no idea what that could be, she knew she could not simply sit at home and wait. She needed to go and see the place herself.

Drawing in a deep breath, Claudia felt her nerves settle once the decision was made. Yes, she would go and look for her son herself. After all, she was his mother, and that was what mothers did, was it not?

When supper was called, Claudia forced herself to go downstairs and eat, knowing that whatever lay ahead she would need her strength. Also, she needed to put her family at ease in order to gain a head start. Her brother would never allow her to travel to the inn, and so she had simply decided not to involve him in her plan. She had followed his lead thus far, and it had led her nowhere. Now, she would do things her own way.

After bidding her family a good night, emphasising her exhaustion, Claudia retired to her room where she slipped into her most comfortable riding habit. She found a small bag and stuffed it with a few garments as well as a purse with her small savings. Then she sat down to wait for the house to fall asleep.

Chapter Eight
A WATCHFUL MAN

Atop his horse, Garrett once more stood beneath the large oak outside the viscount's townhouse and gazed up at the darkened windows. The last light had been extinguished only moments ago, and Garrett was trying to convince himself to head back to Lord Tynham's residence. Although he knew he needed sleep, he also knew that it often eluded him these days. If he slept, it was only for a short while and always fitful. He woke unrested, his head still filled with all the questions that had already plagued him the day before.

His mind had presented him with many reasons why he ought to hold back and not confront his wife directly about why she pretended not to know him. However, slowly, Garrett was coming to realise that what truly held him back was the fear that she would reject him.

What would he do then? Would he simply return home? Or would he fight for her? Was there any use in fighting for a woman who did not want him? A woman who had made her disregard for him known by looking right through him?

Perhaps on the morrow-no matter the outcome-he ought to call on her and let the cards fall where they may. He needed to know the truth. Before long, all these unanswered questions would drive him insane.

Sighing, Garrett nodded, somewhat relieved to finally have decided. His heart felt a bit lighter when he pulled on the reins, urging his horse down the street. However, his mount had barely taken a few steps when something caught his eye.

Again, he pulled on the reins and then turned his gaze back to the viscount's residence. At first, he saw nothing in the dim light, but then movement caught his attention, and he squinted his eyes to see better.

A shadow moved beside the large building approaching the street. It was a rider leaving the viscount's property.

A frown drew down Garrett's brows before a second later his eyes opened wide when he recognised the rider was a woman. She kept glancing over her shoulder as though trying to reassure herself that her departure was going unnoticed.

Claudia!

The realisation hit Garrett so abruptly that he almost groaned, his hands tensing on the reins. What on earth was that lunatic woman doing now? First, she sought out a solicitor, and now she was leaving her brother's house in the middle of the night without an escort?

Garrett shook his head, wondering if he had been misinformed about the conduct of English ladies or if he had found the only woman in all of England who possessed the courage to go against convention. It was either that or she had lost her mind.

Keeping his distance, Garrett once more followed her down the street, his mind conjuring all kinds of reasons for her unusual behaviour. However, when she continued onward and eventually crossed over into a less savoury part of town, Garrett felt his concern grow in spades.

Glancing around, Garrett took note of the taverns lining the street, loud voices echoing through the night while his wife up ahead seemed to be completely unaware of her surroundings. At the very least, her posture gave no indication that she was aware of the fact that she was potentially placing herself in harm's way. What on earth drove her to ride across town in the middle of the night?

Only when a group of drunken men, their slurred singing drifting through the night air, stumbled out of a tavern and onto the street, effectively blocking her way, did Garrett see signs of alarm in her.

One man tumbled over another, and in no time a fight broke out among the two while the others cheered them on. At least until one of the spectators took note of the young woman upon her horse only a few paces away.

Within moments, the men swarmed around her like moths drawn to a flame.

Finally alarmed, Claudia kicked her horse's flanks, urging it onward, but one of the men stepped into her path, snatching up the reins, a satisfied grin on his face. "What've we here?" he slurred, his words grotesquely mangled. "A mighty fine lady."

Another man joined his drinking companion in the front, his eyes raking over her. "Wanna join us, darlin'? Promise we'll show ye a real good time."

Although his honour urged him to interfere, Garrett held back, wanting to see what she would do. Perhaps it would do her some good to be frightened out of her wits so she might learn her lesson and not do something so foolish again.

Still, Garrett could not say that he was surprised when she did not cower or plead, but squared her shoulders, lifted her chin and said with utter disdain, "Unhand my horse immediately, you filthy brute, or you'll pay for it!" Her right hand-as of yet hidden to the men-tensed upon her riding crop as she slowly moved it forward in the shadow of her horse's neck.

Despite the severity of the situation, Garrett could not help but smile, the sight of her here this night reminding him of the woman he had met almost a year ago.

Gone were the paleness of her cheeks and the sadness clouding her eyes. Now, her fierce character shone through, and Garrett remembered well the vivaciousness he had so admired in her. Whatever had happened to change her so, the woman he had known-if only for a short few hours-was still there, hidden deep inside!

Perhaps all she needed was to be reminded of who she was.

Kicking his horse's flanks, Garrett left behind the shadows and came out into the dim light of the lit street lamps, urging his mount to her side. "May I assist ye?" he asked, feeling his skin tingle at simply being near her.

At the sound of his voice, her head snapped around and her eyes met his, and Garrett fell for her all over again.

Chapter Nine

A LADY AND A HIGHLANDER

C ursing her own foolishness, Claudia glared down at the man holding on to her reins.

With only her son on her mind, she had not noticed the changes around her, had not been aware that townhouses no longer lined the sides of the street, but instead taverns and presumably other establishments unsuitable for a young woman.

Her attention had been focused inward, and her thoughts had circled around what to do once she reached the *Prancing Pony*. Now, it looked as though even reaching the inn was rather unlikely.

Still, she would not give up at the first sign of trouble.

Squaring her shoulders, Claudia gritted her teeth, ignoring the icy chill that slowly crept up her spine and met the man's stare with a disdainful one of her own. *Do not show fear,* she counselled herself, *for a pack of wolves always goes after the weak. Be strong!*

"Unhand my horse immediately, you filthy brute," she hissed, the look on her face underlining each word, "or you'll pay for it!" Her fingers tensed around the riding crop in her hand, and she lifted it slowly, wondering how best to respond should the man laugh in her face.

He did not though.

Still, at the very least, her words seemed to surprise him for he stared at her with a rather bewildered look on his face. Unfortunately, his confusion only lasted for a moment, and he continued to hold tightly to her horse's reins.

What now?

Wracking her mind, Claudia considered kicking the man in his leering face. Would that make him release the reins? Or only serve to anger him? Or perhaps she ought to use the riding crop in her hand? Or kick him first and then strike him?

Before Claudia could make up her mind, the sound of hoof beats on cobble stone reached her ears, and she noticed her attacker's attention drift from her and to someone behind her left shoulder.

"May I assist ye?"

The man's voice sent a strange shiver down Claudia's spine, and she turned in her saddle, squinting her eyes to see in the dim light.

Separating from the shadows around him, the man urged his large mount forward, and for a rather unsettling moment, he appeared like a phantom, not quite there, solid or corporeal.

Claudia blinked as her gaze swept over him, taking note of his fine clothing and noble steed, relieved to conclude that he had to be a gentleman of high social rank and, therefore-hopefully-a man of respectability and honour. Someone who would feel compelled to assist her in her current predicament.

His black mount stood on tall legs, making the stranger appear even taller. He sat upon his horse with ease, his broad shoulders drawn back, and his chin slightly raised as he glared down at the men before her.

In the dark of night, his hair seemed almost pitch black, and his narrowed green eyes held a threat that would have sent her cowering into a corner if it had been directed at her. Fortunately, it was not, and she could see the effect of it upon the men's faces.

The drunk holding her reins took a sudden step back, his gaze drifting from the stranger's face and lower.

Frowning, Claudia allowed her gaze to follow, down the man's strong arm to his hand which was resting leisurely on his thigh. Just below, she spotted the hilt of a dagger protruding from his knee-high boot.

Claudia swallowed. She could only hope that he truly was a gentleman.

The men crowded around her seemed to have drawn a similar conclusion for the triumph that had been on their faces only moments ago had turned into wariness. They took another step back, their gazes a little sharper as though fear had sobered them.

"We were only jestin'," said the drunk who held her reins. His hands opened and he dropped the leather straps, then he lifted his palms in surrender and tipped his absent hat in imitation of a farewell gesture. In the next moment, the group quickly dispersed, soon swallowed up by the night as though they had never been there.

"Are ye all right, Lass?" the stranger asked, urging his horse alongside hers.

Once more, the sound of his voice sent a shiver down Claudia's back, and her mind felt suddenly crowded as though filled with thoughts she could not quite grasp. His dark green eyes held hers in such a familiar way that Claudia experienced a rare moment of speechlessness.

All she could do was stare.

Moments ticked by, and his gaze softened, bringing with it a gentle smile that warmed her heart.

Your son! Her mind suddenly screamed, ripping through the fog and bringing Claudia's attention back to the here and now.

Clearing her throat, she smiled at the stranger. "I thank you for your assistance," she said kindly, picking up the reins. "If you hadn't come, it might have proven difficult for me to rid myself of these men. Thank you." She gave him a nod in acknowledgement of the service he had done her and then urged her mare onward. "I bid you a good night."

A frown descended upon the man's face, and although he barely moved, his steed reacted to his silent intentions and stepped forward, effectively blocking her way. Bewilderment hung on his face, and a hint of anger shone in his green eyes. "Do ye truly intend to pretend that we dunno know each other?"

Taken aback, Claudia blinked, her gaze once again shifting over the man's face.

Indeed, he was ruggedly handsome with his almost black hair and piercing green eyes. Despite his fine clothing, he looked more like a warrior about to ride into battle than a man asking a lady to dance. His instincts appeared sharp, and his attention was fully focused on her. Indeed, he was a man who would draw all eyes to him.

And yet, her mind drew a blank. Try as she might, she could not place him. However, it had been a long time since Claudia had last taken note of any man around her. Had she not spent the past months locked away from any opportunity to mingle with society? The only time she had set foot outside and-

The ball!

A smile drew up the corners of her lips, and she sighed. "Yes, now I do remember," Claudia said laughing. "I apologise for not recognising you sooner. We met at...the ball a few days back." For the life of her, Claudia could not remember whose ball it had been, but then again, she had barely paid any attention that night. "I'm sorry. I did not catch your name."

For a moment, the man stared at her as though her words had stunned him beyond comprehension. His lips thinned, and the anger in his eyes seemed to blaze from a spark into a raging flame. Still, he remained calm, inclining his head to her. "Garrett MacDrummond," he said, his voice even, and yet, highly unsettling, "of Clan MacDrummond in the Scottish Highlands."

Swallowing, Claudia returned his icy greeting, not certain what to make of him. "Pleased to meet you," she said, her voice strong, unwilling to allow him to intimidate her. "I'm Claudia Davenport, sister to Lord Ashwood."

At her words, his lips thinned even more as though she had displeased him simply by stating her name.

"I bid you a good night, Mr. MacDrummond," Claudia said, lifting her chin as she looked at him rather haughtily. Who on earth was he to treat her thus?

Pulling on her reins, she made to guide her horse past him when he once more blocked her movement. "I will see ye home," he objected,

his eyes rather hard on hers. "'Tis not wise for a woman to travel alone at this time of night."

Claudia gritted her teeth, anger rising to warm her chilled bones. "Thank you for your kind offer," she snapped, the tone in her voice far from polite, "but I'm afraid I must decline for I am not heading home. Good night."

He lifted a hand to stop her. "Then I shall see ye to wherever it is ye wish to go."

Huffing under her breath, Claudia glared at him through narrowed eyes. "Once again, I must decline. I-"

"And I must insist," he interrupted her, the ghost of a smile dancing over his face as though he was enjoying their argument.

Shaking her head, Claudia stared at him. "Not to insult you, Mr. MacDrummond, but it is none of your business where I'm headed." He opened his mouth to object, and Claudia quickly added, "I ask you kindly to let me pass."

He grinned. "I'm afraid I cannot."

"But I insist!"

Still grinning, he lifted his brows. "I canna in good conscience leave ye out here on yer own, Lass." Then the grin vanished; the look on his face sobered. "Ye saw what almost happened." He shook his head, his green eyes all but drilling into hers. "Nay, I canna leave ye."

Inhaling a deep breath, Claudia pondered what to do as it seemed clear that Mr. MacDrummond could no sooner be moved than a mountain could. Either she allowed him to escort her home and risk being discovered by her family or she allowed him to escort her to the inn and hope that he might get discouraged once he saw that they were headed out of London. In fact, ...

Shrugging, Claudia gathered up the reins. "Fine, if ye insist," she said, mocking his Scottish lilt. "However, I am headed out of London and have no intention of returning any time soon." Glancing at him out of the corner of her eye, she took note of the tension that gripped his jaw and silently congratulated herself. "And so, I ask you, do you truly wish to follow me across England? Or would you rather go home and forget you ever met me?" Turning to look at him, she smiled, a glimmer of mischief in her eyes. "I promise I shall not breathe a word of our encounter. Your honour would not suffer."

For a moment, he held her gaze, his own all but expressionless. Then, however, he leaned forward, bringing his face closer to hers. "Ye canna dissuade me, Lass," he said, his voice almost a growl speaking to the anger that boiled under his calm exterior. "Ye might as well accept that."

Gritting her teeth, Claudia cursed.

The right corner of his mouth twitched ever so slightly as though in amusement. "Where are ye headed? Ye might as well tell me, for I'll see once we get there."

Claudia sighed, then kicked her mare's flanks and set off. "To an inn north of London," she said, resigning herself to her fate. "The *Prancing Pony*."

Catching up with her, Mr. MacDrummond then slowed his horse so that they were riding side by side. "May I ask what leads ye there?" His voice had tensed once more.

Claudia scoffed, keeping her eyes straight ahead. "You may ask as I may choose not to answer."

If she was not thoroughly mistaken, the man had the nerve to roll his eyes at her. However, as she refused to look at him, she could not be certain. In any case, without another word, Mr. MacDrummond stayed by her side, his eyes watchful and his senses alert. Unlike her, he often let his gaze sweep over their surroundings, his ears attuned to the smallest sounds, which became apparent when he suddenly gripped her reins, pulling her horse to a stop.

"What the blazes-!" Claudia began, ready to hurl a string of curses at his head when she took note of the small pack of dogs that suddenly dashed across the lonely street.

The breath caught in her throat, and her hands tightened on the reins as her horse neighed in alarm.

Still holding on to her reins, Mr. MacDrummond brushed a gentle hand over her mare's neck, whispering soft words of comfort in his Gaelic tongue. When her mare had calmed sufficiently, he looked up, his green eyes meeting hers. "Are ye all right, Lass?"

Claudia swallowed. "I'm fine," she replied curtly, hating him for proving her wrong. "Thank you." Glancing down the side street to ensure that no more wild animals would come dashing out of it, Claudia then directed her mare onward, unwilling to meet the man's eyes. Would they be full of triumph? At least, he refrained from saying *I told you so.*

Oddly enough, a moment earlier, she had wondered if it would be safe for her to allow him to escort her. After all, she had met him only once and could not say who he truly was or what character he possessed. Still, even before he had gripped her reins, Claudia had dismissed her concern. She could not say why, but for some odd reason, she felt safe with him.

He riled her, certainly, but she did not doubt that he would do everything within his power to ensure her safety.

Shaking her head, Claudia swallowed, wondering where on earth that certainty had come from.

Chapter Ten

THE PRANCING PONY

Once they left London behind, darkness engulfed them. Only the moon overhead shone bright and clear illuminating their path. The road was deserted, and Garrett wondered if it was merely luck that they were able to see their feet in front of them or if she had intentionally chosen a night with an almost-full moon.

Glancing at his wife, Garrett doubted it very much. There was a strange air of urgency, of desperation about her as though her mind was clinging to one thing alone, unable to focus on anything beyond that, ignoring all else. What on earth was she doing riding to an inn in the middle of the night? And on her own?

That question as well as many others circled around in Garrett's head as he rode beside his wife. Anger still burnt in his veins that she would pretend not to know him, and yet, his heart told him that she was not pretending. Was this possible? How could she not remember him?

When he had met her that night in Gretna Green, they had shared a few drinks. Still, he had not even woken with a headache the next morning. Could the alcohol truly have robbed her of her memory? Dimly, Garrett remembered that in his earlier years, he had woken now and then with a throbbing head and a rather hazy memory of the night before. Was she so unaccustomed to spirits that they had such a shattering effect on her?

Sighing, he glanced at her out of the corner of his eye, taking note of the way her hands were almost clenched around her reins. She sat straight, her shoulders back, and yet, every so often her eyelids drooped as though she was fighting to stay awake, determined to reach her destination. What did she hope to find at the *Prancing Pony*?

"Do ye do this a lot?" Garrett asked when her eyes closed and remained so, her head slowly sagging forward.

As though a jolt had gone through her, she snapped to attention, her lids blinking rapidly. "W-what?" she stammered, turning to look at him before she rubbed a hand over her face. "What did you say?"

Garrett grinned, unable to ignore the little dance his heart did every time he looked at her, every time she looked at him. "I asked if ye did this sorta thing a lot? Riding through the night on yer own?"

"I..." She cleared her throat. "I don't."

"Then why tonight?"

She sighed then, and for a moment, Garrett thought to see a tear glistening in the corner of her eye. Instantly, his heart tightened, and as his gaze swept over her, he cursed himself for not seeing the vulnerability that clung to her features.

Her strength had been nothing but smoke and vapours, a tool to keep him from standing in her way. Clearly, she was desperate to reach this inn, but why? What did she fear so?

"I need to find someone."

Her voice had been so soft and faint that for a moment Garrett wondered if he had merely imagined it. Still, the effect it had upon his heart left him without doubt. "Who?" he asked, not certain if he wished to know.

Her jaw clenched, and she pressed her lips together.

Gritting his teeth, Garrett cursed inwardly. Why had he asked? Was she on her way to meet up with another man? Had she taken a lover since they had parted ways? Had he been so mistaken about her character? She had seemed so vivacious, like someone starved for adventure, and yet, she had been no fool. Her mind had been sharp and her thoughts provocative, challenging. Garrett had glimpsed an iron will, but also a kind heart, yearning for love. She had swept him off his feet, and the thought that she had so easily forgotten him-worse, replaced him-pained more than anything he had ever suffered.

An hour later, they finally reached the inn, a two-storey house of simple structure with a stable situated in the back. Faint lights shone through the shutters, and an old wooden sign swung in the wind.

As soon as the building came into view, Garrett noted a change in his wife. Her hands gripped the reins tighter, and her breathing increased as though she was about to face her greatest fear. If she indeed were to meet a lover here, would she be this nervous? This afraid?

The terror that gripped her shoulders and sent a tremble along her jaw stirred Garrett's protective side. No matter what had happened, this was his wife, and he would not let anyone harm her.

With ease, she slid from her saddle and quickly tied her mare to a post out front. Then her feet carried her toward the door, her hands trembling before she balled them into fists.

Hurrying after her, Garrett grabbed her by the arm, pulling her back. "Talk to me, Lass. Ye look the fright. Who are ye meeting here?"

Her chest rose and fell with rapid breaths as she stared up at him, her jaw quivering and tears standing in her eyes. For a moment, she seemed ready to sink into his arms and allow him to hold her.

But she did not.

Swallowing, she took a step back, her hand brushing his away. "I'll only be a moment," she whispered, her voice barely audible, her face white as a sheet. "Wait here." And then she was gone.

Cursing under his breath, Garrett pulled open the door and stepped inside after her, finding her only two steps ahead of him as she stood in the entry, her eyes taking in the scene.

Only a few men lingered in the taproom this time of night, receiving their drinks from a fatigued serving wench with dark circles under her eyes. The atmosphere was calm and pleasant as most guests kept to themselves, nursing their drinks near the open fire in the hearth. The flames sent a warm glow about the room, offsetting the mild stench of many travellers stepping across the threshold.

After his perusal of the room, Garrett directed his gaze back at his wife. He crossed his arms and leaned back against the wall, watching as she inhaled a deep breath and then stepped up to the counter. Her hands were trembling, and he wondered if it might only have been fatigue that caused it. Still, the look of utter fear in her eyes had been burnt into his mind, and he knew he would never be able to forget it for as long as he lived. Why on earth was she here?

From a door in the back, the innkeeper emerged. A tall man, thin and lanky, he wiped his hands on his vest when he saw Claudia approaching the counter. A polite smile came to his face, and he offered her a greeting. Beyond that, Garrett could not guess what words were exchanged for their voices did not travel far enough to reach his ears. Still, he watched through squinted eyes as they spoke to one another. He took note of the faint look of surprise on the man's face before he replied, and the blood nearly froze in his veins when he saw his wife's reaction to the innkeeper's answer.

Even from across the room, Garrett could see her drawing in a sharp breath, her right hand flying up to her chest as though in shock. Then a smile of utter relief lit up her face, chasing away all fatigue and giving her a gentle glow as though the light suddenly came from within her.

Garrett was thunderstruck, overwhelmed by how much she affected him. It had been months since he had last seen her, and yet, right then and there, it felt as though she had been with him every day of his life.

Blinking, Garrett shifted his attention from his wife to a man sitting by himself off to the side. His gaze was no longer directed at the drink in his hand but had travelled upward and was now sweeping over Claudia's assets in a fairly intimate fashion. In the next moment, the man staggered to his feet and sauntered over, eyes fixed on her.

Pushing himself off the wall, Garrett gritted his teeth, willing his body to relax. Then he strode forward, cringing when the man reached Claudia's side before him.

The man half-leaned onto the counter as he addressed her, his eyes nowhere near her face. "Do you travel alone, dearie?"

Frowning, Claudia turned toward the man who was so rudely interrupting her conversation with the innkeeper. Her eyes narrowed into slits as she looked at him like one would look at a bug.

Despite his anger, amusement tickled the corners of Garrett's mouth, and once again, he knew exactly why she was the one for him.

Before Claudia could utter any kind of reply, Garrett reached her side, placing a hand onto the small of her back. Then he turned to look at the innkeeper. "Do ye have a free room for my wife and me?"

As the innkeeper nodded his head in affirmation, Garrett noticed the way the drunkard's eyes dimmed before he stepped back and disappointedly sauntered back to the small table in the corner where he had left his drink.

Next to Garrett, his wife turned, her blue eyes meeting his, a hint of confusion in them. Her features, however, held sheer stubbornness as she seemed to dig in her heels, squared her shoulders and met his eyes. "I'm not staying here," she hissed in a hushed tone. "I need to go. There's no time to lose."

Taking a step forward, Garrett brought his face closer to hers. "'Tis not safe to travel onward," he hissed back, one arm still resting comfortably around her middle as though it belonged there. "Not in the dark. Ye need sleep, Lass."

Her eyes hardened, and Garrett could see that she would not yield easily. So, when she opened her mouth in protest, he pulled her in close, her chest pressed against his. She gasped at the sudden contact, but to his surprise, she did not struggle to free herself from his grasp. "Ye will get some sleep, Lass," he whispered against her lips, "if I have to tie ye to the bed. Dunno test me."

Pulling back a little, she looked up at him, a slight frown on her face. "You called me your wife."

"Aye," was all Garrett said as he held her in his arms for the first time in almost a year. It felt utterly right.

Rolling her eyes at him, she groaned in annoyance. "Why?" she snapped. "Why would you tell him I'm your wife?"

Because ye are! His mind whispered, and yet, Garrett did not say so out loud. Something in her eyes made him hold back, knowing that right here and now she was not ready to hear it...if indeed she truly did not know.

"Ye will have noticed the place is full o'lonely men," he whispered, his gaze shifting around the room before returning to hers. "I thought ye wouldna care for their company."

Claudia frowned before understanding crossed her features. "I would bolt my door."

A low chuckle left his lips. "I've no doubt ye would, Lass, but ye see there are always ways around a lock."

Holding his gaze, she inhaled a deep breath, and he could see that she wanted nothing more but to lash out at him, to tell him to go to hell and do things her way. But she did not. He could see her mind work. He could see reason overcome the urge to tell him off. He could see her calculating gaze study his face.

Then she sighed, a hint of vulnerability back in her eyes. It almost stole the breath from his lungs. "Will I be safe with you?" she asked quietly, her blue eyes wide and trusting as she stood in his arms looking up at him.

Garrett sobered. "Aye," he promised solemnly, no mockery in his voice now. "Aye, Lass, ye'll be safe with me. I swear it."

Again, she inhaled a slow breath before nodding her head. "All right then." Leaning back, she stepped out of his embrace, her blue eyes holding his as though still needing the reassurance of his promise.

Clearing his throat, Garrett took the offered key from the innkeeper and asked the man to have someone see to their horses. Then he offered Claudia his arm and escorted her up the stairs, wondering if any woman would share a room with a stranger if she truly did not know who he was. If only he could be certain.

"Did ye get the answer ye sought?" Garrett asked as they walked down the small, dimly lit corridor.

For a moment, she frowned before understanding came to her eyes and a true and honest and utterly captivating smile lit up her face as though the sun had risen in the dark of night.

Garrett was speechless, cringing at the thought that another man had put it there. Who else could she be looking for?

Chapter Eleven
THOSE WHO ARE LOST

Stepping into the small room, Claudia's mind was reeling with the innkeeper's words.

After a moment's hesitation that had nearly stopped her heart, he had told her that a few days ago a man and an infant had stayed at the *Prancing Pony* and had then headed farther north the following day. In that moment, Claudia could have sagged to the ground with relief, with joy, with utter exhilaration.

Then a frown had chased away her joy, and she had wondered why her brother had not told her that. Was he still searching, following this clue, without her knowledge? If so, why? Did he believe she would break if she knew? Why would he think that?

Or did he truly not know?

Claudia drew in a slow breath as she approached the window and glanced out into the dark, barely aware of the man who stepped into the room behind her and closed the door. She remembered her brother's words to her only too clearly. Indeed, he had spoken to the innkeeper as well as everyone else they had met, and yet, they had discovered nothing. How was this possible? Had her brother lied to her? Or had the innkeeper lied to her brother? But why? What reason could either of these two men have to lie?

Turning around, Claudia faced yet another man of unknown loyalty.

Standing by the door, Mr. MacDrummond looked at her, his green eyes holding hers as though they had known each other for years and possessed that often unsettling ability to communicate without words. Claudia did not know what to make of him.

Indeed, she had expected him to turn back long before now. Never would she have expected such commitment. Even gentlemanly conduct had its limits. Then why was he here? After all, they were strangers. He owed her nothing. She was no duty or responsibility of his. Why was he still here?

Swallowing, Claudia wondered if he might have an ulterior motive. Had she been a fool to agree to this? To share a room? Had he truly insisted she pretend to be his wife only to protect her? Could she trust him? Or had she just invited the devil into her room?

Squaring her shoulders, Claudia cleared her throat. *Do not show fear,* she counselled herself for the second time that night, *for a lone wolf always goes after the weak. Be strong!*

"Why are you helping me?" she asked into the stillness of the room, her voice almost deafening to her own ears. "Why do you insist to stay?"

He shrugged. "Because ye canna do this alone, Lass. Ye've proved that more than once tonight. Dunno deny it."

Pressing her lips together, Claudia glared at him for reminding her of the fact that she had indeed needed him that night, that without him she might not be standing here. "While that might be true," she bit out, "it does not answer my question. I cannot believe that any man would follow a stranger merely out of the goodness of his heart."

To her surprise, a teasing grin came to his face. "I've never met a Lass who would insult the man who has gone to great lengths to help her. Is this yer way of showing yer gratitude?"

"I did not insult you!" Claudia snapped. "I merely-"

"Aye, Lass, ye did," he interrupted, his long legs carrying him closer to her. "Ye questioned the goodness of my heart. Is that not an insult to yer mind?"

Gritting her teeth, Claudia glared at him. "I merely meant to point out that your behaviour does not make sense."

"Neither does yers," he said chuckling.

Ignoring his interruption, Claudia rested her hands on her sides, feeling her blood begin to boil. That insufferable man! "I am no one to you," she snapped, pointing an accusing finger at his chest. "Why would you go to these lengths-as you put it-to help me? I'm a stranger to you. I've never met a man who would abandon his own plans and follow an unknown woman out of town in the middle of the night."

"If ye recall, I offered to take ye home."

Exasperated with his evasiveness, Claudia could have smacked him on the head. "Why will you not answer me? It is a fairly simple question, and I do believe I have a right to know." Holding his gaze, she raised her brows. "Why are you helping me?"

His face sobered as they looked at one another. Then finally, he drew in a long breath and said, "'Tis the way I was brought up. 'Tis the way of the clan to look after each other. No one is ever truly alone. There's always someone there to turn to for help." Taking a step closer, his green eyes studied her face, a question hanging in the air. "'Tis a question of honour to guard one's family, those within one's circle."

Claudia swallowed, feeling the weight of his gaze as though she was back in his arms, enveloped and safe. "But I'm not family," she whispered, unable to look away. "You have no reason to protect me. I'm not your responsibility."

"Then where is yer family? Why are they not here? By yer side?"

Claudia dropped her gaze, her hands clasped around her arms. "It's...complicated."

Silence fell over the room as she kept her eyes on the floor, feeling her hold on her nerves slipping as she thought of her family. Had they already discovered her absence? What would they think once they found her note? Unable to explain herself, she had simply penned a few words of apology, saying that she could not sit at home and wait. She had to go and find her son.

"Who are ye looking for, Lass?"

Claudia's head snapped up, and she found Mr. MacDrummond standing merely an arm's length away from her, his green eyes gentle as they searched her face. And yet, there was an almost desperate need in those eyes to have her answer his question. Why did he care?

Swallowing, Claudia shook her head, unwilling to risk offending him. How would he react if she was to tell him that she was looking for her bastard child? As a gentleman with a high code of honour, he would most likely desert her on the spot.

Was that not what you wanted since your paths first crossed? A traitorous voice whispered. *This is your chance. Rid yourself of him.*

And yet, to her great dismay, she could not.

The thought of him turning from her and leaving her behind, alone, brought an aching pain to her chest. Oddly enough, his presence was reassuring, comforting. Despite the fact that they were strangers, she felt safe with him.

"I'm...I'm looking for a friend," she finally said, carefully glancing up at him. "That is all I can tell you."

His green eyes remained on hers, and she could see that he was disappointed. Still, he nodded, a shadow falling over his face. "I'm looking for my wife."

Stunned, Claudia stared at him, momentarily speechless. "Your wife? You're looking for your wife?"

Sighing, he nodded.

"What happened?" Claudia asked before she could prevent it, reminding herself that they were in fact strangers and that such a question might be too intimate in nature. Still, her eyes remained on his, all but begging him to answer her. Why was it that *she* cared so much?

Mr. MacDrummond shrugged. "I dunno know," he whispered, his green eyes fixed on her face as though he was the one waiting for an answer. "One morning, I woke up and she was gone. I havena been able to find her since."

Claudia swallowed, seeing honest pain on the man's face. "How long has it been?"

"Almost a year."

Claudia's eyes widened at his words, and the thought of not finding her son any time soon-perhaps not ever-brought tears to her eyes. "I'm so sorry," she whispered, blinking them away. "You must be devastated." Was that why he was helping her? Hoping that his wife, too, would receive help from a stranger, should she ever need it?

His jaw tensed, and she could see that he was gritting his teeth as sadness fell over his face. "I wish I knew why she left," he whispered, and his gaze rose to meet hers. "She didna say a word nor leave a note. It eats me up not knowing."

Swallowing, Claudia looked at him. Utter love shone in his eyes, and it was all too obvious how much his wife still meant to him. For almost a year, he had been searching for her with no success, and yet, he was far from giving up. If he never found her, it would haunt him for the rest of his life. She could only hope he would be spared that fate.

And yet, a small stab of pain assaulted her heart at the thought that his had already been claimed. If she was not thoroughly mistaken, he was indeed a true gentleman, and any woman would have been fortunate to call him her own.

Only his wife seemed to have been blind. Why on earth would any woman have left such a man?

Frowning at herself, Claudia wondered about how quickly he had won her over when only moments ago she had yelled at him. It seemed her mind and heart were constantly at war when it came to him. While her mind counselled her to be cautious-suspicious even-her heart all but urged her back into his arms. When he had pulled her into his embrace down in the taproom, it had taken all her willpower to step back. She was not certain she would be able to do so again.

A knock on the door shook them both from their thoughts, and Mr. MacDrummond walked across the small room to open it. A maid greeted him, handing him Claudia's hastily-packed bag, then bid them a good night.

"I see ye came prepared," he said, the hint of a teasing grin back on his face, as he put her bag down on one of the two chairs set around a small table.

Claudia returned his smile, but found herself feeling suddenly uncertain, not knowing how to continue.

"I shall head downstairs for a wee drink," Mr. MacDrummond said, his gaze dark as it held hers. "Go ahead and slip into bed. I promise I'll be quiet and not wake ye." He took a step backwards and collided with the door, and yet, his eyes stayed on hers as though he could not bring himself to look away.

Claudia nodded, feeling his gaze almost like a caress travelling over her skin. "All right then," was all she could manage as she tried her best to calm her thoughts. Who was this man? And why did he have such an overwhelming effect on her?

Swallowing, Mr. MacDrummond finally turned and left the room. However, before he closed the door behind him, their eyes met yet again, and Claudia felt heat shoot through her body, hot enough to singe her hairs. The thought of undressing in a room that they shared was utterly scandalous but tempting all the same.

Warmth filled her heart, and a smile claimed her face.

Then as though to punish her, her mind conjured the images of another room at another inn where she had woken after a reckless night spent with a stranger and then found herself unmarried and with child. It had been these feelings that had brought her all this heartache, that had put her in this place.

A place where she was alone and searching for her son. What if she never found him? What if she did? Would she be able to give him up again?

Claudia doubted it very much, and yet, it would be the right thing to do.

Why did the right thing never feel right? And why on earth could not the wrong thing feel as wrong as it was?

Chapter Twelve
BEHIND A NAME

After an hour spent downstairs staring into the dancing flames in the hearth, Garrett finally returned to their room. His hands trembled as he opened the door and stepped across the threshold into the darkened room. She had extinguished the candle, and all he could see were vague shadows as he slowly made his way across the floor to where the two chairs were set around a small table in the corner by the window.

His breath quickened as his senses reached out to her. After a moment, he could hear her soft breathing from the back of the room where the bed stood against the wall. His heart thudded wildly in his chest, and every fibre in his body urged him to slip into bed with her and pull her into his arms.

As though it had been yesterday and not almost a year ago, Garrett remembered the night he had spent holding her in his arms, watching her sleep, her head resting on his shoulder, her soft breath brushing over his skin. It had felt heavenly, and he had ached for her ever since.

Alone in his bed, he had felt abandoned, utterly lonely. How often had he reached out in his sleep searching for her? How often had he woken to feel the memory of her loss like a punch to his stomach?

And now she was here, across the room, sleeping.

Inhaling a deep breath, Garrett shed his coat and hung it over the back of a chair. Then he pulled off his boots when the sound of their steps on the wooden floor suddenly seemed all too deafening. Carefully and with the greatest of care, he approached the bed, his eyes searching for her in the dark.

At first, he only saw the soft rise of the blanket covering her body before his gaze wandered upward and then finally touched her face. In the dim light from the window, her skin seemed pale, and yet, the silvery light of the moon gave her face an ethereal glow. Her thick lashes rested gently on her soft skin, and her mahogany curls lay strewn about the pillow, wild and untamed.

Garrett smiled, remembering how she had told him that she hated to put it in a plait. Even in sleep, the small tugs on her scalp whenever she turned had always felt like a confinement. He had run his hands through her wild curls then and told her he never again wanted to see it bound. Had she slept without a plait ever since that night? Or was it only now, away from the boundaries of her old life, that she dared to unleash her inner self?

A small sigh left her lips, and she turned onto her back, one hand resting against her forehead as though she was in deep thought.

Garrett's fingers itched to touch her, to brush the stray curl from her temple and run the tips of his fingers down the long column of her neck.

Still, he resisted that urge for he knew that whether she remembered him or not, something had changed. Something had happened. Something that was currently the only thing on her mind. Had she truly met another? Had she lost her heart to him? Had he then deserted her? Was he the one she was looking for?

The thought alone brought physical pain to every inch of Garrett's body, and a part of him wanted nothing more than to shake her awake and demand an answer. She was his wife, for goodness sake! He deserved to know if her heart had been claimed by another!

Rubbing his hands over his face, Garrett stopped when he heard her stirring. Only now, it was not the languid movement of someone lost in deep slumber or losing herself in a pleasant dream.

No, now, her fingers curled into the blanket as though seeking help.

Her breathing quickened, and she tossed her head from side to side, her eyes pinched shut. Then she rolled over and curled into a ball, her jaw quivering as tears escaped the corners of her eyes and painful sobs tore from her throat.

"Lass," Garrett whispered, sensing her distress. "Lass, wake up. Ye're dreaming." Sitting down on the side of the bed, he reached out and gently touched her shoulder, giving it a little shake. Her skin was warm even through her shift, and yet, her muscles felt tense like those of someone fighting for dear life.

"Claudia!" he called when she did not react, when her sobs continued. His heart clenched painfully at the sight of her misery. What on earth plagued her so?

And then one word left her lips. One word that changed everything. One word that felt like a bullet to his heart. One word uttered with such heart-breaking longing that Garrett knew all his hopes to be dashed. "Aiden."

The name echoed in Garrett's heart, confirming his worst nightmares, and for a long moment, he sat on the bed beside her, unable to move, unable to think, feeling pain flood his body sob by agonising sob.

And then the world around him returned as though a veil had been lifted.

Despite his own, very acute grief over the woman he now knew he had lost, his heart still went out to her as she cringed in her sleep. The other man's name flew from her lips again and again, pleading, begging, and Garrett knew that he could not leave her to her misery.

Ignoring his own pain, he reached for her, gently pulling her into his arms as he settled back on the bed. He held her tightly, brushing a hand over her wild curls, up and down her arm and back as he murmured words of comfort into her hair. His own eyes filled with tears for her as much as for himself, and he wondered if this would be the last time he would get to hold her in his arms.

Savouring the feel of her soft, warm body against his, Garrett returned to his memories of the few hours they had spent together in Gretna Green. The way they had talked, open and without restraint. The way they had laughed together, danced together. The way they had made love in the dim light of their room. The way she had felt in his arms as though she belonged there, as though he had been made to hold her cradled against him.

Slowly, her sobs calmed, and her breathing evened. Garrett felt her muscles relax and the tension leave her body. He knew he ought to rise, and yet, he did not. He stayed where he was, holding her in his arms, feeling his lids close as fatigue overwhelmed him.

Soon, he was fast asleep, and for the first time in months, he slept through the night peacefully: his heart calm and beating evenly in the knowledge that the woman he loved lay safe and warm in his arms.

The next morning dawned bright and early, and Garrett woke to feel her head on his chest and her curls tickling his nose. For a short moment, he was at a loss, blinking his eyes rapidly, before his memories returned and he could not help but smile.

Unwilling to wake her, Garrett lay still, feeling her heart beat against his own. He turned his head a little in order to get a better look at her face as she lay sleeping, her left hand on his chest. She seemed peaceful, and he could not help but chuckle when she snuggled closer, a soft murmur of contentment leaving her lips.

Abruptly, she stilled, and Garrett cursed himself.

Her breathing changed, and her muscles tensed as she left the realms of deep slumber behind, her mind slowly returning to a state of wakeful awareness.

Looking down, Garrett took note of the slight flutter that came to her lashes. Her fingers curled against his shirt before she stretched them, a deep sigh leaving her lips.

Then her eyes opened.

Bracing himself for what lay ahead, Garrett inhaled a deep breath. "Good morning, Lass," he greeted her, allowing his hand to run over her back one last time.

As expected, she shot upright in the blink of an eye, her jaw dropping and her eyes wide as she stared down at him. For a moment, words seemed to fail her as her mouth closed and opened and closed again. Then she scooted back, suddenly aware that their bodies were still touching. "What are you doing in this bed?" she demanded, her voice slowly growing in intensity as her face took on a look of outrage. Crossing her arms in front of her chest, she glared down at him.

Garrett chuckled, overwhelmingly reminded of the woman he had fallen in love with. "I thought that was obvious," he replied grinning. "I was sleeping, same as ye."

Her eyes narrowed. "But why here? Why in this bed?"

Garrett shrugged. "In my country, people sleep in beds. Is it different in yers?"

Groaning in frustration, she suddenly lunged herself at him, her eyes murderous as her hands clawed at his face.

Seizing her wrists, Garrett held her at bay, strangely delighted to see such fire in her. "Ye seem upset, Lass," he commented dryly, knowing it would only rile her into doubling her efforts.

"You beast!" she shrieked, struggling against his hold on her. "I should have you arrested!"

Garrett frowned, amused with how she alternately tried to pull her wrists from his grasp and then lunged forward again, hands straining to reach his flesh. "If I'm not at all mistaken, Lass, ye're the one attacking me. Not the other way around. What grounds would ye have to have me arrested? I dunno believe even the English would arrest a man for sleeping in a bed." Again, he chuckled, and when she lunged at him once more, he flipped her over, pinning her with his body and holding her hands safely tucked into the mattress, one on each side of her head.

Feeling his weight on top of her, she stilled, her chest rising and falling with each rapid breath as she stared up at him. "You said...," she began, then swallowed. "You said I'd be safe with you."

Garrett sobered, feeling the hammering of her heart against his chest. "I did," he replied, no teasing in his tone now, "and I meant it. I swear I didna touch ye. Ye've nothing to fear."

Holding his gaze, she seemed to consider his words. "You did touch me," she said then. "You held me." A deep breath followed, and she held his gaze. "Why?"

Garrett swallowed, sensing a shift in the air as their conversation slowly turned to touch on what had happened last night, on what he had learnt. Still, unable not to, Garrett teased, "To keep ye from falling out of bed, Lass. Ye tossed and turned quite a bit. I was afraid ye might hit yer head."

Her eyes narrowed, and yet, there was a slight twitch to her lips, drawing his gaze. The sudden urge to kiss her overwhelmed him, and he lowered his head to hers without thinking.

Instantly, her eyes widened, and she struggled against him.

Garrett stilled, cursing himself. "I'm sorry," he whispered, fearing his foolishness had finally destroyed the last shred of trust she could have had in him. After all, what woman would trust a man who promised he would not touch her and then tried to kiss her a moment later?

Releasing her wrists, Garrett rose from the bed. "I'm sorry," he mumbled again. "I dunno know what came over me."

Scrambling into the far corner of the bed, she pulled the blanket up under her chin, her eyes watching him intently. And yet, there was no fear in her eyes, merely distrust. Her blue eyes were wide and curious as they slid over him, briefly lingering on his lips as though she, too, had felt the same temptation, but had merely managed to resist it better than him.

Garrett held his breath as they looked at one another, and he wondered what her heart was whispering to her in that very moment. Almost a year ago, she had wanted him, desired him. Even if she truly could not remember, had her body recognised his, remembered something that her mind could not grasp? Had their closeness felt familiar to her?

Last night when she had snuggled deeper into his arms, Garrett could have sworn that a part of her knew who he was, that the arms that had held her felt familiar, reassuring, that she had calmed because somewhere deep down a part of her had recognised him.

Now, the look on her face told him the same as though she was trying to place him, to remember the moment he had last made her feel like this. Perhaps if he were to kiss her...?

In the next moment, she shook her head in frustration, and a frown descended upon her face. Her features hardened, and the softness in her eyes vanished. "I would ask you to leave," she hissed, jerking her chin toward the door. "I need to dress."

Garrett nodded, reaching for his boots and pulling them on one after the other. Then he strode toward the door. Still, when he reached for his coat, he stopped, turning back to look at her.

Instantly, she tensed, eyeing him suspiciously.

As much as he wanted to, Garrett could not ignore what he had learnt last night. He needed to know. He needed to confront her. "Who is Aiden?" he asked without preamble.

At his question, her eyes widened in shock and her face paled in such a way that he feared she would faint.

"Is he the man ye're looking for?" Garrett prompted when she remained silent. "Is he the one ye're after?"

Slowly, she swallowed, her gaze fixed on his, before she licked her lips, her breath strangely laboured. "Leave," she said, anger and pain darkening her voice, "and never speak that name to me again."

Garrett frowned wondering if he had been mistaken. Perhaps she had not lost her heart to another. Perhaps he was someone who had hurt her. But if that were so, then why was she looking for him? Why would she go anywhere near that man if she feared him?

Disappointed, wanting to know the truth and yet fearing it all the same, Garrett nodded and then turned to go. Still, as he descended the stairs, he remembered the way she had called out the man's name last night. Her voice had been full of sadness, but also filled with longing. No, whoever that man was, she did care for him. Of that, Garrett was certain. The only question was: could Garrett win her back? Could he conquer her heart yet again? Could he help her remember their time together? Or was her love for that other man so complete and possessive that Garrett would not stand a chance?

Breakfast was a quiet affair as they each dwelt on their own thoughts, and so before long, they swung themselves back into the saddle. Without a look at him, his wife turned her mare down the road heading north.

Sighing, Garrett followed. Anger and disappointment still boiled in his veins, but he knew that he could not abandon her. That, he would regret for the rest of his life.

Hearing the sound of his gelding's hooves on the dry road, she turned to look at him over her shoulder. "There is no need for you to follow me," she said brusquely, her gaze barely meeting his. "Return to London and your own life. I'm certain you have better things to do than follow me to an unknown place." Then she gave him a curt nod, seeking to dismiss him, and dug her heels into her horse's flanks.

Gritting his teeth, Garrett watched her race off, knowing beyond the shadow of a doubt that she was running away because she *had* felt something. It frightened her not to know, and yet, to be reminded of something she could not grasp. Well, he would simply have to remind her again and again until not only her body remembered him, but her heart and soul as well.

Digging in his heels, Garrett raced after her.

Again, she looked over her shoulder when she heard the sounds of his approach. "What are you doing?" she yelled over the thunder of their horses' hoof beats. "Go back! I don't need your help! I'll be fine on my own!"

Shaking his head, Garrett laughed when he saw her curse, her eyes narrowing and shooting daggers at him. As much as her stubbornness riled him, he loved the fire she possessed, the passion that often flared up in her eyes.

"Blasted man!" she muttered, spurring on her mare to gain ground.

Laughing, Garrett followed. He leaned low over his horse's neck, feeling the morning's cool wind brush over his face as he came up beside her. His eyes met hers, and his heart jumped at the small twitch that came to her lips before she turned her head away to hide it.

Side by side, they thundered down the road, which lay deserted this early in the morning. Again, and again, their eyes met across the dusty path, and the slight twitch in the corner of her mouth grew into a large smile that reached up and touched her eyes. Then laughter spilled from her lips, and she threw back her head, momentarily closing her eyes as the sun touched her face.

Thunderstruck, Garrett stared at her. While his mind screamed at him that she was being foolish, stupid, reckless to be closing her eyes at such speeds, his heart revelled in the sight of her, brave and strong and free.

Free of the sadness that always clung to her.

Free of the tension that had dug its claws into her.

Free of the life she had always found restricting.

"The tree is the finish line!" she yelled all of a sudden, pointing ahead at a gnarled monster of a seemingly ancient oak, its thick branches reaching across the expanse of the road.

Garrett nodded, digging in his heels once more as he tried to keep up. On they flew, smiles clinging to their faces, their eyes shifting back and forth between the old tree and their opponent. And then they were side by side, their eyes locked, as the shadow of the monster's arms fell over them.

Laughing, Claudia pulled up her reins. "It would seem I cannot rid myself of you."

Garrett shook his head, his eyes unable to leave hers. "Never," he replied, seeing a spark of recognition momentarily light up her eyes.

Perhaps all hope was not lost.

Perhaps he could make her remember him after all.

Chapter Thirteen

THE JOURNEY NORTH

T he weather was pleasant this time of year. Not too warm, and not too cold. The sun shone through the few clouds dotting the blue sky, and there was no rain in sight, only a mild breeze touched her face and tangled with Claudia's long hair.

That morning, she had not bothered to pin it up tightly. Neither had she plaited it into a long braid going down her back as she hated the soft tugs that came with it. Instead, she had taken a few loose strands and drawn them back from her temples, then tied them in the back to keep them out of her face. The rest of her wild mane hung loosely down her back, and she could feel it dancing on the wind as they raced onward.

After their first race toward the gnarled tree standing like a lone sentinel by the side of the road, they had slowed their horses, giving them a respite. Silence had fallen over them as they had continued down the road, and yet, it had not been the kind of silence that became awkward and uncomfortable. No, something had changed since they had set out. If only Claudia knew what it was.

Every once in a while, Mr. MacDrummond would look over to her, his green eyes shining in the brilliant sun, and there would be something there in the way he gazed at her that...

Frustrated, Claudia turned her head away, feeling as though she had looked into his eyes before, as though they had looked into hers before. Not now or the day before, but...

"Call me Garrett," he suddenly said, breaking the silence.

Turning to look at him, Claudia found him lifting his brows at her teasingly, and yet, the look in his eyes betrayed how important his offer was to him. "I do not believe that would be appropriate," she replied, knowing her brother would have fits if she did. Then again, he would not have approved of a myriad of things she had done in the past day.

As though reading her thoughts, Mr. MacDrummond laughed, "I do believe 'tis too late to stand on proper decorum." A wicked glint came to his eyes. "After all, we spent the night together in the same room, in the same bed, in each other's arms."

Claudia gritted her teeth at his teasing, and yet, she realised she was not truly angry. In truth, he was a man after her own heart. Someone who did not feel the obsessive need to follow each and every rule. Someone who said what he thought. Someone who acted on a whim, on a moment's flaring passion.

A shiver went down Claudia's back as she remembered his body pinning her to the bed. He had almost kissed her then. It had been so unexpected that it had spooked her. Her heart had hammered in her chest, and yet, a moment later she had regretted her actions. The look of regret and disappointment on his face had touched her, and for a moment, she had allowed herself to believe that he truly cared about her.

Although he was still a stranger, his presence continued to comfort her, put her at ease as though he was a trusted friend. Something about him felt eerily familiar as though they had met before. Her body had responded to his touch in a strange way, not bothered in the least by the stranger in her bed. In fact, Claudia had slept like a rock. She had felt safe and cared for, at peace, and her dreams had once again taken her back to the night spent in Gretna Green.

Again, she had heard her child's father whisper to her in the dark, his words bearing a strange lilt, their meaning lost to her. And yet, she had felt in her heart that his words had not merely been words, but endearments. He had cared for her, at least, in her dreams, Claudia was certain of that.

"Well then?" Mr. MacDrummond pressed as his gelding drifted closer and his knee brushed against hers. "Do ye have the courage to break a rule?"

Frowning, Claudia looked at him. Had she spoken out loud? Sometimes it felt as though he could almost read her thoughts. "Fine," she relented, realising that she not only wanted to break a rule, but she truly wanted to call him by his given name. "However, only when we do not have company. Understood?"

Grinning, he nodded. "So, when we're alone?"

Claudia scoffed, rolling her eyes at him. "Perhaps this is a mistake," she mumbled more to herself than to him.

"I doubt it," Mr. MacDrummond-Garrett-replied to her thoughts.

"Of course, you wouldn't think so," Claudia snapped. Shaking her head, she frowned at him. "You do what you do for no good reason, at least not that I can see, and then you criticise me for-" Clamping her mouth shut, she dropped her chin, belatedly realising that she had been about to reveal more than she had intended. What on earth made her speak to him so freely? Without restraint?

"We all have our reasons," Garrett said, his voice now gentle as he tried to catch her eye. "Whether they are deemed reasonable by another is a different matter. I do what I think right, and I try not to concern myself much with what others think of my reasoning. After all, 'tis my life, not theirs."

Closing her eyes, Claudia felt a smile curl up her lips. Then she turned to look at the man riding beside her. "I've never met a man like you, Garrett," she said without restraint, knowing that he would not fault her for it, "but I've always wanted to."

For a moment, he stilled, and his eyes grew darker in intensity as he held her gaze. She could see that her words had affected him as he inhaled a slow, almost torturous breath. She could see that he wanted to say something, that there was something on the tip of his tongue, and yet, he remained quiet for a long time.

"Neither have I met a woman like you, Claudia," he finally said, his gaze holding hers as though watching for her reaction, "not since the night I met my wife."

His words felt like a punch to the stomach, and for a moment, Claudia thought she would be ill.

His wife! Of course, he had a wife!

How could she have forgotten that? How could she have forgotten that the man who was endearing himself to her more and more with each passing minute was already married? No matter how she was beginning to feel about him, nothing could come of this.

Not only his heart but also his hand had already been claimed. As much as he acted like her knight in shining armour, he was not hers. She would do well to remember that!

Digging her heels in, Claudia urged her mare into a gallop, unable to look at the man beside her. Her eyes remained on the road ahead and then shifted to the structure appearing on the horizon. Another inn! Perhaps it would mean another clue. Another clue that would lead her to her son. That and nothing else was what she ought to think about.

When they reached the inn sometime later, Claudia felt her breath come in fast gasps. Her mare, too, seemed ready for a break.

"We should rest here," Garrett said beside her. Not since he had mentioned his wife had they said one word to each other. "The horses, too, could do with a wee bit of a break."

Claudia nodded. "Will you see to them?" she asked, handing him the reins. "I will go inside and...make enquiries." Not waiting for his reply, Claudia simply headed toward the door, unable to even look back at him over her shoulder. She knew he wanted to know more about who she was looking for. He had made that abundantly clear. The only thing she did not know was why. Why was it so important to him to know who she was looking for?

Pushing all these thoughts aside, Claudia opened the door and stepped inside.

Once again, she found herself at an inn, hoping that the innkeeper could tell her what she needed to know. She told herself that the chances of that happening were slim. She told herself that he would shake his head and tell her he had not seen a man travelling with an infant. She told herself that there would be other ways to learn what had happened to her son.

She tried her best not to get her hopes up. A fall from such heights would be devastating.

To Claudia's great surprise, she did not fall.

"A man and a babe, yes, they were here," the innkeeper confirmed, scratching his head. "Thought it a bit odd that they were travelin' alone, but who am I to judge?"

"Do you know where they headed?" Claudia asked, feeling her heart dance and her head grow dizzy as her emotions threatened to overwhelm her.

"North," the innkeeper replied without a moment's hesitation. "They headed north."

In that moment, Claudia paused-although she could not say why. "North?" Claudia replied as the situation she found herself in reminded her too closely of the one at the *Prancing Pony*. "Did he tell you that?"

The innkeeper frowned. "I suppose."

"You suppose?" Claudia's eyes narrowed. "What did the man look like?"

The innkeeper shrugged. "He was...eh...tall...and...eh...wore dark clothes." He shook his head. "Sorry. I don't remember more. There're so many people coming and going here. It's hard to remember them all."

And yet, you remembered that they were headed north, Claudia thought. The same as the last innkeeper. Oddly enough, it felt as though the man who had taken her child was leaving bread crumbs for her to follow.

At the *Prancing Pony*, the innkeeper had not spoken to her brother about a man with an infant. Claudia was certain now that her brother would not have lied to her about something so important. That would mean that the innkeeper had lied? But why? And why had he told *her* without a moment's hesitation? Had he been told or rather paid to give this message to her and her alone?

Claudia's thoughts raced, and she barely took note of Garrett as he appeared by her side, telling her that he had stabled the horses. Then he guided her to an empty table and ordered a hearty luncheon. Claudia ate, but her mind remained elsewhere.

Who would take her child and why, and would they then lead her to them? How would the kidnapper even know that she would follow? If she had not, then all his messages would have been for nothing.

"Are ye all right, Lass?" Garrett asked, brushing a hand over her arm in order to get her attention. "Ye havena said a word in over an hour, and I'm beginning to worry." A tense smile crossed his face as he tried to look into her eyes. "What's on yer mind, Lass?"

Claudia blinked, his words belatedly finding their way to her mind. "I'm fine," she said, trying to smile at him. "It's nothing."

Frowning, he sat back in his chair. "Quite obviously, no one has ever told ye this," he began, crossing his arms in front of his chest in a rather annoyed gesture, "but ye're not a good liar. If ye dunno wish to tell me, then say so, but dunno lie.

Seeing the sincerity in his eyes, Claudia nodded. "You're right. I'm sorry." Sighing, she leaned back in her chair, her eyes on the man who continued to watch her like someone trying to decipher an ancient text. "Don't look at me like that."

His brows rose. "Like what?"

"Like you know me."

A teasing grin came to his lips. "Do I not?" Leaning forward, he rested his arms on the table top, his green eyes rather unnervingly fixed on hers. "Ye feel trapped in a life ye did not choose. Ye wish and ye dream, but ye force yerself to abide by their rules. Yer head and yer heart rarely agree so ye often feel torn about what to do. And yet, yer heart still has hope, and so ye speak yer mind, doing at least that if nothing else." He grinned. "Until now. Now, ye've chosen to walk yer own path and damn who disagrees." His gaze narrowed. "Why? Why now?"

Overwhelmed, Claudia could do little else but stare at the stranger across from her. The stranger who seemed to know her almost as well as she knew herself. Had he truly been able to learn all that from what little time they had spent together?

His hand reached across the table and gently settled on hers. "Claudia?"

Claudia flinched, instinctively jerking her hand back. "I-I need to go," she stammered, pushing back the chair and rising to her feet. She was already halfway to the door when his hand came around her arm, pulling her back.

Urging her sideways into a corner of the room where they were hidden from the other guests, Garrett looked down at her, his green eyes strangely compelling. "Whether ye like it or not," he whispered as he towered above her, "there's something between us, Lass." When she dropped her gaze, he reached out and grasped her chin, forcing her to look at him. "I know ye can feel it. I can see it in yer eyes. Why will ye not admit to it?"

Trying to catch her breath, Claudia stared up at him, knowing beyond the shadow of a doubt that his words were true. There *was* something between them. She could feel it every time he looked at her, every time the sound of his voice reached her ears, every time he touched her.

"You have a wife," she finally said, her voice hard. If she did not break the spell now, she might lose her heart to him, and her heart was in no shape to withstand another loss. She simply could not risk it. She needed him to leave her alone. She needed him to stay away from her. "I doubt she would care for the way you speak to me." Then she jerked her chin from his grasp, shoved him aside and rushed out the door, tears stinging her eyes.

Chapter Fourteen

A WALL IN-BETWEEN

When the sun began to lower itself below the horizon, they reached the next inn on their way north.

Despite her best efforts, Garrett had not abandoned her. Even though his face had held barely-controlled anger, he had saddled his horse and followed her as before. Claudia did not know if she was relieved or not. His presence still calmed her, put her at ease, and yet, it also did things to her heart and her body that frightened her.

He is married! She kept reminding herself, wishing her heart would listen and abandon its pursuit. *He has a wife!*

Once more tossing him the reins of her mare, Claudia headed inside yet another inn without another look back, welcoming the distraction as her mind once more focused on what had led her here. Wondering what would happen, she approached the counter and waited for the innkeeper to hand a key to a young couple before addressing the man.

Strangely enough, the same thing happened again. It was as though the man had been all but expecting her so he could deliver his message and be done with it. His words, too, largely resembled those she had heard at the previous inns. They'd all spoken of a man and a babe, staying one night and then heading north the next morning. That seemed to be the extent of their knowledge. No more and no less.

In that moment, Garrett walked in the door, heading straight to her side. However, before he could utter a word, Claudia once more turned to the innkeeper. "Do you have rooms available?" she asked, keeping her gaze sternly forward. "One for myself and another for my companion?"

The innkeeper nodded and turned to a wall full of keys.

All the while, the man beside her said not a word, and yet, she could almost feel his anger coming off him in red, hot waves. His body had tensed at her words, and he had dropped her bag.

Good, Claudia thought. Perhaps now he would keep his distance. Perhaps now he would leave her as she had made it clear that there would be nothing between them.

Claudia swallowed, but then forced a smile back onto her face, not caring in the least whether or not he would be able to see through her lie. "Are you hungry?" she asked lightly. "I admit I'm quite famished. Shall we sit down and have some supper?" Without awaiting his answer, she picked up her bag, took the proffered key from the innkeeper and then headed into the taproom.

Settling at a table, Claudia exhaled the breath she had been holding when she found him following her into the room and taking the seat across from her. Still, she could not help but be disgusted with herself for seeking the company of a married man.

As before, they ate in silence, only the occasional glance exchanged between the two of them. And yet, Claudia found that she had never been more aware of another person than she was now in that very moment of the man who sat across from her. The hum of voices from the guests around them wrapped them in a world of their own, and it seemed as though no one and nothing else existed.

The emotions she could read on his face changed from anger to something softer then back to a steely glare directed at her. Sometimes his mouth would open as though he wished to say or ask something, but it was only near the end of their meal when he finally spoke. "Who is Aiden? And why are ye looking for him, Lass?"

Claudia froze and was about to shoot to her feet when his warm hand reached out and settled on hers, grounding her to her seat. "Ye need to tell me for I do believe I deserve to know," he whispered, and yet, his voice held a touch of anger, of urgency and the will not to be denied.

Ignoring the feel of his hand on hers, Claudia shook her head, her eyes holding his, taking note of the small flare that lit them like burning embers.

"Was he yer lover?" he forced out through gritted teeth, his hand tensing on hers. "Did he desert ye? Is that why ye're looking for him?"

Annoyed with his overbearing attitude, Claudia jerked her hand free. "As I've told you before, this is none of your concern." Then she shot to her feet. "If you cannot accept that, then you should leave. Good night."

With quick steps, she crossed the room, heading for the staircase. The hairs on the back of her neck stood on end, and she could all but feel him following her with his eyes. Anger fuelled her movements, and she stomped up the stairs, earning her looks of bewilderment from the other guests. Claudia could not have cared less. Hastening along the dim corridor, she located her room, unlocked the door and headed inside, slamming it shut.

Or she would have...if Garrett had not silently followed on her heel, his hand catching the door as it was about to swing closed.

Spinning around, Claudia stared at him as he stepped across the threshold, his face dark with anger. He closed the door with a kick of his boot and then tossed her bag into the next corner.

Claudia had forgotten all about it. Too preoccupied had she been with the man in front of her. "Out!" she shrieked, only too aware of the anger that sent a tremble up and down his arms. "Get out of my room!"

His lips pressed into a thin line as he came stalking toward her, his green eyes dangerously dark as they held hers. "Answer me," he snarled. "Who is Aiden?"

Gritting her teeth against the tears that threatened, Claudia shook her head, tapping into her anger rather than her grief. "You have no right to an answer," she snapped, glaring at him despite the shiver that ran down her spine. "I never asked you to come. *You* were the one who insisted. I told you to go, to leave me alone before we even left London. I told you again and again, but would you listen? No, of course, not." Shaking her head, she stemmed her hands in her sides. "Men always think they know better." Claudia was only dimly aware that his mouth opened a couple of times in order to reply, but she could not stop herself. Her anger and confusion and fear came pouring out of her. "If you had listened to me, then none of this would have happened. You would be back in London, doing whatever it is that you do, and I would be well on my way to-" Clamping her mouth shut, Claudia stomped her feet, annoyed with herself for almost saying more than she had intended - again.

"On yer way to what?" Garrett asked as he took a step closer, his gaze not wavering from hers. "Or to whom?"

Again, Claudia shook her head. "As I've told you before you may ask-as annoying as that is-while I may choose not to answer."

His jaw tensed, and she took note of his hands balling into fists. "I swear," he forced out through gritted teeth, "if ye dunno tell me, I will tie ye to my horse and take ye back to London."

The breath caught in Claudia's throat. "You wouldn't!"

"Try me!" he hissed, lowering his head to hers. "As I've told ye before, I canna in good conscience have ye roaming the countryside on yer own, Lass."

Stomping her foot, she glared at him. "You wouldn't!" she hissed once again.

Taking another step toward her, he grasped her chin, his face now only an inch away. "Try me! I dare ye!"

Chapter Fifteen

THE MEMORY OF A KISS

Anger held Garrett rigid as he stared down at his wife. Her eyes were wide, and he could see the small tremors that shook her. She was holding on by a thread, one that would snap at any moment. Did she truly think he would leave her alone? And in this condition?

Cursed woman! Why could she not simply tell him the truth? After all, she did not know that he was her husband. Why should she fear to upset him if she revealed the truth about the man named Aiden? Why could she not simply be honest?

"Did he leave ye?" Garrett asked again, feeling her chin begin to quiver. Still, her eyes were as steely as before, and a part of him was impressed by the strength she showed. "Did he leave ye, Lass?"

A small sob escaped her throat before a lone tear rolled down her cheek and onto his hand. "He was taken from me," she whispered, her voice breaking. "Highwaymen took him."

Never would Garrett have expected her to answer thus. "He was taken," he repeated, a lump forming in his throat, one he could not dislodge no matter how often he swallowed. "Who was he to ye? Who...who *is* he to ye?" Again, he tried and failed. "Did ye...do ye love him?"

Longing stood in her eyes, bright and clear, and yet, a cloud descended upon her face before the steel returned to her gaze. Her eyes hardened, and her lips thinned before she pushed his hand away, removing it from her chin. "I've answered your question," she hissed, her lips quivering. "I will tell you no more."

Garrett gritted his teeth. He was so close to the truth, the complete truth in all its devastation. He could not stop now.

Again, before he could speak, she cut him off though. "What reason do I have to trust you? Why should I-?"

"What reason?" Garrett growled. "I've done nothing but help ye, Lass. I-"

"But why?" she interrupted, her hands gesturing wildly as her anger overwhelmed the pain he had seen in her eyes. "Why would anyone do what you did?" She shook her head. "No, there has to be an ulterior motive. One you conceal. One you refuse to name."

"Blasted woman, I-"

"No gentleman would feel obligated to assist a stranger in such a way," she hissed, her eyes narrowed as though that would help her understand his motivation. "You've done more than anyone could have expected. It makes me wonder. It makes me wonder what you're hiding."

Garrett snorted, "What I'm hiding? What about-?"

"You cannot deny that you're keeping something from me," his wife snapped, her blue eyes ablaze as she stepped toward him, an accusing finger pointed at his chest. "You're not being forthright. You're concealing something, and I demand to know what it is!"

Staring down at her, Garrett suddenly found himself reminded of the night he had first laid eyes on his wife. She had sat in the taproom of the inn, a drink in her hand and a scowl on her face. A group of men had been crowded around her. However, as she had begun to lament about what insufferable beings men proved to be, the small crowd had quickly dispersed.

Only Garrett had remained, drawn to the fire in her eyes.

Words had flown from her mouth without pause, and as much as he had tried to make himself heard, to have her notice him, see him, she had been too lost in her tirade. Outrage over having been abandoned in Gretna Green had made her blind to everything around her, and he had known from the way her eyes had glazed over that she was barely aware he was right in front of her.

Now, here, she *was* seeing him. Her blue eyes held his, demanding an answer, and yet, her mouth never ceased speaking as though she, too, did not know whether or not she truly wanted to know. Therefore, Garrett did what he had done then, almost a year ago.

Reaching for her, he pulled her into his arms and his mouth closed over hers, cutting off her words.

Instantly, she stilled, and he could feel her surprise in the way her body tensed in his arms.

Still, he did not retreat. Instead, he deepened the kiss, one arm holding her tightly against him while the other traced down the line of her jaw until it settled in the nape of her neck.

He kissed her the way he had kissed her before, the way they had kissed before. His lips knew hers. His hands were familiar with the terrain of her body. And yet, it had been a long time.

Overwhelmed by the feel of her, Garrett barely noticed when her body softened in his arms. Her mouth opened, and she returned his kiss, her hands tentatively travelling up his chest. A soft moan escaped her lips, and he groaned deep in his throat, daring to hope that despite everything she was still his.

Then she broke their kiss, and her eyes stared up at him, wide and deep, the blue in them more intense than he had ever seen it before. "How...?" Her eyes narrowed in confusion as she tried to put into words what her heart had just realised. "This...this was not our first kiss, was it?"

Still holding her tightly in his arms, Garrett shook his head. "It was not."

A rush of air escaped her lips, and her eyes blinked rapidly. "How?"

Caught up in her confusion about this stranger who knew her better than anyone ever had, Claudia did not see his intent before it was too late. She saw his gaze shift lower and touch her lips a mere second before his mouth claimed hers.

Shock froze her limbs, and yet, the touch of his lips upon hers stirred something deep inside her.

A memory.

Only, like in her dream, this memory did not come with images. She did not see his face. Perhaps a faint shimmer of his green eyes looking into hers. But nothing more.

What she remembered was the feel of him. He felt...familiar. So very familiar. His hands on her, gentle, and yet, powerful. His mouth on hers, caressing, teasing. She felt her heart leap with joy as he held her close.

She felt safe and...loved.

Without thought, Claudia's body responded to him, to the sensations he invoked within her. She kissed him back, and it seemed as though her lips knew exactly how to meet his, how they fit together. She moaned at the familiarity of their encounter and heard his answer in the low groan, rumbling deep in his throat.

Then she pulled away, staring up into his face. A face that no longer seemed to be that of a stranger. He looked as he had before, and yet, when their eyes met, it was as though she was taken back to a time... when they had met before. A time when they had known each other. "How...?" she gasped, overwhelmed by the emotions and thoughts pulling her in all directions. "This...this was not our first kiss, was it?"

He shook his head, and his arms tightened on her as though he feared she would slip from his grasp. "It was not."

The breath she had been holding escaped in a rush, and she blinked her eyes, trying to clear her head. Was she dreaming? "How?" she asked once more, not certain what exactly it was that she wanted to know when another memory drew her attention.

A memory only a day old.

Again, Claudia saw the faint light spilling out of the tavern. She heard men stumbling along the street, their voices slurred. She felt her skin crawl with what lay ahead.

And then *he* had come.

Blinking, she looked back up at Garrett, her eyes focusing on his.

"When you came to my aid in London," she whispered, shock tinging her voice, "you asked if I truly meant to pretend that we had never met before."

Holding her gaze, Garrett nodded.

A cold shiver went down her back. "We've met before," she whispered, staring up at him for confirmation.

"We have."

"And you did not mean the ball, did you?"

He shook his head.

She swallowed, and her gaze drifted lower, touching his lips. "We've kissed before."

"We have," he replied, a hint of wickedness in his eyes as he grinned at her. Still, it seemed that he, too, was overwhelmed by everything that had passed between them and sought to lighten the burden by pretending that it did not exist. "Do ye not remember, Lass?" he asked, and she could see the tension that held him as he waited for her answer.

All of a sudden, Claudia realised that the fact that she had forgotten about him pained him greatly. He cared for her, remembered everything there was to know about her while she had not even been able to recall his name.

Guilt stole into her heart, and she smiled up at him. A peace offering. "Yes and no," she finally replied. "My mind cannot seem to remember, but when you kissed me..." Shaking her head in disbelief, she stared up at him. "Would you kiss me again?"

He chuckled, and the corners of his mouth rose into a dazzling smile. "How could I refuse such a request?" he whispered as his gaze darted to her lips.

Unlike before, he moved slowly now. His eyes remained on hers as he leaned down, and she could feel his warm breath teasing her lips, speaking of the fulfilment of a promise. His arms tightened on her, pulling her ever closer, as his eyes held hers captive.

Only in the last moment before his mouth touched hers did Claudia close her eyes.

His warmth engulfed her, and as her lips began to tingle at the feel of his, something stirred in a far and distant corner of her mind.

Flashes streaked across the blackness that had always blocked her view, refusing to allow her the knowledge of what had occurred.

Responding to his kiss, Claudia strove against him, reaching for the memory that lurked on the horizon of her conscious mind. She knew it was there. She could feel it. And yet, it always retreated out of reach whenever she came close. It was nothing more than a flash. There one second and gone the next.

Claudia gasped when she suddenly felt his hand move from its position in the back of her neck. The tips of his fingers grazed her jaw before travelling down the column of her neck, sending shivers into every region of her body.

Abandoning all thought, she turned to his touch with all her being, knowing beyond the shadow of a doubt that she had done so before. She felt his lips on hers, felt them move down to the line of her jaw until they reached her ear. She felt his teeth against her skin before he whispered to her.

It was the word from her dream, and her eyes flew open at hearing it from his lips.

No more than a murmur, she could feel it all the way to her toes. Her mind could not understand its meaning, but her heart knew it to be an endearment.

In a flash, images tumbled into Claudia's mind, and she gasped.

As she sank into Garrett's arms, her mind suddenly remembered her frustration when William had abandoned her in Gretna Green. She remembered seeing Garrett's green eyes across the taproom. She remembered speaking to him, drinking and dancing with him.

Pulling back, Claudia stared up at him as her mind conjured the moment he had first kissed her. Then, too, she had been cursing and yelling at him, barely giving him a chance to say a word, let alone two. She remembered the way his lips had curved into a wicked smile before he had seized her, kissing her speechless.

"It was you," Claudia gasped, unable to believe that after all this time she finally knew who she had been with in Scotland. "It was you. In Gretna Green, it was you."

For a moment, his eyes closed, and she could see utter relief falling over his face. Then he looked at her again and nodded. "Aye, Lass, 'twas me." Smiling, he brushed a gentle hand over her cheek and down along her jaw to her chin, giving it a little pinch.

Breathless, Claudia tried to grasp the faint images floating in her mind. "We...we kissed. We..." Breaking off, she stared up at him, her mind unwilling to provide more than it had. "Did we...?" Her body tensed as she held her breath.

When she strained away from him, Garrett pulled her back, his eyes holding hers without the smallest sign of hesitation or regret. "Aye, we did, Lass. A lot happened that night, and it drove me nearly mad that ye did not remember."

Closing her eyes, Claudia pushed his hands off, and this time he did release her. She staggered backwards, her heart and mind overwhelmed. The thought that she had been intimate with this man, a man she had not been able to remember until a moment ago, knocked the air from her lungs.

Glancing up at him now, Claudia could remember bits and pieces, but there was still something that eluded her. They had kissed and danced and laughed, but how had they ended up in the room where she had awoken the next day? And why had he not been there? If he had, then-?

The blood froze in her veins, and her right hand fell down to rest on her flat belly. *Aiden!* Her heart and mind screamed, picturing the beautiful face of her son. The son she had had to give up because she had been foolish. Because she had shared a stranger's bed.

But he was no longer a stranger, was he?

Lifting her gaze, Claudia looked at Garrett, shock freezing her tongue when she realised that she finally had her answer.

At least one.

Now, she knew who her child's father was.

Chapter Sixteen

UNSPOKEN WORDS

S tanding back, Garrett watched his wife. He saw her mind race as her pale blue eyes darted around the room, unseeing, before staring into the distance, her inner eye too preoccupied with what she had just learnt. Her cheeks were pale, and her hands still trembled as she blindly staggered about the room.

"Do ye truly not remember?" Garrett asked, but his voice held no accusation. Seeing how distraught she was, he felt his heart soften. Perhaps she had had more to drink that night than he had thought. Perhaps it had truly erased him from her mind. From the look in her eyes, it was clear that she was still in shock, that she had truly not known. Still, considering everything that had happened, he had to ask.

Swallowing, she stopped in her tracks. Her eyes blinked before they turned to him, focusing on his. Then she shook her head. "I remembered nothing between arriving in Gretna Green with William and then waking up the next morning." For a brief moment, she closed her eyes. "I've been wracking my mind ever since, trying to remember. Sometimes I saw things in my dreams, but nothing tangible." Tears glistened in her eyes, and Garrett could see the pain she had been through. "I remembered the feel of your hands," she whispered, her eyes drifting over his body as though to familiarise herself with him again. "The feel of your lips on mine. I remembered the words you whispered to me without knowing what they meant." She inhaled a deep breath, blinking away her tears. "I remembered all that, and yet, nothing that could have told me who you were. If I had..." Her voice broke off, and yet, her gaze remained on his.

Silence fell over the room as they looked at each other. Her eyes studied his face and then slid down to his shoulders and farther over his chest. A slight blush came to her cheeks before she dropped her gaze, suddenly unable to look at him.

"What is it, Lass?" Garrett asked, taking a careful step toward her.

For a second, she pinched her eyes shut before her chin rose, and she looked at him once more, a hint of shyness in her blue gaze. "It is strange for me to know that...we have been intimate with each other, and yet, I do not remember."

A smile teased the corners of Garrett's mouth, and he chuckled when he saw her blush deepen. "I've never seen ye blush before," he whispered, gazing down at her. "Ye've always been so certain of who ye were and what ye wanted."

A smile claimed her lips, and he could see a touch of pride gleaming in her eyes. "You do not know what it means not to remember, to have a part of yourself that is lost to you."

Garrett drew in a slow breath. "Do ye want to remember?"

Suppressing a grin, she dug her teeth into her lower lip. "I think I do, but...how? I've tried for months to remember. However, whenever I woke, my dreams vanished and only the faintest echo of them remained."

A teasing grin came to his lips as he reached out and pulled her back into his arms. "Ye remembered when I touched ye, Lass, when I kissed ye." Perhaps if she remembered everything that had happened that night, it would loosen the hold that other man had on her. Perhaps she would remember that she had loved him that night.

Her eyes widened slightly when understanding found her. However, instead of dropping her gaze or blushing even more, a dazzling smile claimed her lips and her eyes shone like two stars in the night sky. "I see," she whispered, her gaze dipping lower and touching his lips.

Feeling his body begin to tingle with anticipation, Garrett lowered his head towards hers. "Ye have to admit 'tis a sound plan," he chuckled, delighting in the hint of wickedness that came to her eyes.

Smiling, she ran her hands up his arms and onto his shoulders. "I find myself unable to disagree, Mr. MacDrum-"

Suddenly, her voice broke off, and her eyes went wide as though someone had struck her. Her body tensed, and for a moment, she stared up at him in shock. Then her body reawakened, and she shoved hard against his chest, her eyes narrowing in anger, and yet, her face paled until she was as white as a sheet.

Feeling his heart thudding in his chest, Garrett tried to understand what had happened. "What's wrong, Lass?" he asked, reaching for her, but she shrank away, her eyes hardening as she looked at him.

"You...you spoke of your wife," she stammered, shaking her head as she backed away from him. "You said you were looking for your wife." Her eyes closed. "Oh, God, you're married."

Sighing, Garrett stepped toward her, relieved that finally all would be out in the open. "Listen, I-"

"Don't touch me!" she hissed, crossing to the other side of the room. Still shaking her head in disbelief, she stared at him with accusing eyes. "I cannot believe this. I...I slept with a married man. I..." Her jaw clenched. "Is this why your wife left? Because you were unfaithful to her?"

Overwhelmed by the absurdity of this conversation, Garrett inhaled a deep breath before he approached her again. "Listen, I-"

"Was she at the inn?" Claudia interrupted, her eyes shooting daggers at him and her lips twisted into a hateful snarl. "Was she there? Did she see us together? Is that why she left?"

"Will ye let me explain?" Garrett growled, grabbing her wrist and pulling her toward him. "I swear I'll-"

"Let go!" his wife snapped, completely unaffected by the way he towered over her. Courage and determination shone in her eyes, and Garrett knew that she was in no mood to listen. "Was she there? Or did she hear of it later? Is that why she-?"

Fed up, Garrett yanked her forward and cut off her accusations with a desperate kiss. He held her to him with an iron grip as fear surged through his being that she would not listen, that she had made up her mind and would not hear a word he could say in his defence. She was as stubborn as a mule, and he knew he had to break through her defences before she closed her heart to him for good.

To his utter surprise, she answered his kiss as she had before. Her body softened, and her lips met his with equal fervour, demanding as much as giving. Unfortunately, it seemed to be no more than her body's desire for him, something instinctual, for a moment later, she began to struggle in his arms.

Her hands balled into fists, and she shoved against his chest, trying to free herself, determined not to be affected by him.

Garrett marvelled at her strength, for he doubted he would have been able to stop himself if she had been the one to kiss him like this, wanting him in her arms.

"Stop!" she snarled, straining as she tried to hold him at bay. "Stop kissing me!"

Not releasing his hold on her, Garrett glared down into her face. "Then shut up!" he growled, relieved when she finally ceased struggling. Her eyes narrowed as she looked up at him. "Shut up so I can talk, or I swear I shall kiss ye all night."

"Fine," she relented, and he could feel some of the tension leaving her body. Still, she held herself away from him. "Say what you will, but it does not matter." With her lips twisted into a snarl, she glared up at him. "You don't matter," she hissed. "All that matters now is that I find Aiden. Say what you wish, but I do not care."

Gritting his teeth, Garrett shoved her away as red-hot jealousy gripped his heart. His hands balled into fists, and as the pressure built inside him, he spun on his heel and let them rain down onto the door to her room. Dull thuds echoed through the stillness as the wood shook with impact.

Garrett's breath came hard and fast before resignation fell over him, and he rested his forehead against the door, panting as he closed his eyes. "Will ye never forget about him?" he whispered, feeling suddenly exhausted. Even though he had been searching for her for so long, he would never have expected this.

"Never," she said from behind him, her voice still tinged with anger and resentment.

Unable to even look at her, Garrett yanked open the door before slamming it shut behind him. Then he strode along the corridor, his boots thudding loudly on the floorboards, and headed down to the taproom and ordered himself a drink.

His body ached with the struggle inside, and he sank onto a chair and stared into the dancing flames in the hearth. Why on earth had he not simply told her the truth? He wondered. But would she even have believed him? She was as stubborn as they came, and if she did not want to see something then there was no changing her mind.

Then what? Ought he give up? Return home and forget about her? As much as he wanted her, would it not be better to give her up than to force her into a marriage to him when her heart belonged to another? What was he to do?

Groaning, Garrett buried his face in his hands.

Chapter Seventeen

SUSPICIONS

After a restless night, Claudia pulled herself into the saddle the next morning. She had eaten quickly, her eyes constantly darting around the taproom. However, they had come up empty. Garrett had been nowhere in sight. Perhaps he had left in the night, finally giving up, and returned to London. She would be glad if he had, Claudia told herself, ignoring the painful stab to her heart at the thought of never seeing him again.

"He is married," she mumbled under her breath, reminding herself of his betrayal. "You'll be better off without him."

Patting her mare's back, she hugged her trusted steed for a quick moment, needing the feel of her warmth as last night's chill seemed to have settled in her bones, unwilling to leave. "Off we go," she mumbled and placed her foot in the stirrup, then pulled herself into the saddle.

As she turned down the road, heading north, another set of hoof beats echoed from behind her. Pulling up the reins, Claudia turned to look over her shoulder.

There he was.

Garrett.

His green eyes were hard as he looked at her, and yet, he was here, at her side, despite the scowl on his face. Anger still held him in its grip, but it was the utter sadness that stood in his eyes that squeezed Claudia's heart painfully.

Forcing her eyes to the front, Claudia tried her best to ignore the painful ache in her chest. But the more she succeeded, the more strongly she felt utter longing to be back in his arms, to have him smile down at her, to see his eyes glow when he looked at her.

Cursing her traitorous heart, Claudia dug her heels into her mare's flanks and quickly made her way down the road, hoping to put some distance between them. However, he would not allow her that reprieve. Only moments later, she heard the sounds of his approach and knew he was there.

Silent, but there.

Forcing her thoughts away from the man who rode beside her, Claudia reminded herself why she was here.

Her son. He was the one she needed to find. He was the one who mattered.

With her eyes on the road and her mind firmly fixed on the task at hand, Claudia found that time passed quickly, and they covered more ground than she would have expected. Around midday, the next inn appeared on the horizon and Claudia wondered what she would learn here.

Sliding off her mare, she did not toss her reins to her silent companion, but instead tied them to a post out front. Then she headed inside.

With every word exchanged with the innkeeper, Claudia's sense of a deja-vu grew. He spoke the same words and gave the same answers as the others before him. No more and no less. Indeed, she felt like Gretel following a trail of breadcrumbs. But where would they lead her? And who had left them for her?

Back in the saddle, Claudia mulled over the question of who might have taken her son for it seemed to become clearer with each stop that the man who took him was known to her.

Her cousin, Mr. Lambert, had spoken of two attackers; whereas, the innkeepers insisted that it was only one man and a babe. Whoever that man was, had he merely hired the other to help him abduct her son? Had that other man been paid and returned to his life?

If that was indeed the case, then there was only one man she needed to uncover. As he was not after ransom, she wondered what it was that he wanted. Clearly, he did not want to keep her son for himself, to raise as his own with a wife who might not be able to bear him any children. If that was the case, he would not have left all these breadcrumbs for her to find.

And if he wanted her to find him, then he had to be someone she knew. Someone who knew her. Someone who knew about her son.

Since her brother had gone to great lengths to hide her condition and keep the existence of her son a secret in order to allow her to return to society and make a favourable match, only a handful of people knew Aiden even existed. Apart from a few old friends, only trusted servants whose assistance they had required had been told.

Out of nowhere, her mind conjured an image of a young footman. A man who had come to Farnworth Manor and worked diligently to prove himself to the family. Eventually, Claudia's brother had entrusted him to watch over her as Richard constantly feared that she might do something foolish.

Gritting her teeth, Claudia shook her head as she remembered the time she had spent locked away, her every step watched. And yet, she could not blame her brother. At least not now. He had only done what he had deemed right, and she *had* given him cause to distrust her, running off to Gretna Green and then turning up unmarried and with child.

Could it have been him? Claudia wondered. Mr. Adams?

As diligent and trustworthy as he had appeared, later they had discovered his true identity when he had tried to poison Richard at Christmas. He was in fact the illegitimate son of their father's elder brother. Had he been born in wedlock, he would have been the one to inherit the title and not Richard. Unfortunately, he had been the child of his father's mistress, a bastard.

Like Claudia's own son.

Learning of her circumstances, he had somehow thought of himself as her champion, blaming her brother for all her troubles. And so, he had tried to take Richard's life...in order to protect her.

Claudia frowned. Could it have been him? It was certainly not far-fetched to think that he would have had the motivation to take her child and then lure her to them, hoping...? What exactly did he think he could accomplish by doing all this?

But then Claudia shook her head, remembering that Mr. Adams had been handed over to the authorities. He was awaiting trial or had already been tried-she could not be certain as her mind had been elsewhere these past few months. If he had already been tried, he could already be dead, hanged for his crime, or in prison or shipped to the colonies.

If not him, then who?

Closing her eyes, Claudia sighed as her mind came up empty.

Chapter Eighteen

A SILENT VOW

L ater that afternoon, they stopped at a stream to water their horses. It wound leisurely through the countryside, its banks lush and green, and wildflowers growing everywhere. The sky was a brilliant blue, dotted with fluffy white clouds, like a family of rabbits chasing one another in the meadow.

Garrett jumped out of the saddle, stretching his legs before he walked over to his wife.

Sighing at the beautiful sight before her, Claudia made to drop to the ground when she found him standing there, holding up his hands to assist her. For a moment, her eyes held his and she inhaled a slow breath before she dropped her gaze to the ground. "I can do this on my own," she whispered, no anger but rather determination in her voice.

Hope flared in Garrett's heart that she might not be as immune to him as she wanted to be. "I insist," he said, his voice strong but with a teasing tone to it.

For a short moment, he thought to see her lips curl up before she forced her features back under control. "Fine," she mumbled. Without meeting his eyes, she leaned forward and slid into his arms.

Garrett heard her suck in a sharp breath when her chest came to rest against his, and he gently allowed her to glide to the ground. Still, his arms remained where they were, holding her against him, forcing her to acknowledge him if she wished to be released.

"Unhand me," she whispered, keeping her gaze somewhere below his collar bone. "Please."

The pleading tone of her voice squeezed Garrett's heart, and yet, he knew if he granted her request they would eventually lose one another. He could not allow that to happen. He would not give her up without a fight. He knew he would come to regret it for the rest of his life.

"Why do ye fight me, Lass?" he asked in a whisper, his hand gentle as he lifted her chin, forcing her to look at him.

The blue in her eyes was filled with sadness, and she blinked them rapidly to will back the tears that lingered. "I have to," she whispered back, her strength falling from her like a heavy cloak.

Lowering his head, Garrett placed a gentle kiss on her forehead. "There's something between us," he whispered, urging her to look at him. "I know ye can feel it. Ye gave in before, why not now?"

One of her hands rose and closed around his wrist as he held her chin in his grasp. "It was a mistake," she said, her eyes unblinking as she looked at him. Then her hand tightened its hold and removed his hand from her face. "It was a mistake, and I will not make it again." Then she pushed past him, took her mare's reins and walked toward the stream.

Giving his gelding free rein, Garrett followed after her, willing himself to remain calm despite the turmoil in his heart. "I've asked ye this before," he said, seeing the way her shoulders tensed as he spoke, "but ye did not answer me. So, I'll ask ye again." He inhaled a deep breath, preparing himself for the worst. "Do ye love him? That man, Aiden?"

A sob left her lips, but she did not turn to look at him. "With all my heart," she whispered, and Garrett fought the overwhelming need to crumble into a thousand pieces.

When she finally looked at him, tears were streaming down her face, and despite his own pain, Garrett's heart ached for her. Never in his life had he seen such sadness before. And yet, a part of him sensed that at least some of her tears were for him.

As they stood facing one another, Garrett realised that there was one thing he had not asked her. Swallowing, he stepped forward, his gaze intent on hers.

Seeing his approach, his wife turned her head away, then pulled on her mare's reins and tried to stalk past him. However, he caught her arm and pulled her back. "Please let me go," she all but begged, and Garrett's heart nearly stopped at seeing her so vulnerable.

"I canna do that, Lass," he whispered, once more forcing her chin up so she would look at him. "There's something else I need to ask ye, and I need ye to be honest for my sake as well as yer own. Will ye promise?"

He felt her jaw tense as she weighed his words. Then she nodded.

Garrett swallowed, feeling his heart beating wildly against his ribs. "Do ye feel something for me, Lass?"

As soon as the words had left his lips, she dropped her gaze and began squirming in his arms, struggling to free herself.

"Ye promised," Garrett reminded her, a small smile claiming his lips when he saw how she fought to ignore the truth, to pretend that there was nothing in her heart that felt for him. "Ye promised."

Her blue eyes met his then, and there he saw everything he needed to know.

His hand slid from her chin to the nape of her neck, and this time when he lowered his head to hers, she did not fight him, but lifted her head to receive his kiss.

For a long time, they stood in the clearing, their arms wrapped around each other and their lips touching, gently and carefully, testing the bond that connected them. "I know that ye're torn, Lass," Garrett whispered, tucking a wild curl behind her ear, "but know that I willna give up." His arms tightened on her. "We were meant to find each other, and I willna let ye go without a fight."

Tears misted her eyes, and for a short moment, her lips curved up into a hesitant smile. Then she sobered and stepped out of his embrace, her head down as she walked past him.

Turning to watch her mount her mare, Garrett drew in a shuddering breath. As devastated as he had been the night before, now he had hope. She did care for him. He had seen it in her eyes and felt it in her kiss.

As he gathered up the reins of his gelding and pulled himself into the saddle, Garrett vowed that he would reclaim his wife's heart. He wanted her to want him, and not remain by his side because she found herself tied to him.

Smiling, he watched her urge her mare back onto the road. "I swear, Lass, I willna make it easy for ye to refuse me." Then he spurred his horse on to catch up with her.

Chapter Nineteen
RETURN TO GRETNA GREEN

As they rode across the border into Scotland, Claudia found Gretna Green to be an adorable little village, settled into green hills. It looked different in the daylight as it touched the few clay houses, the parish kirk and the large inn where she had awoken almost a year ago with no memory of what had happened the night before.

Shaking her head, she sighed. Why did life lead her back here? Was there a connection between her failed elopement and her son's kidnapping? Never would she have thought to set foot into Gretna Green yet again.

Still, here she was, riding side by side with the man with whom she had shared that fateful night. The man who was her son's father. The man who seemed determined to claim her heart.

Even though he already had a wife.

What did he want from her? Did he truly think she would ever agree to be his mistress?

Looking about her, Claudia felt distant memories stirring. Faintly, she remembered the small village, the smell of the river nearby, the cheers from the inn rising into the night sky.

Pulling up the reins, Claudia slid out of the saddle, her eyes unable to leave the large inn where countless couples had been wed in a simple, yet life-altering ceremony. And yet, even without a ceremony, sometimes life changed abruptly, catching one off guard and turning the world upside down. Was her son here? Claudia wondered, feeling the heart ache at the thought of his little hand wrapped around her finger. Or would she find yet another clue? Where would these clues end? Or would she forever follow her son across the world, always hoping but never finding him?

"Go on inside," Garrett spoke out from behind her. "I'll see to the horses."

She heard his boots churn on the ground as he stepped forward and took her mare's reins from her hand, his tall frame momentarily blocking out the sun. She lifted her head to thank him, but found her words cut off when his lips claimed hers in a quick, but thorough kiss.

Despite her shock, Claudia could not help but admit-at least to herself-that this gesture of affection felt overwhelmingly normal as though they were an old married couple who had spent the past twenty years with one another and were still in love. As though his lips belonged on hers like the sun belonged up in the sky.

When Garrett pulled back, a small grin stood on his face. "Do ye remember this place, *mo chridhe?*" He briefly turned his head and looked at the comparatively tall structure of the inn. "I spent the best night of my life here," his green gaze returned to her, "with ye. Never forget that." Then he stepped back and guided their two horses toward the stable, casting her another meaningful glance over his shoulder.

Staring after him until he was swallowed up by the large stable doors, Claudia felt her limbs tremble with the emotions that came rushing back. All day, she had done her utmost to distance herself from him, to gain control of her heart, to be reasonable as her brother had always demanded she had to be. And yet, one word, one kiss brought down her defences completely.

Mo chridhe, she whispered the word she had heard countless times in her dreams, but never knew what it meant. Again, Garrett had addressed her thus, and more than ever Claudia was certain that it was an endearment.

Had he called his wife thus as well? She wondered, trying to clear her head and force her heart to see reason. As much as she longed for him, there was no future for them. He belonged with his wife while she needed to find her son.

Their son.

Ought she to tell him? Claudia wondered. Clearly from the way he had spoken to her, he believed Aiden to be a man who had claimed her heart. A competitor in his own quest. If he knew the truth, would he ever leave her alone? Or would he claim her son, insist to raise the boy himself? Perhaps with his wife, should he ever find her?

Claudia felt her stomach turn, and so she pushed all these thoughts aside and hastened toward the door. There would be time to dwell on these things later. Now, she first needed to find her son before she could consider his future.

The moment she stepped across the threshold, her mind began to spin.

Certainly, there was nothing unusual about this inn. After all, she had seen her fair share in the past two days. To her right, there was a large taproom, crowded this time of day, while a line of new guests stood by the front counter, asking for a room or possibly for direction to the next anvil priest. The air that hung about the establishment was one of merriment and hope. Claudia saw smiling faces of love-struck couples unable to keep their eyes off each other.

Still, when her own eyes swept across the room, her heart jumped here and there, and images floated to the front of her mind. She remembered sitting in an equally crowded room, feeling lonely and abandoned, her heart broken, her hopes dashed. She remembered seeing piercing green eyes from across the room as well as her stubborn determination not to acknowledge them after the heartache she had just suffered. She remembered him approaching her, speaking to her, teasing her.

She remembered smiling up at him, unable not to.

Somehow he had broken through her defences even then. Before she had known what was happening, they had laughed and danced, shared a drink or two-after the ones she had already consumed on her own-and then...he had kissed her.

Kissed her breathless.

Speechless.

At that point, her mind grew hazy again.

Claudia caught glimpses of herself standing with him, holding his hand. She could still feel her lips moving, however, she could not recall what she had whispered. Or what he had said in return. There had been smiling faces around them, and then a cheer had gone up in the room.

And he had kissed her again.

Held her in his arms, his green eyes shining with love and devotion. Could that have been true? They'd known each other only a few hours. Could anyone truly lose their heart in so short a time?

While Claudia's mind reasoned that it was impossible, her heart disagreed, and she could not deny the warmth that claimed her every time she thought of Garrett. Even now when he was out in the stables, not far away, not for long, she missed him. There was something that urged her to his side, an invisible bond, as though that was where she belonged.

With him.

But she did not.

His wife did.

"Seems to be a busy time," came Garrett's voice from behind her, and Claudia flinched, her heart doing a little jump-less with surprise and more with joy. "Shall we have a bite first?"

Swallowing, Claudia nodded and followed Garrett into the taproom and to one of the few unoccupied tables. They ordered a hearty supper and ate quietly. Still, Claudia could feel his eyes on her, and whenever she would break down and look up, his lips curled up into a knowing smile. Her skin began to crawl with the way he looked at her, and she could feel the air grow heavy with words unspoken. Memories lingered everywhere, and she knew he could see their effect on her in her eyes. Everywhere she turned, she felt reminded of him, of them, of their short time together, of what they could have had.

Of what her heart still wanted.

"Wait here and finish yer supper, Lass," Garrett said as he made to get to his feet. "I shall get us a room. It'll only be a moment." And then he walked away toward the front counter, and his words echoed in her mind.

I shall get us a room.

Closing her eyes, Claudia rested her face in her hands, knowing that she ought to stop him, demand he get two rooms. Aware of her own weakness when it came to him, a wall between them seemed like the safest option. And yet, Claudia did not move, did not say a word, but followed Garrett through the crowded room when he returned to collect her.

The sun was slowly setting as they stepped into the small, sparsely-furnished room, and Claudia's heart almost stopped. Her gaze swept over the two lonely chairs set around a small table in the corner by the window and then drifted further to the bed at the back wall. "This is where I woke up," she whispered, feeling her hands grow cold as she remembered that morning almost a year ago. "Alone."

Behind her, Garrett drew in a long breath as he closed the door and then set her travelling bag on one of the chairs. "Aye, I'm sorry for that. I woke early and...went to speak to someone." He stepped around her and drew her cold hands into his warm ones. "I didna want to wake ye, Lass," he said, regret filling his eyes. "Ye slept so peacefully, and I thought to surprise ye with fresh food." He swallowed. "But when I returned, ye were gone."

"My brother," Claudia whispered, feeling her hands begin to tingle as they warmed at his touch. "He came to get me, to take me home."

Garrett nodded. "The innkeeper said as much. I was relieved to hear that ye were safe...at least, but I wish I could've taken ye with me."

Looking up into his eyes, Claudia could have groaned at the desire and devotion she saw there. Her heart ached, and she wanted nothing more than to be in his arms. "What was it that you said to me?" she whispered. "Outside when you took the horses."

"*Mo chridhe?*"

Claudia nodded. "I kept hearing it in my dreams, but I never knew what it meant."

A soft smile touched his lips, and he drew her into his arms, his green eyes never leaving hers. "It means 'my heart'."

Closing her eyes, Claudia all but sank into his arms as his words washed over her. For months, she had heard him whisper to her in her dreams, never knowing what he said. And now, here he was, right before her, a man of flesh and blood, warm and alive, not a ghost in the cold darkness of her chamber.

A weak sigh left Claudia's lips. "Did you call me that before? That night when...?"

When she dropped her gaze, his hand settled under her chin once more, gentle but insistent, urging her to look at him. "Aye," he whispered, his eyes dark pools as he looked down at her. The air around them glowed warmly as the sun drifted lower outside their window, its golden rays painting the world in beautiful colours. "Aye, I said that and more."

A tear rolled down Claudia's cheek as her heart and mind waged a war within her. What was right and what was wrong? Why did wrong sometimes feel so right? How was she to step away from him? Where would she find the strength-

The pad of his thumb gently brushed the tear from her cheek as Garrett leaned down and touched his mouth to hers. Like before in the clearing, it was a tender kiss, restrained and cautious, asking permission.

If he had grabbed her, his mouth hard on hers, kissing her breathless, Claudia might have found the strength to fight him, her innate stubbornness protesting out of habit alone. However, the gentleness and care with which he held her completely disarmed her, blocking out the small voice that whispered of a situation repeating itself.

Opening to him, Claudia kissed him back, her hands travelling up and meeting behind his neck as she strove to be closer. At her response, Garrett's restraint vanished. His kiss became more demanding, and his touch stirred new memories of a shared night long ago.

Lost in the images that flashed before her eyes, Claudia sank into his arms and allowed him to carry her to the bed. Gently, he set her upon the mattress, and she reached up to pull him down to her. Their bodies met, and she could not deny how right it felt to be in his arms. Passion flared, and reason stood in defeat, bowing its head to a deep longing that had grown each day of the past months and would no longer be held at bay.

Chapter Twenty

A FATEFUL NIGHT'S FIRST REVELATION

It was still dark out when Claudia began to wake from her slumber.

A smile hung on her lips, and she felt Garrett's warm flesh under the tips of her fingers. With her head nestled on his chest, she could feel his heart beat, slow, steady and reassuring as his arm held her to him tightly. Her eyelids began to flutter, and her limbs stretched as her mind slowly returned to the here and now.

Wrapped in Garrett's embrace, she was warm and content, feeling her skin hum everywhere he had touched her, and she snuggled closer.

In answer, his arm around her tightened, and he rolled onto his side, his green eyes finding hers. A slow smile tugged on the corners of his mouth before he bent down to kiss her once more.

Every fibre of her body ached for him, and she welcomed his affections and gave them back with equal measure, losing herself in the moment yet again.

When her mind cleared, Claudia could not say. All she knew was that the warmth of Garrett's touch suddenly was no longer able to hold her thoughts at bay. Her mind reawakened, and with it, the doubts and regrets and restrictions of the previous day returned.

Loud and clear.

Almost deafening.

He had a wife!

How could she have forgotten this? How could she have ignored this? It was a betrayal of the worst kind. Not only on his part, but on hers as well.

Somewhere out there was a woman with a broken heart because her husband had betrayed her, because he had been unfaithful to her, because he had taken another woman to his bed.

Her.

Claudia.

Cringing at the thought of what she had done, of what she had allowed to happen, Claudia groaned, pain and guilt chasing away the lingering feelings of warmth and contentment.

"Lass, are ye all right?" Gently, Garrett brushed the wild curls from her temple, his eyes seeking hers. "What's on yer mind?"

Closing her eyes, Claudia shook her head, unable to look at him. Then she shoved against his chest, suddenly anxious to put some distance between them. Was it not his touch that made her forget everything around her? The depth of his green eyes that made her long for something that she had no right to want?

Fleeing from the bed, Claudia found her shift lying near the foot of the bed and snatched it up. With trembling hands, she pulled it over her head, seeking to cover herself as the chilled night air rose goose bumps on her skin.

Sitting up, Garrett watched her, his forehead in a frown. "Talk to me, Lass," he whispered as he rose from the bed and stepped toward her.

Spinning around, Claudia forced her eyes to the other side of the small room. "Will you put something on, please?"

A low chuckle rumbled in his throat before she heard clothes rustling behind her back. A moment later, something soft descended upon her shoulders and she turned to find him wrapping the blanket from the bed around her. "Ye're shivering," he said, his arms seeking to pull her back into his embrace. "Let me warm ye."

"I'm not cold," Claudia insisted, relieved to see that he once again wore a shirt and breeches. "I'm fine." Retreating into the far corner of the room, she saw his eyes darken as he watched her, his mind no doubt wondering what had sent her fleeing from his bed.

Anger surged through her veins. How could he not know? Did it not bother him in the least that what they had just done had broken his marriage vows? Did he not care? If his wife meant so little to him, then why had he been searching for her all this time?

"Talk to me, Lass," he said once again, his jaw set determinedly as he looked at her.

Gritting her teeth against the shivers that suddenly seized her, Claudia shook her head. "I-I need to g-go," was all she could manage before she clamped her mouth shut.

Stepping into her path, Garrett gripped her by the shoulders, his face rigid, and yet, a hint of fear lurked in his eyes. "I willna let ye. Ye belong with me."

Staring up at him, Claudia laughed hysterically. "How can you say that?" she demanded, shaking her head in disbelief. "Release me! Now!"

His jaw tensed, and his lips pressed into a thin line. "No! Not until ye explain yerself."

"Explain myself?" Scoffing, Claudia shoved against him, but his hands held her like iron shackles. "My brother was right," she laughed, feeling hysteria threaten to claim her whole. "He was right. I have no self-control, no sense of right and wrong. I do what I want, and I don't even consider the consequences." Her throat closed up as tears rolled down her cheeks. "Perhaps he was right to restrict my choices, to give me no free rein, to lock me away."

Garrett's gaze darkened, and his hold on her lessened. "He locked ye away?"

"He was right to," Claudia whispered, "for I cannot be trusted to do the right thing. I've proved that yet again. Here. Tonight." Repulsed by her own weakness, her own character flaws, Claudia shoved against him once more, and this time, Garrett did take a step backward, his hands falling from her arms. "Do not touch me!" she hissed, stumbling backwards until her back collided with the wall.

Taking a careful step toward her, Garrett stopped in his tracks when she all but flinched. "Tell me what has ye so upset, Lass, and I swear I will help ye. I'll protect ye." His jaw clenched. "What has yer brother done? What has he done to ye?"

Again, Claudia laughed, knowing that he could not understand, and yet, unable to see the world through his eyes. "Nothing," she whispered, shaking her head. "He's done nothing but protect me."

A deep frown descended upon Garrett's face.

"It is I who has failed," Claudia sobbed as all her life choices came crashing down upon her.

Running off to Gretna Green with William.

Refusing to return home upon being discovered by his brother.

Ending up in a married man's bed.

Giving up her child.

Losing her heart to that man.

Perhaps the last one had not been a clear choice, but it had led her to where she was, back to the moment that had determined the past year of her life. "I'm an awful person," she sobbed, lifting her gaze to meet his. "I slept with another woman's husband." She swallowed. "Again."

At her words, Garrett closed his eyes, his jaw tensing. "Listen," he said, stepping toward her. "There is something I need to tell-"

"No!" Claudia yelled, backing away. "There's nothing to say. Nothing to explain. Nothing that would change what is." Shaking her head, she sidestepped him when he tried to reach for her yet again. "I'm a horrible person, and I've done something unforgivable."

"No, ye havena," Garrett objected. "Would ye calm down so I can explain-?"

"I need to go!" Storming toward the door, Claudia could only focus on one thought alone: to get away. "I need to be alone!"

"Will ye calm down?" Garrett roared, grabbing her by the arm and yanking her back against his chest.

Staring up at him, Claudia felt her skin crawl. "How can I? Tell me that! How can I calm down after what I've done?"

"Ye-"

"You're married!"

"Aye, to ye, Lass!" he ground out, his green eyes burning into hers. "To ye!"

Shock froze Claudia's body as she stared up at him, her mind slow to process what he had said, and yet, her heart rejoiced, unhindered by doubt or logic or the need to understand.

Only basking in the knowledge that he was hers after all.

Chapter Twenty-One

A STROLL DOWN MEMORY LANE

Looking down into her wide blue eyes, Garrett swallowed, trying to calm himself as he felt his pulse thudding in his neck. "I'm married to ye, Lass. 'Tis the truth. I swear it."

Her face grew frighteningly pale, and she remained stock still, her eyes beginning to water as she continued to stare up at him. Then she blinked, and tears spilled over and ran down her cheeks. Her lips moved then as though trying to speak, but unable to utter a sound.

"Here," Garrett whispered, afraid to spook her. "I can prove it to ye, Lass." Gently, he removed his hands from her arms and took a step back, praying that she would not turn and bolt for the door. Then he dropped his gaze to the floor and searched for his jacket.

For a terrifying moment, he could not find it, and the little hairs on the back of his neck stood on end with fear of what she might do. Luckily, a heart-stopping moment later, he spotted the garment half-hidden beneath the bed. Bending down, he retrieved it and reached into the inner pocket, withdrawing a folded sheet of parchment. Tossing the jacket onto the bed, he stepped toward her. "Here, look at this."

With shaking hands, she took a hold of the parchment, her eyes wide and her jaw quivering, and began to unfold it. Then her gaze dropped to the writing on the page.

"'Tis our marriage certificate," Garrett said into the deafening stillness of the room. "Ye signed it. Do ye see?"

From his vantage point, he could see her eyes tracing over the lines written there until they reached her signature. Seeing her own name, she suddenly clasped a hand over her mouth as a heart-breaking sob escaped her lips.

"'Tis true, Lass," Garrett said, gently placing a hand on her arm, praying that she would not push him away again. "'Tis true. Ye're my wife, and I'm yer husband."

Blinking, she looked up at him, fresh tears trailing down her cheeks. "How?" she gasped, her voice almost breathless with shock.

Taking her hand, Garrett guided her back to the bed and all but pushed her onto the mattress, fearing her legs might not hold her much longer. Then he sat down beside her, noting the way her fingers curled around the parchment in her hands as though holding on to a lifeline. "We met here, downstairs in the taproom," he began, his voice quiet, almost reverent, as he spoke of the moment that had changed his life. "Do ye remember that?"

Swallowing, his wife nodded. "I do," she whispered and then turned her head to look at him. "I remember seeing you. Not in detail, but..." She inhaled a deep breath as she tried to capture the memory of that night. "The way you looked at me, it...it frightened me."

"Frightened ye, Lass?" Garrett asked, a frown darkening his face as his body tensed with apprehension.

A soft smile flitted across her features, allowing him to draw another breath. "I don't know if I can explain it," she whispered, "but I think a part of me might have known even in that first moment that I would lose my heart to you." Almost shyly, she looked at him. "And that frightened me."

Relief spread through Garrett, and he smiled at her. "I know what ye mean. I felt it, too, as though something had hit me right in the chest. It was painful, aye, but also utterly compelling, drawing me to ye." He sighed, "What do ye remember after that? Ye said that ye remembered me kissing ye."

A smile drew up the corners of her mouth, and she traced the pad of her thumb over the spot on the parchment where he had signed his name. "I do remember that. You kissed me to silence me." A little laugh escaped her, and when she looked up at him, her blue eyes were glowing.

Never had she been more beautiful.

"Aye, I did," Garrett confirmed chuckling, "but 'twas not the only reason I did so. 'Twas nothing but a welcome excuse."

Again, she laughed, her eyes teasing as she looked at him. "Is that so? And what about yesterday? Then, too, you kissed me because-"

"Because I wanted to, Lass," Garrett interrupted her, his eyes holding hers, a wicked gleam in them. "For no other reason, but that I wanted to."

Smiling, she nodded. "I wanted to as well."

Garrett's eyes narrowed. "Is that why ye never let me speak? To get me to kiss ye?"

Again, her laughter echoed through the room. "I'm not admitting to anything," she said with a twinkle in her eye, reminding him of the woman he had met under this roof almost a year ago. "However, I have to say it is a fairly well-thought out plan. I might consider using it in the future."

"Will ye then?" Garrett asked, feeling his heart thudding against his ribs. "Share yer future with me?"

Her face stilled, and the look in her eyes sobered. "I want to," she whispered, hesitation in the way she dropped her gaze. "But I...I need to know what happened. Is this true?" Holding up their marriage certificate, she looked back up at him, her eyes slightly fearful as though she did not dare believe for fear of having her heart broken yet again.

"'Tis true, Lass," Garrett assured her. "It happened right here at the inn. Downstairs in the taproom. Ye told me about that cad who had abandoned ye here, and I thought to myself I'd better claim ye for myself before another might snatch ye away." Smiling, he shrugged. "I was certain I would regret it for the rest of my life if I let ye go, so I asked ye to be my wife; ye agreed and we were married by an anvil priest right there on the spot."

As he had spoken, her eyes had become distant, and he could see that a memory stirred within her. "I remember us facing each other, holding hands," she whispered slowly, tentatively. "Others were watching and then cheered when you kissed me." She blinked, and her gaze returned to him, a touch of awe in her blue eyes. "We're married."

Garrett nodded. "Aye, we are."

Rising to her feet, she began to pace the room, her eyes once again distant as her mind worked.

Garrett sat back, watching her, giving her the space she needed to feel at peace with what he had told her, with what her mind had finally chosen to reveal to her.

"You said," she suddenly spoke, her gaze returning to meet his, "that you were looking for your wife." A question clung to her words, and yet, she did not say more.

"I did," Garrett confirmed, rising from the bed to stand in front of her. "When I saw ye at the ball, and ye looked right through me, I..." He shook his head, grasping for words to explain how he had felt in that moment. "It knocked me off my feet. 'Twas as though the world had turned upside down, and nothing made sense any longer. I couldna believe that ye truly didna remember me." He sighed, hoping his words would not offend her. "I told myself ye lied because ye had come to regret yer decision and wanted to rid yerself of me. I was angry."

Inhaling a deep breath, she nodded. "I was angry, too, when I woke up and found myself alone. I thought that whoever I had been with did not care about me. I was hurt, and I felt foolish." Her eyes narrowed slightly. "Why were you not there when I woke up?"

"I had no intention of leaving ye," Garrett said, reaching for her hands. "I came to Gretna Green with two of my clansmen to retrieve a couple of lovesick fools who thought that running off together would solve all their problems." He chuckled. "I dinna expect to lose my heart that night, but ye swept me off my feet, and so my companions were left alone to handle something that was my responsibility." He sighed, relieved to see her gaze soften. "So, when I woke, I went to see them to apologise-we were set to return home that morning. They laughed and congratulated me. They told me to hurry as Cormag was expecting us back."

"Cormag?" she asked, a slight frown drawing down her brows.

"Our laird," Garrett explained. "He's a good friend of mine, but he has a clan to consider and so I needed to return." He sighed, remembering his shock when he had returned to their room to find her gone. "I went back to speak to ye and ask ye to come home with me, but ye were gone, without a note or a message. Now, I know why." Sighing, Garrett shook his head. "But back then, it hit me hard. I mean, I knew ye were safe because it was yer brother who'd come to fetch ye home, but I couldna help but wonder why ye had left without a word."

"I'm sorry," she said, her gaze gentle as she looked up at him. "I wish with all my heart that I could have, but..."

"I know, Lass," Garrett whispered as he pulled her into his arms and held her tightly. "I know that ye couldna. It wasna your fault. Perhaps I should've woken ye. Perhaps then we wouldna have lost one another for so long."

Sighing, she snuggled closer into his embrace, her head resting against his shoulder, her hands soft on the front of his shirt. "You said you were looking for your wife," she whispered, the fabric of his shirt muffling her words. "Did you come to England to look for me?"

Her shoulders tensed, and Garrett knew she was holding her breath, waiting for his answer. His heart rejoiced to know that she cared that much, that she had wanted him to come and find her. "Aye," he finally said, and she inhaled a deep breath.

Lifting her head off his shoulder, she smiled up at him. "I wish I had known."

Garrett nodded. "I wish I had known about ye as well, Lass. I..." He sighed, remembering months of wondering, of not knowing, of fearing the worst. "Well, frankly, it took weeks for the issue with the runaways to be resolved, and I couldna go to look for ye before 'twas. Cormag asked me to be present and use my influence to help find common ground. 'Twas a delicate matter, and it took longer than expected." Taking his wife's hand, he walked back to the bed and bade her sit down next to him. Then he simply held her hand in his, feeling the soft beat of her pulse as he looked up and met her eyes.

"When I went to England," he began, remembering only too well the hope he had harboured in his heart, "'twas as though ye'd vanished,

Lass. No one seemed to know where ye were. I even went to yer broth-er's estate and asked for ye, but I was told ye were travelling." He shook his head. "Where were ye, Lass? 'Twas as though the earth had opened up and swallowed ye whole. Ye weren't even in London for the beginning of the Season. A friend of mine helped me navigate the treacherous sea of London upper society and invited me to accompany him to many events. He said ye'd be there. Everyone I spoke to said ye'd be there. But ye weren't. All of London was abuzz with yer absence, whispering about ye and that cad who'd abandoned ye here. It drove me mad to listen, not knowing what was true and what not." Squeezing her hands, Garrett sought her gaze. "I know ye did not remember me or what happened between us, Lass, but where on earth were ye?"

Chapter Twenty-Two

A FATEFUL NIGHT'S SECOND REVELATION

Touched that he had searched the whole of England for her for so long, Claudia inhaled a trembling breath. Never would she have thought, dared to dream to be that important to someone, that he would still come for her after all this time. Never giving up.

Hanging her head, she remembered the past year and all that had happened. Of course, no one had told Garrett where she had been as her brother had kept her under lock and key in order to hide her condition. She had even left Farnworth Manor after Christmas and retreated to a smaller, remoter estate toward the end of her pregnancy. Crestwood House had been in the middle of nowhere, and it had served her well. No one had found out that she had given birth there.

At least no one of London's upper crust.

However, someone had to have found out. Someone who had then stolen her child and was now leaving bread crumbs for her to follow. Would she ever see Aiden again?

Glancing at Garrett, Claudia knew she ought to speak to him about her son. Their son. The thought pulsed through her being like a wildfire. Garrett was Aiden's father. He was her son's father, and he was her husband.

Ready to tell Garrett everything, Claudia suddenly froze when-belatedly-her mind put two very important pieces together, and the puzzle suddenly looked nothing like it had in the beginning.

Garrett was Aiden's father and her husband. They had gotten married here in Gretna Green almost a year ago, and Aiden had been born nine months later.

Claudia's eyes closed, and the air rushed from her lungs.

Her son was not illegitimate! He was not a bastard! He had not been born out of wedlock!

Claudia's hands began to tremble when she realised how differently her life-all their lives-would have turned out if she had known. If only she had known!

Never would she have had to give up her child. She could have been happy. They all could have been. After all, they were a family. They belonged together.

Her chin quivered when she turned to look at Garrett. Concern and incomprehension covered his face as he watched her, watched all these emotions play over her face. And yet, he remained quiet, giving her the space she needed to make sense of them.

Then doubt suddenly claimed her heart.

Garrett MacDrummond was a wonderful man, but did he love her? Had he truly come because he could not live without her? Or had it been more of an obligation?

Inhaling a deep breath, Claudia finally dared to admit to herself that her heart beat for him. He was the one man who had ever touched her in this way, made her feel like a rare woman and never tried to restrict her, to change her. No matter how aggravating he found her, he had never once demanded she be someone she was not.

Did that mean that he loved her?

"Lass?" he whispered, his hand gently squeezing hers. "What's on yer mind? Do ye not wish to tell me where ye were?" His eyes darkened, and Claudia could see pain and suffering, doubt and regret as well as the determination to hold them at bay and not demand she give him an answer.

Clearing her throat, Claudia rose from the bed and took a few steps back, needing room to breathe. "Before I can tell you," she began, "there's something I need to know."

Holding her gaze, he nodded.

"Why did you come for me?"

His eyes narrowed, and a dark frown descended upon his face. "Because ye're my wife."

Claudia swallowed, her hands tense as she wrung them. "I see," she mumbled, her gaze dropping from his as she tried her best not to keep her hopes up. "So, you came because we're bound to one another?"

Again, Garrett nodded, a hint of suspicion in his eyes as he slowly rose to his feet.

Nervous, Claudia took a step back. "I mean, you came because it was your duty to see to your wife, to-"

"I came," he said, and his voice was like a flash of lighting cutting through the clouds, "because ye're my wife, Lass." His gaze grew heated as he stalked toward her. "I came because every day that ye were gone, I felt as though half my soul was missing." His hands reached for her then, pulling her back into his arms. "I came," he whispered as his fingers grasped her chin once again, forcing her to meet his penetrating gaze, "because I love ye, and I have since the moment I first saw ye. I wondered if it might wane over time, but it hasna. I want ye today as much as I wanted ye then, if not more."

Staring up into his face, Claudia felt her knees go weak, and her heart beat so wildly in her chest that she feared it might break through her ribs. Could this be true? Was it possible to be this happy? To feel this complete?

The only one missing now was Aiden.

Against all odds, his parents had found one another again, and now, they needed to find him and bring him home. And then, Claudia vowed, they would never lose sight of each other again.

"Garrett," she began, her voice shaking as she fought for control. "There's something I need to speak to you about. There's something you don't know." Blinking back tears, she cleared her throat and took a step back so as not to have to crane her neck. Then she took his hands into hers and held his gaze. "I need to tell you about Aiden."

Instantly, the light vanished from his eyes and his hands tensed.

Garrett felt her words like a blow to his body, and his heart shrank away from the name he had come to loathe.

And yet, his wife's face was glowing as though she was bathed in sunlight. Utter joy rested in her eyes, and her hands squeezed his tightly, full of strength and hope.

Garrett hung his head. In the very moment he had confessed his love to her, all she could do was think of another man.

Steeling himself for what lay ahead, Garrett met her gaze, determined to know the truth once and for all. He would no longer hide and hope, no longer accept half-truths and believe what he wanted simply because it was what his heart desired. No, here and now, he would accept the truth-whatever it was-and then he would find a way to live with it. "Do ye love him?" he asked, surprising himself with his boldness, and yet, it was the one question that would determine his life from here on out.

When her smile deepened, Garrett released her hands. "I do," she whispered, awe in her voice as though her love for that man had surprised her as well. "I love him with all my heart and soul. He is my life, and I should never have given him up."

Gritting his teeth against the pain and disappointment that shot through his body, Garrett wondered why on earth she would look so elated when speaking to him of her love for another man. Could she not see what this was doing to him? Did she not know that this was destroying him? A moment ago, she had seemed so terrified of hearing that he did not love her, that she was only a duty to him, that he had only come because it was a husband's responsibility to look after his wife. Was it possible that he had misunderstood her?

"Garrett," she whispered, her face still glowing as she stepped toward him.

Unable to look at her, Garrett dropped his gaze, trying his best not to feel the way her hands ran over his chest and then up his neck. Her hands cupped his face, and he could feel her breath brush over his skin.

"Look at me," she whispered, her hands urging him to comply.

Swallowing, Garrett lifted his gaze.

The blue of her eyes deepened, and she smiled up at him. "Aiden is my son. Do you hear me? He's my son." Tears pooled in her eyes, but she blinked them away. "I know you thought I had given my heart to another, and I let you believe that to keep you at bay, but now," she swallowed hard, "I need you to listen to me."

Staring down into her eyes, Garrett felt suddenly numb. "Yer son?" he whispered, overwhelmed by this sudden revelation. Had she ever mentioned a son? Had he simply been a dolt and not been listening? Or had she truly kept this from him? How could she not have told him? "Ye have a son? Ye never mentioned-"

"He's yours."

If lightning had struck him in that moment, Garrett could not have been more stunned.

All the tension that had held him before suddenly fell from him. His arms were dangling limply by his sides. His jaw went slack as he stared at her, and his heart seemed to have stopped altogether. "Mine," he whispered, trying to swallow the lump that had settled in his throat. "How?" Blinking, he tried to focus his mind.

His wife heaved a deep sigh, and her voice was thick with emotions as she began to tell her tale. "After returning to England, I soon realised that I was with child. I told my brother-I didn't know what else to do-and he kept me hidden so that I could give birth in secret and then return to society as though nothing had happened."

Garrett's eyes widened as his mind began to catch up, slowly realising what she was trying to tell him.

"I was unmarried and with child," she said, sobs rising in her throat, "the ton would have eaten me alive. I would have been ruined. My son would have been a bastard, never to be received anywhere, always looked down upon." With pleading eyes, she looked up at him. "I didn't know what to do. But I knew I couldn't be reckless again. I had to think of what was best for him, of his happiness. He didn't deserve such a fate. As much as I wanted him, I couldn't do that to him, and so I agreed. I tried my best to keep myself separated from him throughout the pregnancy. I tried not to think about him, not to feel him. I tried not to care, but...but I couldn't." Tears poured down her face, and she let them fall. "No matter how hard I tried, I came to love him. I couldn't help it. Still, it didn't change what was, and so I brought him into this world, and then...I let him go." Her jaw quivered, and Garrett felt his own heart break. "I returned to London and tried to forget. I tried to pretend that nothing had happened, that he had never been." Shaking her head, she clenched her teeth. "But I couldn't. I couldn't forget him. He's my son. How could I've...?"

She broke down then, all her heartache pouring out of her. Garrett caught her as she sank to the floor, and together, they sat on the wooden floorboards, wrapped in each other's arms, and mourned the loss of their son.

Chapter Twenty-Three

NOTHING BUT THE TRUTH

S inking deeper into her husband's arms, Claudia allowed herself to break down as she had never done before. All her defences came down, and her heart ached with such acuteness that she thought it surely must break. All the pain and loss of the past year came pouring out of her, sobs wrecking her body as she clung to Garrett.

Dimly, she heard his voice, soft and gentle, as he murmured words of comfort into her hair, his hands brushing over her back and down her arms as he held her to him. Like in her dreams, she felt a sudden wave of warmth and love wash over her, and her sobs began to calm.

Brushing at her tears, Claudia lifted her head and her gaze swept over Garrett's face, seeing an answering look of pain in his eyes that she knew to be in hers as well. Shock still clung to his features, and he looked tense and rather pale as he tried his best to work through the chaos into which her revelations had plunged him.

For a long while, they sat on the floor, eyes locked, not saying a word. Then Garrett cleared his throat, one hand gently brushing over her cheek. "Where is he now? Yer...Our son," a gentle smile came to his face, "where is he?"

Bowing her head in defeat, Claudia swallowed hard as fresh fear squeezed her heart.

Garrett sucked in a sharp breath. "Where is he?" he said again, panic tinging his voice. His hand reached out and grasped her chin, bringing her gaze up to meet his.

The green in his eyes looked dark and thunderous, and the muscles in his jaw stood out as he clenched his teeth. "Ye said..." He took a deep breath, his teeth grinding together. "Ye said that Aiden," he spoke their son's name carefully, "that he had been taken. By highwaymen." His fingers tightened on her chin. "Where is he?"

Unable to keep fresh tears from falling, Claudia sniffled. "I don't know. I've been trying to find him. That's why I set out that night. That's why I came here."

Garrett closed his eyes and his face hardened, his lips pressing into a thin line as he fought for control. Then he looked at her again, his hands reaching for hers. "Tell me what happened. Everything."

Taking a deep breath, Claudia nodded. She began her tale the day she was parted from her son, telling him how she had returned to London a fortnight later, unable to bear the solitude at Crestwood House any longer. She told him how only a few days later her brother had told her that her son had been taken, that the carriage had been ambushed on its way to the boy's new family. She told him about speaking to Mr. Lambert, her cousin, about the nurse she had sought out and who had been able to recall that the highwaymen had mentioned an inn. She spoke to him of her brother's return from said inn and the heart-breaking conclusion that it had to have been a ruse by the highwaymen in order to throw anyone following off their trail.

"No one demanded ransom?" Garrett asked, his eyes narrowed as his mind worked to take everything in. "No letter arrived? No message delivered?"

Claudia shook her head, feeling her heart grow lighter at being able to share her heartbreak with someone who felt it as acutely as she did. "No, nothing."

Cocking his head, Garrett looked at her. "Why did ye go to that inn, Lass? Did ye not believe yer brother?"

Sighing, Claudia tried to explain the desperation she had felt that night. "It wasn't that I thought he was lying to me, but rather...I...I had to do something," she finally said, her eye suddenly dry as a new wave of determination washed over her. "I couldn't simply sit back and wait. It occurred to me that Mr. Lambert had believed that the nurse would not be of help, and so he never even spoke to her again. But then I went, and she was able to remember the name of the inn." Shrugging, Claudia looked at him. "I thought perhaps they'd overlooked something. I thought if I went myself, perhaps..." Again, she shrugged.

Understanding shone in Garrett's eyes as he squeezed her hand. "Ye did right, Lass. Ye went and ye looked for him as a mother would. I'm proud of ye."

Blinking back fresh tears, Claudia smiled at him, and for the first time since she had found out she was with child did she truly feel like Aiden's mother. She had said the words before, thought them before, and yet, it had not been until this moment that she could feel the bond between her and her son.

"What did ye find?" Garrett asked, drawing her attention back to him. "Ye spoke to the innkeeper?"

Claudia nodded. "I did, like my brother had, but while he found out nothing, the innkeeper told me that a man with an infant had passed through, travelling north."

Garrett's eyes narrowed. "I'm guessing the same happened at the next inns?"

"It did," Claudia confirmed. "It felt like someone had left bread crumbs for me to find as though these were messages for me alone, and when my brother asked, he was not told."

For a moment, Garrett remained quiet, his gaze distant as his mind worked. Then he met her gaze once more. "This feels personal," he whispered. "No ransom demand was made, and whoever took our boy is leading ye to them." He shook his head. "'Tis a man ye know, Lass. Perhaps someone who cares for ye and thinks he's doing this for ye."

"I've thought of that, too," Claudia said, wishing she had listened whenever her family had discussed the issue of Mr. Adams. If only she knew what had happened to him.

Garrett's eyes narrowed, and the hands holding hers tensed. "Ye know who it is, do ye not?"

Claudia inhaled a deep breath. "I might."

"Who is he?"

"He was a footman at my brother's estate."

Garrett's jaw clenched. "How well...did ye know him?"

Claudia scoffed, "I can see what you're thinking, and the answer is no." Slapping him on the arm, she shook her head. "He was nothing to me. I barely knew him. I barely noticed him. I was too preoccupied with..." Absentmindedly, her hand brushed over her middle, remembering the feel of her child.

"I'm sorry," Garrett said, his hand reaching for hers yet again. "I didna mean to suggest that-"

"Yes, you did," Claudia interrupted, feeling her blood boil. She grabbed him by the front of his shirt and brought them closer. "I know I did a foolish thing running off with William, but that was one time. I always tried to do what was expected of me, but that night, I..." Sighing, she closed her eyes, remembering. "I so wanted it to be real." Her fingers on his shirt loosened as she saw the green in his gaze soften. "I wanted to feel something, adventure, excitement, love. I wanted to feel something, something more than..." Shaking her head, she sat back. "I just wanted to feel."

Smiling, Garrett brushed a wayward curl from her forehead. "I know," he whispered, "and I'm glad ye did, Lass. Otherwise, we would never have met, and Aiden would never have been."

Pulling herself onto his lap, Claudia wrapped her arms around him, her eyes searching his. "I followed the wrong man to Gretna Green," she whispered, "to find the one I was meant to be with."

Garrett's eyes were dark as they held hers, and for once, there was no humour in them. His hands reached up and gently cupped her face. Then he brought her down to him, his lips touching hers with the lightness of a feather. "When I returned home after Gretna Green," he whispered then, his green eyes looking deep into hers, "Cormag wasna surprised to hear I was married. He said that Moira had seen it in her dreams."

Claudia frowned. "Moira?"

"People whisper that she has the sight," he explained, his lips coming back to brush against hers every so often, "that she sees things before they happen. Cormag told me she insisted he send *me* to retrieve the runaways."

"She knew I would be here?" Claudia asked, overwhelmed by the thought that destiny had guided their steps. "And he believed her? Is she his wife?"

Garrett chuckled, "Nah, she isna, but sometimes I wonder if he might want her to be." He shrugged. "He treats her differently than the rest of the clan. They meet her with distrust because..." He sighed, "Well, 'tis a long story, but he always stands with her no matter what, as though he knows more than the rest of us do. As though he trusts her."

Claudia smiled. "Perhaps they belong together...like we do."

"Perhaps," Garrett whispered against her lips before kissing her gently. "As much as I want to kiss ye, Lass," he murmured, "we need to find our son first." Smiling, he brushed yet another untamed curl from her face and tugged it behind her ear. "Tell me about this footman. Why do ye think it might be him?"

Nodding, Claudia forced her thoughts to return to one of the darkest moments of her life. "At Christmas, he tried to poison my brother."

Garrett's eyes widened with shock...and fear for their son.

"If it hadn't been for Evelyn, his wife, we would have lost him. She's a doctor, the best I've ever met. She saved his life."

"Why?" Garrett asked. "Why did he do it?"

"We didn't know it at the time, but later we learnt that we are related."

"Related?" Garrett growled. "He would kill his own kin."

Claudia sighed. "He is the son of my father's elder brother and thus ought to have inherited my brother's title instead of him."

"Then why didn't he?"

"Because he is illegitimate," Claudia explained, thinking of her own child and wondering what kind of life Mr. Adams had led. "He was the son of my uncle's mistress, and he never even acknowledged him. I believe he wanted to get back at the family who rejected him."

Garrett nodded, a glint of understanding coming to his eyes. "So, yer...situation reminded him of his own? Of his mother and himself?"

"I believe so. He wanted to free me of my brother because he thought Richard was forcing me to give up my child. He thought him cold-hearted and only seeking to protect his reputation." Despite many misunderstandings throughout their lives, Claudia now knew beyond the shadow of a doubt that her brother loved her dearly. "Richard decided for me because he knew I couldn't do it myself. But if I had told him that I wanted to keep my son, he would not have fought me. Especially then. Especially after Evelyn helped him...understand me."

"But I suppose Mr. Adams didna believe that."

Claudia shook her head. "I didn't speak to him after the poisoning, but I suppose it is very likely that he still believes as he did before. However, I'm not certain if it even can be him for my brother had him handed over to the authorities. Before I left for Crestwood House, I heard that he was to face trial. I'm certain he was convicted, but I don't know what happened to him after that."

Rubbing a hand over his face, Garrett exhaled loudly. "Perhaps he escaped. Perhaps he had help. Ye said that there'd been two men stopping the carriage?"

Claudia nodded.

"Of course, we canna be certain that 'tis him," Garrett admitted, "but I believe 'tis very likely. Somehow, he got away, but instead of running away and hiding, he came back and took yer child, and then he left clues so ye would find him."

"But how could he have known that I would search for him?"

A gentle smile came to Garrett's face. "'Tis what mothers do, Lass. 'Tis what mothers do." He sighed, "Perhaps 'tis a test to see if ye're worthy to be reunited with yer son, to see if ye would put him above yer own reputation, yer family, yer prospects."

Claudia felt her insides tense. "Do you think he will give him back to us?"

Garrett's shoulders tensed, and his lips thinned as he thought for a moment. "I dunno think so, Lass. For one, he doesna know about *us*, and I worry what he might do if he learns that we're married. It would destroy his carefully-laid out plan."

"What if I find him on my own?" Claudia asked, afraid to discover her son's whereabouts only to lose him all over again. "What if I go to him on my own and-?"

"I dunno think he's planning on returning the boy to ye, Lass," Garrett objected, his eyes dark with anguish. "It wouldna make sense to take the boy and then simply return him. Even if ye were to keep him, he would still be a bastard and face the same life Mr. Adams has suffered." Gritting his teeth, Garrett shook his head. "Nah, I dunno think he will return our son to ye. I think he wants to take ye both away."

Chapter Twenty-Four

A MESSAGE

Claudia's eyes opened wide with shock. "Take us away? But where? How?"

Willing himself to remain calm despite the fear and pain rolling through his middle, Garrett shook his head. "I dunno know, Lass, but I think he has a plan where to hide ye, where to live. I think he plans to keep ye with him." He swallowed, pulling her closer into his arms. "Do ye think he might have taken a shine to ye?"

A gust of air rushed from her lungs as her eyes widened. "That is ridiculous. I barley spoke a word to that man. He only ever followed me like a shadow. On my brother's behest, of course."

Pressing a quick kiss to her lips, Garrett felt his heartbeat slow a little. Even if Mr. Adams had fallen for her and was now under the illusion of turning her and their son into a new family for himself, at least Claudia had never looked at the man with love in her heart.

"Have ye had a chance to speak to the innkeeper downstairs?" Garrett asked, forcing his thoughts back to the task of locating their son.

Sadness came to his wife's eyes as she shook her head. "It was too crowded. He couldn't hear a word I was saying." Her eyes narrowed. "How did you get this room?"

Garrett chuckled, "I didna speak to him, Lass. I only tossed him a few coins, and he tossed me a key."

Suddenly rising to her feet, his wife looked down at him, impatience in her eyes. "We need to speak to him." Then she turned her head toward the window where a faint glow appeared on the horizon. "The sun is about to rise. I'm certain he will be up soon."

Nodding, Garrett got to his feet. "Get dressed, Lass," he said before a devilish gleam came to his eyes, "for I willna let ye walk out that door half-clad as ye are."

Returning his smile, Claudia went to retrieve her clothes. They both dressed quietly, exchanging a glance here and there. Garrett's heart rejoiced at the silent understanding that suddenly seemed to exist between them. Only a few hours ago, there had been doubts and questions building a wall between them, and now, he only needed to look at her to know what she was thinking.

Now, all they needed was their child, and then life would truly be perfect.

Their child!

Whenever that thought entered his mind, it still knocked the air from his lungs.

He had a son!

Once dressed, they rushed downstairs, and Garrett banged on a few doors-disturbing a maid or two-in the process of locating the innkeeper.

Grumbling, the old man finally appeared, scratching his head and mumbling curses under his breath. "Could ye not have allowed me a wee bit more sleep?" he said yawning. "The sun's barely up. This better be important." Apparently, in a village with only one inn, there was no need to treat their guests kindly as they had very little choice when it came to accommodations.

About to speak, Garrett thought better of it and stepped back, gesturing to his wife.

Nodding her head, Claudia approached the innkeeper. "I'm terribly sorry to have woken you. However, this is a truly important matter," she said sweetly, a dazzling smile on her lips to which the innkeeper was not immune.

Grinning back at her, he leaned closer. "What can I do for ye, dearie?"

"I need to know," Claudia began, her hands trembling, and she clenched them in the fabrics of her skirts, "if a man with an infant has come through here recently. The boy would have been only a few weeks old."

A frown descended upon the man's face before his eyes suddenly opened. "Are ye Miss Davenport then?"

Garrett's heart stopped, and he saw his wife's face turn ash-white. "Yes," she said almost breathless. "I'm Claudia Davenport. Do you have a message for me?"

Claudia MacDrummond, Garrett thought grimly, but with no small amount of pride. However, there would be time later to point that out.

Rummaging behind the counter, the innkeeper soon reappeared, an envelope in his weathered hands. "I was asked to hold this letter for ye, dearie. I'm sorry. I saw ye yesterday, but I didna catch yer name."

"It's all right," Claudia whispered, the smile on her face becoming more and more strained. "Thank you." Then she reached out a trembling hand and took the envelope. "Good day." Turning on her heel, she strode past Garrett back toward the stairs leading to the upper floor.

Hurrying after her, Garrett felt his heart beat wildly in his chest as fear and hope clawed at it for supremacy. Fast steps carried him up the stairs, and he closed the door behind them with a loud bang, his eyes fixed on his wife as she sank onto the bed.

Her eyes rose to meet his, and then she returned her attention to the envelope in her hand, ripping it open. Her breath came fast as her eyes flew over the parchment, and her face grew ever paler. "It is him," she whispered, her voice almost inaudible over the loud pulsing of his blood. "It's Mr. Adams."

Every muscle in his body tensed as Garrett watched his wife, saw the tears form in the corners of her eyes and felt her heartbreak as much as his own. "What does he write?" he asked, unable to control his need to know any longer.

Looking up through a veil of tears, she held the letter out to him. "Read for yourself."

Sucking in a deep breath, Garrett stepped forward and took the parchment. Then he began to read.

My dearest Miss Davenport,

I apologise for the heartache I have caused you. However, there was no other way to ensure your son's well-being. Let me assure you that he is well and that you shall be reunited with him soon.

I have no doubt that my deeds must seem confusing to you, but they were necessary. I assure you. This ruse was the only way to liberate you and your son from your brother's clutches. I had to be certain that you truly wished to have your son in your life and saw him as a blessing and not a curse. He deserves that and more.

As do you.

In my heart, I knew that nothing-not even your brother-could prevent you from coming after your child. You've shown true strength and devotion in following my leads, and I am proud to know that your little boy finds himself loved by his mother.

Meet me in Port Glasgow in two days' time. Do not worry. I shall find you.

My sincerest regards,

Maxwell Adams

With each written word, anger rose in Garrett's heart, and he crushed the parchment in his hand. His teeth grit together painfully as he cursed the man who would steal his wife and child and deem himself a hero for doing so. "Why Port Glasgow?" he asked Claudia, doing his best to silence his anger and allow rational thought to take over.

It was easier said than done.

"I do not know," she replied, her eyes darting to his and away from her own thoughts. "I've never been there myself. The only time I ever came to Scotland was..." She left the sentence unfinished, but a deep smile lit up her face and she stepped closer to him.

Cupping her face in his hands, Garrett kissed her gently. Then he sighed, holding her tight, as he tried to determine how to proceed. "There is only one reason he would ask ye to meet him in a harbour town, Lass," he said slowly, not wishing to frighten her. "He plans to take ye away on a ship. Perhaps to Ireland or the colonies."

A long sigh left his wife's lips, and she dropped her head, resting her forehead against his shoulder. "Do you think Aiden is safe?" she whispered, her voice muffled by the folds of his shirt. "Do you think he will harm him?"

Tightening his hold on her, Garrett closed his eyes. "I do believe that Aiden is safe right now," he said, praying with all his heart that he was right. "I dunno think Adams will harm him as long as he sees him as innocent."

"What if he finds out that he's not a bastard after all?" Claudia asked, lifting her head and meeting his gaze. "What then?"

"I dunno know, Lass."

"He must not find out," his wife said with vehemence as her spine straightened and she stood taller, her muscles no longer slack. "We will go to Glasgow, but once we reach the town, we'll go in separately." She glanced at the letter Garrett had tossed to the floor. "He wrote he would find me, so we don't know when he'll be watching. But he'll have to be. How else will he know where I am?"

A proud smile drew up the corners of his lips. "Ye've quite the strategic mind, Lass," he whispered, grasping her hands and holding them up to his chest, right above the place where his heart beat for her. Then he lowered his head, and his eyes held hers with silent intensity. "Are ye ready then, Lass? Or do ye need more rest?"

Inhaling a deep breath, Claudia nodded. "I'm ready," she said, her voice strong and full of determination. "Let's go get our son."

Before he allowed her to step away from him, Garrett pulled her into his arms once more, holding her tightly. He did not know what the next few days would bring. With any luck, they would see his wife and him reunited with their son. But what if something went wrong?

What if Mr. Adams somehow found out about him, Garrett? Would he see him as a threat to his plan? To how he saw the world? Would he no longer feel bound to protect Aiden and Claudia? Would he become a threat to them?

Garrett wished that there was time to send a message to his clan. After all, they did not know if Mr. Adams had help. Had he hired men to assist him in his plan? Garrett frowned. In all likelihood, he believed Claudia to have come alone as he had laid out these bread crumbs only for her. Perhaps he would not deem it necessary to seek assistance. Perhaps he was truly working alone.

Still, Garrett would have felt more at ease if he had a handful of men from his clan by his side. He had no doubt that Cormag would send help if only he asked for it. However, to send a message to *Seann Dachaigh Tower* would take too long. They needed to be in Glasgow in two days. There was simply no time.

His heart ached with doubts and uncertainty, and yet, there was no other choice but to take a step forward. There was nothing else to do but to go to Glasgow and do what he could to retrieve his son. To put him back in his wife's arms where he belonged.

Sighing, Garrett rested his chin on the top of Claudia's head. *My son*, he whispered silently to himself, his heart swelling with pride and joy at the thought of his little boy. If only he knew what he looked like. If only he knew what it felt like to hold him in his arms and feel his little fingers wrapping around one of his own.

But he would.

He would go and get Aiden back no matter what the cost, and he would look into his son's little face and he would know that it had all been worth it.

Aiden.

A beautiful name.

Chapter Twenty-Five

PORT GLASGOW

The weather was fine as they set out for Glasgow after a hearty breakfast.

A part of Claudia wanted nothing more than to race the distance, to urge her mare to a gallop and thunder along the road in order to reach Port Glasgow as fast as humanly possible. It was that side that ached for her son and knew nothing of caution and reason and consequences. The side that only desired to have him in her arms, to look upon his little face and know him to be safe.

Her body ached with actual physical pain, and Claudia was astounded by the bond she felt to the young life she had never even held in her arms.

Garrett, too, seemed lost in thought, and Claudia could only imagine how he felt. Within a short few moments, she had shared the news with him and made him a father. Father of a little boy who had been taken by a madman.

Certainly, it was enough to turn one's world upside down and throw one off balance. And yet, Garrett remained as steady and calm as before, despite the tension she saw in his shoulders and the line of his neck. Occasionally, he would smile at her or gently squeeze her hand in comfort and reassurance. Still, they hardly spoke as they continued along the road, each lost in thought, dwelling on their own hopes and fears.

"I thought it rained a lot in Scotland," Claudia remarked simply in order to have something to say, to hear his voice and be reminded that she was not alone. She gazed toward the horizon, the bright sun sparkling down at them from a brilliantly clear, blue sky before turning her gaze to meet her husband's. "Don't people often complain about the weather in Scotland?"

A low chuckle rose from his throat, and Claudia felt herself relax. "I wouldna know, Lass," he replied, the same relief in his eyes she felt in her own heart. "I canna say I've spoken to the English a lot about the weather. If they spoke to me about it, I must admit I wasna listening." His gaze deepened as he urged his gelding closer to her. "My thoughts were focused on nothing but finding ye."

Claudia sighed, "I'm sorry everything happened as it did. I cannot help but think if only I had remembered you. If only I had had at least a dim memory of you." She shook her head, thinking how easy her life would have been. "None of this would have happened."

"Dunno fret, Lass," Garrett said, his voice determined as he reached for her reins, bringing both their horses to a stop. Then he grasped her chin and slightly ducked his head in order to see into her eyes. "Ye couldna have known, and these thoughts only serve to make ye doubt yerself, to make ye feel lacking." He shook his head. "Nothing good can come from this. Ye must put it out of yer mind. I know 'tis not easy. Believe me." He sighed, rolling his eyes at himself. "I feel the same way, Lass. I keep thinking if only I hadna left ye. If only I had woken ye. If only..." Again, he shook his head, and she could see the depth of his regret. "It willna do us any good to think these thoughts. What is done is done. All we can do now is look ahead and go get our boy."

Warmth seeped into Claudia's heart as she smiled at him. "Our boy."

Garrett nodded, pride sparkling in his green eyes. "Aye, our boy." Then he leaned forward and captured her lips with his. "I swear I will do this for the rest of my life," he said grinning.

Claudia laughed, and a little weight was lifted off her shoulders. It felt good not to be alone. To have someone by her side who would stand with her, fight with her and was willing to risk everything to bring their son home.

Not until this moment had Claudia realised how alone she had felt embarking on her quest alone. How she had struggled to hold her doubts and uncertainties at bay. What if she failed? What would happen to her son then?

Now, she had Garrett by her side, and for the first time, Claudia wholeheartedly believed that she would get to hold her son in her arms after all.

Soon.

After allowing themselves and their horses a little rest at midday, they continued onward, relieved that fate-as well as the sun-was smiling on them. The roads were dry, and the air was fresh and warm when they finally drew near Port Glasgow in the late afternoon.

"I think I can smell the sea," Claudia whispered as she looked toward the horizon and past the harbour town lying at her feet from where they had stopped on a small hill. "The air moves much stronger here."

Garrett nodded. "Do ye remember what I told ye? Head into town, stay on this road and it will lead ye to a large inn, *The Golden Eagle*. Get a room for yerself and wait for me."

Raising her brows at her husband, Claudia willed a glare into her gaze. "Do you truly think I could forget? You told me at least three times." A smile threatened to break through, but she held it at bay, enjoying the way he rolled his eyes at her.

"Ye must admit yer memory has let ye down before, Lass."

Claudia's jaw dropped. "I can't believe you just said that!" she exclaimed, raising her fist in anger as he laughed loudly. "You blackguard!"

"I apologise," he replied, then caught her arm as she aimed her fist at his head and pulled her against him, lifting her clear out of her saddle, and hauled her onto his lap. Before she could utter a single word of protest, his mouth claimed hers in a passionate kiss.

Indeed, she too could do this for the rest of her life, Claudia thought as she strove closer, her arms coming around his neck.

Kissing him back, she marvelled at the faint memories his touch always stirred within her. Although her mind had finally recalled most of what had happened when they had met at Gretna Green, these memories were still hazy and unfocused. They seemed like a dream, and a part of her still was not certain if they had once been more. However, when she lay in Garrett's arms, these memories soared to life, no longer a faint echo of what might have been, but proof of the deep bond that connected them.

"We need to go, Lass," Garrett whispered against her lips, his hold on her not lessening. "We canna sit here all-day kissing." A deep grin stood on his face, and utter delight shone in his green depths.

Claudia narrowed her eyes at him. "Might I remind you that it was you who grabbed me, not the other way around, Mr. MacDrummond. I was about to head down into town when you seized me."

"I apologise, my lady, if I've offended you," he whispered with feigned regret, his eyes betraying that he was far from sorry.

Then again, neither was she. "Oh, not offended," Claudia assured him, smiling sweetly. "Only delayed. Wasn't that the accusation you'd laid at my door?"

Laughing, Garrett helped her back onto her mare before he reached for her hand again. "Be careful, Lass, and keep yer eyes open. I willna be far behind."

Seeing the sincerity in his eyes, Claudia nodded, then spurred her horse on and headed toward Port Glasgow. She allowed her mare free rein and only occasionally urged her into a certain direction, her own gaze travelling over the small town, simple and yet efficient. Tall masts rose into the sky from where ships were moored, and she could hear the distant sounds of them being loaded and unloaded, men striving to move the heavy cargo. The air was salty, and seagulls circled overhead.

All the way, Claudia could feel Garrett's eyes on her, and yet, when she turned now and then to look over her shoulder, he was nowhere to be seen. *Good*, she thought, *at least this way Mr. Adams will not know that I'm not arriving alone.*

Was he here? Claudia wondered. Was he somewhere among all these people moving back and forth along the crowded street, watching her? Or was it simply the thought that he might be that had the little hairs in the back of her neck standing on edge?

Inhaling a deep breath, Claudia did her best to remain calm as she allowed her gaze to sweep her surroundings, always on the lookout, and yet, trying not to seem to eager. A little farther down the road, she spotted a large sign, confirming that she had reached the end of her journey. At least for now.

Arriving at the *Golden Eagle*, Claudia slid out of the saddle and unfastened her small travelling bag. Although she had spent only a handful of days in his company, it was utterly strange not to have Garrett by her side, reaching for her horse's reins and telling her to go on ahead inside. Unable to help herself, she looked over her shoulder, but found the spot where he should have been empty. A small pang of regret filled her heart before she could call herself to reason.

Don't be a fool, she chided herself. *He'll be here in a few moments.*

Handing the reins to a stable boy, Claudia then headed inside.

The taproom was filled; however, the counter was blessedly deserted and so she strode ahead and rang the small bell. A moment later, the innkeeper appeared, and she was able to let a room. Turning toward the stairs that led to the upper floor, Claudia paused, then turned back to the haggard man. "Pardon me, did you see a man with an infant travelling through here?"

A small smile came to the man's face. "Oh, are you Miss Davenport?"

Claudia swallowed, trying her best not to let her shock show on her face. "Yes. Yes, I am. Do you...have a message for me?"

Reaching under the counter, the man retrieved another envelope identical to the one she had received in Gretna Green. "Here you are, miss."

"T-thank you," Claudia stammered, then bid the innkeeper a good day and headed upstairs. Her hands trembled, and by the time she reached her chamber, the letter in her hand was almost crushed. Her muscles were tense, and she had to pry her fingers open to allow it to drop onto the top of the small table in the corner.

Then she sank onto one of the chairs and waited.

An eternity passed before a knock sounded on the door, and Claudia all but jumped to her feet, her heart pounding. "W-who is it?"

"'Tis me, Lass," came her husband's familiar voice. "Let me in."

Rushing forward, Claudia turned the key and opened the door.

Stepping over the threshold, Garrett quickly closed the door behind him before he turned to look at her, his tall stature towering above her. "Are ye all right, Lass?" he asked, his eyes flitting over her as though checking for injuries.

Claudia chuckled as the tension finally left her body. "I am," she breathed, sinking into his arms. "I've missed you."

She could feel him smile against the top of her head as his arms drew her closer against him. "I missed ye as well," he whispered. "I know 'twas foolish, but a part of me feared I wouldna see ye again." Looking down, he tilted up her head. "It feels good to have ye back in my arms."

Sighing, Claudia rose on her toes and reached up to kiss him. Then she pulled back, nodding toward the table in the corner and the letter she had not been able to open.

Garrett's eyes widened as he strode toward it. "From him?"

Claudia shrugged. "I don't know. I guess so. I-I couldn't open it." Her hands still trembled. "Does that mean he knows I'm here? At this inn? Was he watching me?"

Garrett looked up to meet her gaze. Then he reached out a hand to her. When she took it, he pulled her to his side, wrapping his arm around her shoulder. "That I canna say. Perhaps he left these notes at every inn in town. We canna know." He glanced down at the letter in his hand. "May I?"

Claudia nodded, sinking deeper into his embrace as her head began to spin. She closed her eyes and rested her head against his shoulder.

Retrieving the small parchment from the envelope, Garrett unfolded it, holding it up to his face. "Dear Miss Davenport," he read, his voice tense, a small growl rising from the back of his throat. "Cursed man," he muttered before reading on. "Welcome to Port Glasgow. I shall await ye at the docks on the morning of the 26th. Once more, I assure ye that yer son is well. My sincerest regards, Maxwell Adams."

Exhaling the breath she had been holding, Claudia looked up at her husband. "That's tomorrow morning."

Garrett nodded. "Aye." Then he sighed and tossed the parchment into a corner. Turning to face her, he met her eyes. "Aye, tomorrow then. Tomorrow we shall see our son." A small smile played on his lips, and yet, Claudia could see only too well the tension that held him, the fear that would not leave. What if something went wrong?

It was a question on both their minds, and yet, neither one of them dared to say it out loud.

"We should rest," Garrett said, brushing his hands up and down her arms. "We should eat and then rest. 'Tis been a long day in the saddle. Ye must be tired."

Hearing the challenge in his tone, Claudia welcomed the distraction and returned his taunt. "As must you for you've been up as long as I."

Smiling, her husband nodded. "Aye, I'm tired as well." He glanced at the door. "I'll head downstairs and fetch us some food."

Claudia nodded. "That sounds good."

Reluctantly, they parted, not wishing to be seen together. Still, when Garrett finally returned, his arms laden with a hearty meal, Claudia almost sighed with joy. When had his mere presence become so essential to her? She could hardly draw breath when he was not around, her thoughts focused on him alone, unable to find a distraction that would hold them for long.

Seated around the small table, they ate together in comfortable silence. The sun slowly sank lower, and they lit a candle which cast a warm glow over their faces. Their eyes met, never leaving for long, and their hands often brushed against the other as they reached for a piece of bread or cheese. They both sought comfort from the other, their hearts and minds tense as they awaited the next day.

What would happen? They could not know, and yet, their own thoughts painted images of what they most feared.

Unable not to, they soon sank into each other's arms, the warm feel of their bodies soothing the ache in their souls.

Once again, Claudia felt reminded of her dreams. Dreams that had stayed with her throughout the past year. Dreams that had given her a small reprieve from the days that continually broke her heart.

In these dreams, she had felt Garrett's arms around her, had felt the tips of his fingers brush along the line of her jaw and down the column of her neck. She had felt safe and loved with him, and when he had whispered to her in the dark, her heart had been whole.

Now, he was no longer a faceless ghost. Now, he was a man of flesh and blood.

Her husband.

Her son's father.

Her other half.

Throughout the night, they clung to each other, hoping, praying, trying to forget. If only for a moment. A small reprieve.

Chapter Twenty-Six
THE MEANING OF FAMILY

After a quick breakfast filled with palpable tension, Claudia left their room first and headed downstairs. At every step, she had to fight the urge to turn and look over her shoulder, assuring herself that Garrett was there.

He will not leave you! She reminded herself. *He loves you.*

That thought brought a small smile to her face, and she remembered the moment he had pulled her into his arms in Gretna Green, telling her that the time without her had felt as though half his soul had been missing. He truly loved her, didn't he?

Amazement filled Claudia's heart, and she let it grow as it was far better than the fear that sneaked in whenever she was not purposefully locking it out.

Although they had known each other only a matter of days, Claudia could not help but wonder how she had ever lived without him. They belonged together, and now that they had finally found each other, it was so obvious that no other man could ever have conquered her heart.

A chuckle escaped her lips as she stepped out of the inn and into the warm sunlight in the yard. "All my seasons were for nothing," she mumbled, shaking her head. Still, if she had not met William and fancied herself in love, she would never have come to Gretna Green. Then she would never even have met Garrett, and she would never have known what she would have missed out on. Fate truly had a strange way of making itself heard.

Slowly, Claudia made her way down to the docks. Even this early in the morning, the streets were bustling with people. It seemed Glasgow was a town that worked late and rose early. Merchants and sailors were everywhere, stumbling in and out of taverns or going about their business before heading back to their ships. On the horizon, tall masts pointed Claudia in the right direction, and she wondered why Mr. Adams wanted to meet her at the docks.

Was Garrett right? Was the man planning on taking her and her son away? What would they do if that were his plan? Did he simply expect her to board the ship without objection?

Perhaps Mr. Adams truly did not expect resistance from her. Based on everything, she had learnt about him he seemed to be thinking of himself as her knight in shining armour. Perhaps he truly thought she would be grateful to him for freeing her and her son from her brother's clutches. Had those not been his words?

But what would happen once he realised that she did not see him in that light? That she saw him as the villain who had stolen her child?

Claudia drew in a slow breath. She would have to be very careful not to anger him, not to say too much and weigh her words. A snort escaped her at the thought. Never in her life had she weighed her words. They tended to fly off her tongue without seeking her permission.

Perhaps her brother had been right. Perhaps she ought to have learnt what to say and what not to say. Now, it was too late for instructions. She could only hope that her instincts would not lead her astray and put her son in harm's way.

Aiden!

Again, his name echoed in her heart, and she briefly closed her eyes when she spotted the first ship through the throng of people crowding around her.

The docks! What now? Was Mr. Adams around somewhere watching her? In his letter, he had not specified a time, and so, Claudia had insisted on arriving early, afraid he would get tired of waiting and simply leave, thinking she had decided not to come after all.

Seagulls screeched overhead as Claudia let her gaze glide over the tall ships moored along the docks, their sails neatly wrapped and stowed until it was time to leave Glasgow behind. A few sailors climbed in the rigging, but mostly the masts looked calm, birds sitting here and there on the ropes, watching the goings-on below.

Stepping to the side, Claudia retreated into a quieter corner where she was not constantly jostled along by the throng of people heading somewhere or other. Her eyes swept the many faces around her, trying to remember the one she sought. Although Mr. Adams had been in her brother's employ for at least two years-as far as she remembered-Claudia had barely spoken a word to the man. Not even when he had been assigned to guard her after she had returned from Gretna Green. Sometimes, she had glared at him when he had reminded her not to leave the premises, but that had been it.

Shaking her head, Claudia wondered how he had ever taken a liking to her considering how rude she had been to him. If it had been she, she would never have felt tempted to help him in any way. Quite on the contrary, she would have loved to tell him off.

As her eyes swept the crowd, Claudia inhaled a sharp breath when her gaze settled upon a pair of familiar green eyes. A small smile drew up the corners of Garret's mouth as he stood across the shipyard near a two-storey structure, his back to the wall and his head slightly lowered so as not to draw attention.

Claudia's heart skipped a beat at seeing him so close, but then settled into a more normal rhythm as his presence slowly calmed her fluttering nerves. All would be well, she told herself. It had to be.

Walking up and down the small stretch of ground that seemed far enough outside the path people cut across the harbour to give her enough room, Claudia waited and waited and waited, her nerves wrung tight. With each step, each turn, each breath, her mind began to unravel, unable not to dwell on all that could go wrong. She alternately cursed herself for entertaining such thoughts and then allowed them to prepare her for what might lie ahead.

"You look well, Miss Davenport."

The blood in Claudia's veins froze at the sound of her name. Still, Mr. Adams's voice did not sound at all familiar, and as she turned to face him, her mind wondered what he looked like. Dimly, she recalled a young man of slender build, an expressionless face, his hair a brownish shade.

When her eyes finally found him, there was nothing about him that made any kind of impression on her. She did recognise him. However, that was all. What in fact did catch her attention was that he had come alone.

"Mr. Adams," she addressed him, reminding herself not to antagonise him. "Where is my son?"

An appreciative smile came to the young man's face as he stepped closer, his gaze more intrusive than she remembered as it swept over her, studying, assessing. "Do not worry. I assure you he is well."

Fighting down the urge to strangle the man, Claudia willed her voice to remain calm-even though her heart was battling to free itself from her ribcage. "You wrote that you would return him to me."

"And I shall," he assured her as though they were speaking of nothing more important than him returning her handkerchief.

"Where is he?"

"Safe," was all Mr. Adams said before he stepped closer and leaned in conspiratorially. "How did you manage to escape your brother?"

Surprised by his question, Claudia blinked. "I simply left when he wasn't looking," she said, remembering her desperate run out into the night...and how she had come across her husband, not knowing who he was.

Mr. Adams chuckled, "I always knew you were a fighter," he replied proudly as though her courage had somehow been his accomplishment. Then he sobered, and a deep sadness tinged with no small amount of anger claimed his eyes. "I cannot say how relieved I am to see you safely here in Glasgow, Miss Davenport. I also wish to apologise I was not able to protect you from your brother's cold heart until after your son was born."

Claudia gritted her teeth, remembering the night her brother had almost died-poisoned by the man who claimed to only want to protect her. "It was not your duty to see to my protection," she said, trying her best to hide the tone of accusation her statement was meant to have.

"Oh, but I disagree," Mr. Adams objected, his hand briefly coming to rest on hers. "After all, we are cousins. Our fathers were brothers, and, therefore, it is indeed my duty to see to your safety and well-being. I'm saddened to think that your brother does not feel compelled to do so."

Doing her best to hold back the curses that wanted to fly from her lips, Claudia inhaled a deep breath and counted to five before she answered. "Well, all that is in the past now."

Mr. Adams sighed, "Unfortunately, the past has a way of overshadowing the present. As much as we tried, my sister and I were never able to overcome our past and be seen as more than the bastard's society wanted us to be."

Claudia frowned. "Your sister? I didn't know you had a sister."

Mr. Adams nodded. "I do indeed. Sophie is two years my junior and has suffered just as much as I did. Our father never acknowledged us, not deeming us worthy of his attention, his care, his name. Few people know of her existence as our father sought to keep it quiet that he had fathered yet another bastard with his mistress after the scandal that had ensued after my birth. Did your father never speak of it? Or your brother?"

Claudia shook her head. "I do not recall my father ever mentioning anything, and I doubt that my brother knew. When our mother informed us of your existence, he seemed honestly surprised."

"Nonsense!" Mr. Adams snapped, and his gaze narrowed dangerously as he took a sudden step toward her. "He's lying. Just like everybody else. All lies to protect themselves and their precious reputation." For a moment, he closed his eyes and inhaled a deep breath. Then he looked at her again, a hint of regret in his eyes. "I apologise for my outburst, Miss Davenport. I did not mean to frighten you."

"It's all right," she assured him, unable not to feel for him and his sister considering all they had suffered. Still, that did not give him the right to interfere in her life and steal her son.

At her assurance, he gave her a grateful smile. Then his gaze briefly shifted to something beyond her shoulder and his eyes narrowed. "Did you come here alone?" he asked, and his pale blue eyes returned to meet hers.

Claudia swallowed, but forced herself to remain calm. "I did. Why do you ask?"

Sighing, he shook his head. "Nothing. It is of no importance."

Claudia could only hope that he had not spotted Garrett. At Mr. Adams' outburst, she suspected that her husband had been unable to remain calm and driven by his concern for her had acted less than inconspicuous, drawing Mr. Adam's attention in the process. Hopefully, Mr. Adams had dismissed whatever it was that he had seen.

"How did you come to be here?" she asked, seeking to distract him. "Last I heard, you were to be tried for...I can't seem to recall." *My brother's attempted murder.*

An evil snort left his lips. "I was indeed tried and convicted," he spat, venom dripping from each word as though he had been an innocent in all of this and felt rightfully wronged. "I was to be deported to the colonies, but due to my sister's interference, I managed to get away." A small smile came to his face. "That is what family does. They protect each other. Still, it gave me an idea, which is why you are here today, Miss Davenport."

Wringing her hands, Claudia waited to hear what he had planned for her and her son.

"I feel a duty to you and your son," he remarked, and the gleam in his eyes spoke of how highly he thought of himself for feeling thus. "Therefore, I could not have simply left the two of you to your hopeless fate. I felt it was my duty to interfere and offer you the life that had been denied to me and my sister. While it sadly does not lie within my capabilities to change your family's mind and have them accept you and your son as you deserve, I am able to offer you a new life far away from the censure and restrictions of English society."

Claudia felt cold sweat break out all over her body. "What life are you speaking of? I thought I was here to collect my son."

A rather indulgent look in his eyes, Mr. Adams reached for her hands. "I cannot in good conscience allow your son to stay in England. The life he would face would undoubtedly destroy him. No, he deserves more."

Claudia swallowed. "Where...where will you take him?"

Mr. Adams' face lit up. "To the colonies, of course. A new world for people who don't fit in over here." He scoffed, "To hell with all those self-righteous snobs. We shall go and create our own world without the restrictions and prejudices of this one."

Claudia wanted to scream at the man. Did he truly believe that the colonies were any different? After all, they were populated by people who had once lived here in the old world. Certainly, change-if it ever came-could not be achieved that swiftly. A bastard in the colonies would still be a bastard and treated as such.

"The only question is," Mr. Adams said, his eyes looking deep into hers, "do you wish to accompany him? He needs his mother, and I did what I could to ensure that he would have you. Still, the decision is yours. Are you willing to give up your old life, to give up everything and follow your child to a new world?" He smiled at her. "I assure you no one will find us there. We will be able to begin again as a family."

His hands tightened on hers, and Claudia received the distinct feeling that he had matrimonial intentions toward her. Clearly, he had pictured their future in agonising detail, seeing himself as the hero who would save her and her son from her brother and bring them into a new world where they could start over.

As though to prove her right, he added, "I promise I shall raise your son as my own and never treat him differently from other children we might have. I've always looked out for you. Trust me now, and I assure you all will be well."

Wishing she could jerk her hands from his grasp, Claudia pictured her son's little face. The memory was already fading. The brief moment when she had seen his face was slowly slipping away. She needed him back.

Now.

"Please take me to my son," she said, doing her best to give him a genuine smile. "It has been so long."

"Of course," Mr. Adam's nodded, his eyes glowing with triumph as he clearly understood her question as her approval and consent for what he had planned. "I'll take you to him right away."

Taking his proffered arm, Claudia glanced into the crowd as Mr. Adams led her through the throng of people down the docks.

Garrett's eyes, furious and dangerous, met hers, and she could see the tension that held him rigid, and she prayed that he would be able to keep himself under control and not do anything foolish.

Her son was almost back in her arms.

Almost.

All they needed was a little more time.

Chapter Twenty-Seven

ACROSS THE SEA

When Mr. Adams reached for Claudia's hands, Garrett almost lost it.

His own hands balled into fists, and his teeth ground together so tightly that they sounded like mill stones, grinding grain into flour. Heat shot into his face, and his legs quivered with the need to cross the docks and pound that man into the ground.

And yet, he held himself in check.

It was the hardest thing he ever had to do.

With his eyes fixed on his wife, Garrett watched as they spoke to each other, wishing he could hear what was being said. Still, he could see the way his wife leaned back ever so slightly whenever Mr. Adams would step too close. He could see the tension in her shoulders and the way she wrung her hands.

Pride filled his heart that she was able to hold her tongue and speak to the man so civilly. Garrett was not sure he could have done so.

When Mr. Adams offered Claudia his arm, Garrett sucked in a sharp breath, wishing he was not alone, wishing his clansmen were by his side, wishing there had been time to deliver a message.

Meeting his wife's gaze as they walked past him, Garrett nodded to her, assuring her that he was here, that she was not alone, that they were in this together. Then he slowly fell in with the crowd, carefully following without being spotted.

Craning his neck to keep them in sight, Garrett dodged a cart here and there and occasionally had to find his way through a group of sailors boasting about their adventures. Fear held his heart tightly, urging his feet on lest he lose them in the crowd.

Leisurely, they strolled along the docks, his wife's hand tucked into the crook of Mr. Adams' arm, the man's other hand resting possessively on hers. Garrett wanted to wring his neck!

On their way, they passed a number of ships, some smaller and some boasting three masts. Eventually, Mr. Adams halted his step next to a two-masted sloop, sitting low in the water. Sailors scrambled to load the last of their cargo into the merchant vessel's hold, their movements practised and fluid as they prepared the ship for departure.

Garrett's heart thudded wildly in his chest. Was his son on board this ship?

Inching closer, he tried his best to remain inconspicuous. However, in order to protect his family, he needed to know what was going on. Pretending to watch the sailors as they scrambled through the rigging like spiders, he strode closer. Still, he did not dare look at his wife for fear their reaction to one another would give them away.

"This is it, Miss Davenport," he heard Mr. Adams say. "Now, you need to make a decision. The ship will set sail within the hour and take us across the ocean to the colonies. Will you join us? Or will you return to London?"

Garrett's blood froze in his veins.

"My son is on board this ship?" his wife asked, her voice carefully controlled, and yet, he heard with perfect clarity the fear that lived in her heart. "I want to see him."

For a moment, Mr. Adams did not answer, and Garrett felt compelled to turn and look. Moments before he would have lost the battle with himself, the man finally spoke.

"Certainly," he said, a bit of an edge to his voice as though he was disappointed that Claudia did not have complete trust in him. "However, I cannot allow him into your care until you've made your decision."

Out of the corner of his eye, Garrett saw the man raise a hand and wave it back and forth a couple of times, his gaze directed at the deck of the ship.

A moment later, a young woman stepped up to the railing, a small bundle in her arms as she looked down at them. Garrett squinted his eyes, thinking the lass looked familiar. Where had he seen her before?

"The nurse!" his wife gasped, shock and disbelief in her voice.

Garrett's muscles tensed, rooting him to the spot lest he do something foolish and draw her into his arms.

"S-Sophie...Sophie is your sister? She was my son's nurse. She..."

For a short moment, Garrett saw himself standing outside a simple building somewhere in London after following his wife to a solicitor's office and then continuing after them. The door had opened, and for a short moment, a young woman had appeared before she had bid them inside.

It had been the same woman he now saw up on the ship, his son in her arms.

His heart lurched into his throat at the thought that his little boy was only a few steps away. If he were to rush up the gangplank, he could draw him into his arms within moments. But what about his wife? Would Mr. Adams threaten her if he found out that she had not come alone?

Garrett gritted his teeth, glancing at the man out of the corner of his eye. There was something oddly unsettling about him. While he seemed perfectly polite, his manners easy and considerate, something dark lurked under that friendly exterior. Here and there, it had already reared its ugly head if only for a moment. Anger lived in the man's heart, and its constant presence had taken its toll over the years. What compassion and decency he might have possessed once were now grotesque alterations, twisted into his very own ideas of right and wrong.

"Can I hold him?" Claudia asked, her voice trembling as she blinked back tears, her gaze fixed on the small bundle. Wrapped in a soft blanket, their son was all but hidden from their eyes. Only a little hand protruded from the bundle as though waving to them in greeting. His wife's breath caught in her throat, and she clasped a hand over her mouth, fighting to remain strong.

"As soon as you decide," Mr. Adams repeated, a rather triumphant sneer on his face that Garrett would have loved to extinguish.

Every fibre in his body strained to knock the man senseless and retrieve his wife and child. Still, they needed a plan. Who knew what Mr. Adams had told his sister to do should he be attacked? She stood so close to the railing that if she were to release her hold, their son would drop down into the dark waters. Was that intentional? Or was she merely standing so close for them to be able to see the child?

"Who are you?"

The moment Mr. Adams growled the question, Garrett knew that it was directed at him. Still, he remained immobile, glancing at the man out of the corner of his eyes.

"Yes, you!" Mr. Adams hissed, his gaze shifting to Claudia, a loathsome gleam in his eyes. "You said you came alone." His voice sounded like a whiplash, and Claudia flinched. "You lied! Does your son mean that little to you?"

"No!" Claudia exclaimed, turning pleading eyes to the man beside her. "He means everything to me! Please let me hold him."

Staring at her, he shook his head. "How can I believe a word you say?" His gaze rose to meet Garrett's. "Who are you? You've been following us, haven't you?"

Garrett's eyes narrowed as he turned to face the man, his gaze running over him in speculation. How much did he know? How much was merely guesswork? Did he have anyone else working with him besides his sister? Were there others on the docks waiting for a signal from him?

Mr. Adams grinned, his eyes once more lighting up, a look of superiority in them. "Do not look so surprised," he sneered at Garrett. "I've spent years in the service of others, trying my best to remain invisible-as is expected of a lowly servant." He scoffed, his deep-seated anger showing in the snarl on his face. "However, only because no one noticed me does not mean that I was as oblivious as them. I saw. I heard. And I knew more than anyone ever would have guessed." His gaze hardened. "Who are you?"

Squaring her shoulders, Claudia drew Mr. Adams's attention back to her. "He's my husband," she said in a strong, clear voice, her blue eyes determined as she met his. "We've come to retrieve our son."

Instantly, Mr. Adam's face paled, and for a short moment, Garrett thought that he would faint on the spot. However, he regained his composure quickly, anger and betrayal now etched into his eyes as he glared at Claudia. "You lie," he hissed the moment his right hand shot to his side, drawing a dagger from beneath the folds of his coat.

Garrett drew in a sharp breath, cursing himself for not overpowering the man when he had had the chance. "She speaks the truth," Garrett said, carefully taking a step closer, his hands raised in surrender, hoping to appease the man before he could unleash his anger upon Claudia. "We were married almost a year ago in Gretna Green."

Mr. Adams snorted, "If that were true," he hissed, his other hand clamping down on Claudia's arm, drawing her against him, "there would have been no need to hide your indiscretion."

"I didn't know," Claudia hissed back until the blade of Mr. Adams' dagger came to rest against her side, pressing into her flesh through the fabric of her dress. "I couldn't remember. We only met again a few days ago."

Scoffing, Mr. Adams drew her back toward the ship, his eyes fixed on Garrett. "That is ludicrous. You must think me a fool."

Garrett certainly did; however, he managed to refrain from saying so out loud. "The point is," he stated instead, trying to remain calm as that madman dragged his wife toward a ship bound for the colonies, "that we're married, she and I. Aiden is our son, conceived and born in wedlock." He clenched his teeth as he saw the man's eyes narrow. "There's no need for ye to protect him. He'll be safe with us. He'll have everything he deserves, everything that was denied ye. I'll make certain of it. I swear."

"Yes, he'll be fine," Claudia agreed, her blue eyes holding Garrett's as she spoke to the man holding a knife to her body. "I thank you for your concern and...and your devotion toward Aiden. If it weren't for you, I would never have found my husband again, I would never have known that no one would have a reason to think less of my son. I thank you for that. You've done what you could, but now you need to return him to us. He has a family, a mother and a father. He will be well. I promise."

Garrett could see the dark glare in Mr. Adams' eyes as though Claudia had betrayed him by being married, by providing a father for her child and thus robbing him of the opportunity to be her knight in shining armour. The connection that Mr. Adams had seen between them before was now gone, and he glared down at her with all the hatred Garrett had feared.

"Do not come any closer!" Mr. Adams ordered when Garrett had started toward him without even realising that he had moved. "One more step and I'll end her right here and now." Pressing the blade into Claudia's side, he dragged her up the gangplank.

Pain shot through Garrett's body as he stood stock-still, not knowing what to do.

Around him, people moved up and down the dock, sailors called to one another and seagulls screeched overhead. Here and there, someone turned their head to look at him or his wife and Mr. Adams, a slight frown coming to their eyes as they considered the scene. Still, with the blade hidden between their bodies, no one seemed to realise the dire nature of the situation.

Garrett wanted to scream.

No matter what he would do, his wife and child might end up dead...or lost to him across the sea in the colonies. What was he to do?

Panic filled his being, and he felt his heart break as he met his wife's gaze. Her blue eyes held excruciating agony, and tears streamed down her face as she followed Mr. Adams up the gangplank and onto the deck of the ship. Garrett approached the end of the dock, one step short of falling into the water, his eyes never leaving hers. "I will find ye," he called up to her, his voice only loud enough for her to hear as he was still afraid of what Mr. Adams would do should Garrett call attention to them. "I will find ye, Lass. I swear it."

A soft smile came to her lips, and she nodded her head. "I know," she called back. "I'll take care of our son. He'll be fine. I promise."

Tears streamed down Garrett's face as he watched the sailors pull up the gangplank. The sails unfurled, and within moments the ship began to move, gliding through the water like a giant. His eyes remained on his wife's face until the ship turned and headed out to sea.

Then Garrett sank to his knees and buried his face in his hands.

Chapter Twenty-Eight

A MOTHER'S WORDS

Standing at the railing, Claudia felt the muscles in her hands ache as her fingers gripped the wood with excruciating tension. And yet, it was her heart that bled as her eyes held on to the lone figure on the docks, staring back at her. With each wave, the ship was carried farther and farther away, and Garrett's face was soon lost to her. Tears streamed down her cheeks at the thought of losing him again, and when she saw him sink to his knees in despair, Claudia felt an overwhelming need to fling herself into the waters below and swim back to his side.

Still, there was a spark of joy in her heart for never had anyone loved her so fiercely.

All her life, Claudia had gone from day to day, wishing for and dreaming of something that might break through the boring repetition of her daily activities. Never had she felt quite at home or satisfied with her lot in life. Always had she longed for more.

Two nights ago, when she and Garrett had been completely honest with each other and revealed the secrets they had kept, something had changed. The usual restlessness and dissatisfaction were suddenly gone, replaced by a contentedness that was only overshadowed by the loss of their son. Her heart was finally at ease as it suddenly knew precisely what it wanted.

What it needed.

None of her English suitors could hold a candle to her Scottish husband.

Indeed, what might have seemed like thoughtless behaviour on her part had truly been a streak of wisdom, and Claudia sighed in relief that she had possessed the courage-the recklessness as her brother would say-to marry a complete stranger.

For it was that stranger who now made her whole, complete.

With Garrett by her side, every day was an adventure, and right then and there, the greatest adventure her heart longed for was to go home with her son and her husband by her side. All of a sudden, the thought of living peacefully with her little family was enough to make her heart soar into the heavens and set her blood on fire. Perhaps all she had needed, all she had been waiting for had been the one man who could make her feel alive with a single look of his green eyes.

Now that she had found him, Claudia could not imagine a day without him by her side.

Heaving a deep sigh, she hung her head. What would happen now that life had torn them apart again?

He will come for you, a voice whispered in the back of her head. *Like he came for you before.*

"Yes," Claudia whispered. "He will come. He will find a way. He always does."

"If I were you," Mr. Adams snarled from behind her, "I'd forget about him."

Flinching at the sound of the man's voice, Claudia spun around, her eyes narrowed as she glared at him. "You don't know him. You don't know me. How dare you interfere in my life?"

With his lips pressed into a thin line, Mr. Adams stepped toward her. Gone was the gentle smile she had seen on his face before. Gone were the care and concern. In their stead, Claudia saw hatred and betrayal. "I thought you were different," he snarled into her face. "I thought you deserved a second chance, and so I did what I could to ensure that you wouldn't be separated from your son forever." He scoffed, "It's more than your family ever did for you."

Refusing to be intimidated, Claudia held his stare. "If you truly cared, you would have allowed me and my son to go with my husband. Why would you blame me for having a child with a man who loves me? If you truly cared, should you not be overjoyed to hear that Aiden will grow up in a loving family? Should you not be relieved to learn that he will not be looked down upon? That he will not suffer as you did?"

Something flickered in the depth of Mr. Adams' eyes, and for a short moment, Claudia thought to see doubt and regret. However, before they could urge him to realise his mistakes, anger returned in full force. "You betrayed me," he snarled. "I risked everything to free you of your brother, and now you act as though I am the one in the wrong. I'm the one who was wronged."

Claudia gritted her teeth as she felt her blood boil with an anger matching his. Still, reason counselled her to proceed with caution. After all, she was trapped on a ship with this man, heading for the colonies. "Yes, you were wronged," she said, holding his gaze, "but now you're the one wronging another. You're robbing an innocent man of his child. A man who would never abandon his son. A man who would travel to the ends of the earth to see him safe. My husband is not like your father. He is a good man and a good father because he puts his son's well-being above his own."

For a long moment, Mr. Adams stared down at her, his eyes hard, and yet, unmoving as though he had turned into a statue, frozen in time. Then he blinked, and his throat worked, swallowing hard. "Perhaps," he finally admitted, his voice holding less strength than before. "But what of you? You gave up your son without a second thought."

Gritting her teeth against the tears that immediately shot into her eyes, Claudia glared at the man in front of her. "How dare you?" she hissed, her hands balling into fists as she took a step toward him. "You have no idea how it broke my heart to give him away, but I did what I did in order to protect him." Tears now flowed freely down her cheeks, but Claudia did not bother to wipe them away. "Not every decision in life is easy. Some are hard, and some are crippling, leaving you a bare shadow of yourself. And yet, you make these decisions because you love another more than life itself. Have you ever thought of anyone but yourself? All you've done you've done out of anger, out of revenge for what you'd been made to suffer, and yet, you pretended you had a righteous cause, seeking to protect others. Well, you've done nothing but inflict more harm. You're not the knight in shining armour. You're the villain."

In her anger, Claudia had barely noticed the way Mr. Adams' face had paled, his resolve shaken now that he was confronted by how she saw him. A muscle in his jaw twitched, and Claudia could see that he was at a loss for words. Pain came to his eyes as well as a spark of bitter humiliation.

Unfortunately, it was that humiliation that kept him from realising how misguided his deeds had been. If he were to admit his wrongdoings to himself, then he would lose the one thing he had left, his own high opinion of himself.

And he was not willing to do that. "Your brother poisoned you against me," he hissed, once more drawing on his anger to force all doubts and regrets aside.

Claudia scoffed, "Was it not you who poisoned him?" she retorted with equal fervour, unable to hold her anger at bay. "No matter what you say, nothing will change what is true. Now," lifting her brows, she glanced past his shoulder, "I want to see my son. Where did your sister take him?"

With a grim face, Mr. Adams looked back at her. "Very well, you shall see him, but," he lifted a finger in warning, "as you are unfit to make decisions for him at present, I will decide the course of his life. Am I understood?"

Gritting her teeth until her jaw hurt, Claudia glared at him, wishing she could spit in his face and tell him precisely who was unfit to make decisions. "Yes," she forced out. "Where is he?"

Stepping back, Mr. Adams offered her his right arm while his other gestured below deck. "I'll take you to see him."

Reluctantly, Claudia agreed, wishing with every fibre of her being that she could simply push him overboard. Why ever not? She wondered briefly before reason returned, counselling her that she had to think of her son first. There was no way of knowing what the man's sister was capable of. Back in London, she had seemed like an innocent, young woman, truly distraught over what had happened. But had that been true? Was she a reluctant accomplice in all of this? Or was Sophie as devious as her brother?

As they strode across the deck, Claudia glanced around herself, seeing sailors up in the rigging and the captain standing on the quarterdeck.

"Do not do anything foolish!" Mr. Adams hissed as he leaned down to her. "I swear I will see to it that you'll never see your son again if you cause any trouble. Is that clear? All kinds of awful things can befall people on such a long voyage. I would hate for you or him to be counted among those unfortunate souls."

Swallowing her anger, Claudia nodded as she kept her eyes on the horizon, unwilling to let Mr. Adams see the fear that rolled over her in waves. "I would never do anything to endanger my child."

"Good."

Stepping below deck, Claudia squinted her eyes at the dim light that momentarily hindered her sight. Then she moved forward and followed Mr. Adams down a narrow gangway, doors lining both sides. "How many passengers are on board?" she asked, knowing that if she were to have any chance of protecting her child, she would need to know everything there was to know about her surroundings.

"Only the four of us," Mr. Adams replied, then stopped and turned to look at her. "No one will help you. I've already warned the captain that my wife has suffered a traumatic experience and might be a bit frantic, mumbling insane accusations."

"Your wife?" Noting the amused curl of his lips, Claudia shivered at the thought that *he* might be the one out of his mind. She could only hope that he would not completely lose his hold on reality while she and her son were still in his care-if one could call it that.

"Yes," he replied, his gaze hard on hers. "My wife." Then he turned and marched down the gangway. "This way."

Hurrying after him, Claudia suddenly stopped when soft wails reached her ears. Her heart immediately lurched into her throat, and she felt her knees go weak. Then she shot forward, her ears attuned to the quiet whimpers of her son. Pushing Mr. Adams out of the way, she walked on one step, then two, turning her head from side to side, trying to determine where the sound was coming from. Then she approached a door on her right and without further thought opened it and stepped inside.

Sophie's head snapped up as she spun toward the door, her eyes widening slightly before recognition flared in them. "Oh, it's you."

Completely unaware of the woman in the room, Claudia stared at the small bundle in the woman's arms.

Wrapped in a blanket, only her son's face peeked out, his eyes pressed shut and his mouth open as he cried, squirming in Sophie's hold.

Taking a deep breath, Claudia stepped forward, her hands trembling with an emotion she could not name. "Give him to me."

Sophie hesitated, then looked past Claudia before nodding in agreement. "Fine." Crossing the small room in two strides, she stopped and then leaned toward Claudia, gently lifting the boy and offering him to his mother.

Afraid she might drop him or hurt him somehow, Claudia hesitated for the barest of seconds. But then her son's soft cries dug deeper into her heart, and she reached out to him without thought. An old instinct took over, and she gently slipped her arm around him, cradling his head in its crook. Then she stepped away from the other two in the room, and everything else ceased to matter.

Feeling her son's small weight in her arms for the first time, Claudia retreated into a world all her own. Her eyes misted with tears as she gazed down at him and felt his warmth, his strength, his presence. Instinctively, she bounced in her step, rocking him gently as he cried, fighting to free his little hands from the confinement of the blanket. "Hush, hush, little Aiden. Everything shall be fine," she cooed under her breath when the melody of an old lullaby rose in her mind.

Singing softly, she stepped up to the porthole to get a better look at her son. Dark tufts of hair stood on his head, and his rosy skin shimmered, his head slightly red as he continued to cry. His little hands punched the air as though he was eager to share something but could not find the words.

A smile came to Claudia's face when one little hand curled into the fabric of her dress, holding on tightly as though wanting to make sure that she would not leave him again.

A moment later, his cries stopped, and he opened his eyes, looking up at her.

Claudia's lip quivered, and her breath caught in her throat when his blue eyes found hers. Her heart rejoiced, and she knew beyond the shadow of a doubt that he was hers and always would be. And yet, more importantly, she realised that she was his, heart and soul, and that from this day forward she would hold her hand over him until the day she would breathe her last.

Because he was her son.

Her heart.

And he knew it.

Smiling, Claudia brushed the back of a finger across his cheek and over his forehead, her eyes transfixed by the sight of her son. "I'm sorry it took me so long to find you," she whispered, "but I will never leave you again. I promise."

For a short moment, a smile lit up her son's face, and green flecks danced in his blue eyes, a reminder of who his father was.

Belatedly, Claudia realised that she was alone with her son and wondered where the other two had gone and why they would leave her alone. However, a moment later, her son's soft gurgles drew her attention once more, and she sat down on the lower cot, drawing up her legs and leaning her back against the wall as the ship gently swayed. "Life is never easy, little Aiden," she whispered to him. "Unfortunately, you already know that. But if there's one thing I've learnt, it's that great heartache can lead to great joy." Smiling, she leaned down and kissed him gently on the nose. "Your father will come for us. I know he will. So, don't worry." She brushed a hand down his arm, and before she knew it, his little fingers wrapped around one of hers, holding on with a strength she had not expected. "I promise I will do whatever I can to bring you back home," she vowed. "Don't worry, sweetheart. Mama is here."

Rocking her son gently, Claudia closed her eyes, dimly hearing her own mother's voice from long ago. *Having a child is like walking around for the rest of your life with your heart outside of your body.*

It was not until now, until this very moment, that Claudia understood exactly what her mother had meant.

Chapter Twenty-Nine

MEANT TO BE

S till kneeling on the docks, Garrett kept his eyes fixed on the distant horizon where the merchant ship had vanished some time ago. Despair came rushing at him from all sides as he remembered his wife's tear-streaked face, her sorrowful blue eyes looking back into his, and his heart clenched painfully as though it no longer had the strength to continue on.

The worst had happened. Not only had he failed to save his son, but he had also lost his wife in the process. Now, they were both gone, sailing across the ocean to a new world - in the hands of a madman! What would await them once they reached America? What were Mr. Adams' plans?

Garrett's teeth clenched together painfully as he remembered the look in the other man's face, the way he had all but gazed at Claudia, no doubt seeing in her the realisation of his dreams. In his heart, Garrett had no doubt that his wife's cousin would seek to claim her and their son as his own.

A growl of utter and pure anguish and frustration rang from Garrett's throat. His hands balled into fists, and he let his gaze sweep over his surroundings, desperate for something - anything! - to sink his frustration into.

But there was nothing.

Nothing save the far, endless sky and an ocean to match it.

I've never even seen my son's face.

That thought suddenly sprang up in Garrett's mind, and he groaned in agony, fearing that he had lost his only chance. Would he ever see his son? Would he ever get to gaze down upon him? Or would he forever be doomed to remember him as a mere fact alone? Not a person of flesh and blood?

His blood!

Sinking back onto his heels, Garrett drew in a deep breath, knowing that even if he were to find a way to cross the sea and reach the colonies, there was no guarantee that he would find them. From what he had heard, the new world was a vast and equally-endless place. A wilderness yet uncharted.

And what if they never even reached America? The journey was perilous, and many died in their attempts to make a new life for themselves and their families. And his boy was only a few weeks old. Would he even survive the journey?

A surge of protectiveness went through Garrett in that moment as he pictured his infant son as best as he could. It gripped his heart and strengthened his limbs, pushing him to his feet with a strength he had thought lost.

His lips pressed into a thin line, grim and determined, as his gaze returned to the horizon. "I made ye a promise, Lass," he whispered, "and I willna fail ye."

Lifting his head, Garrett squared his shoulders, ignoring the doubts that ran through his head. He would find a ship to the colonies. He would buy passage on it. And once in America, he would do everything humanly possible to find his family.

He had found them once.

He could do so again.

"Garrett!"

Tensing, Garrett blinked, certain he had imagined the voice calling his name. Still, in his mind, he saw his friend Finn, his dark auburn curls framing a laughing face with startling green eyes that more often than not spoke of some kind of mischief.

As children they had gotten into all kinds of trouble, always thinking up one daring plan after another. How often had their mothers thrown up their hands in surrender? How often had they chided them to no avail? How often had they called the laird to speak to their boys?

Foolish, their mothers had called them. Daring, they had called themselves.

No one and nothing had ever been able to separate them, to sever their friendship.

After finally claiming his own true love after a lifetime of foolish pranks, Finn had been the one to urge Garrett to return to England and look for Claudia for as long as it would take to find her. He had been the one to persuade Cormag to listen to Moira and let Garrett go.

With hope in his heart as well as the knowledge that it could not be, Garrett slowly turned around, only to have his breath knocked from his lungs.

Right there striding down the docks toward him was Finn.

Garrett blinked, certain that his eyesight had to be impaired. Certain that he was hallucinating. But then he spotted fair-haired Ian by Finn's side. Ian was an old friend as well, who, however, had always had the good sense not to go along with all their childhood mischief making. Always cautious-suspicious even-he tended to question just about everything.

There was no reason Garrett's mind-under any circumstances-would conjure up an image of Ian. Thus, the man had to be real, which also meant that Finn was as well.

Staring at his two friends, Garrett felt his forehead crease into deep furrows, trying to understand how on earth his friends had found their way to Glasgow.

And today of all days.

When they saw him, saw the look on his face, the joyous expressions on theirs soon changed into something darker, filled with concern and a hint of dread. Immediately, they quickened their pace, rushing toward him as Garrett continued to stand rooted to the spot, unable to move for fear they would simply vanish into thin air.

"Ye look like ye've seen a ghost," Ian observed, his gaze narrowed as he cast suspicious glances around them. "What's going on?"

Garrett inhaled a deep breath as utter relief flooded his heart. "Ye've no idea how glad I am to see ye."

"What's happened?" Finn asked, clasping a hand on Garrett's shoulder. "We didna know ye were back from England."

Garrett shook his head, unable to contain the slightly hysteric laugh that spilled from his lips. "Then what on earth are ye doing here? When I heard ye calling my name, I was certain I was seeing things."

While Ian's face darkened, a scowl claiming his features, Finn laughed, his green eyes shining brightly as though he had seldom had such a good time. "Cormag sent us."

"Cormag?" Garrett repeated, trying to understand. "But how would he-?"

"Did ye find her?" Finn interrupted, eagerness in his voice as he searched Garrett's face. "Yer wife? Is she with ye?" After allowing his gaze to sweep their surroundings, it returned to meet Garrett's. "Come, man, do not keep us waiting!"

Feeling a new sting in his heart, Garrett sighed, and Finn's face immediately darkened. "I found her, aye. Her and my son."

Both men's eyes widened. "Yer son?" they asked in unison.

Pride fought its way to the surface of Garrett's being until a deep smile claimed his features. "Aye, I have a son. Aiden." He inhaled a deep breath. "'Tis a long story, one better told around a roaring fire."

"Congratulations!" Finn beamed, slapping Garrett on the shoulder. Now, that he himself had tied the knot, he seemed particularly happy when others did as well. "Where are they?"

Garrett hung his head, and yet, the anger that swelled in his chest-anger born out of helplessness-tightened every muscle in his body. His eyes narrowed, and he was pleased to see that his friends knew him well enough to understand that what he was about to say was of the utmost importance. "There's a madman in my wife's past," he began, noting the way Finn's jaw twitched. "He stole my son days after he was born, and now he's forced my wife on board a ship to the colonies, threatening our son if she refused him." Gritting his teeth,

Garrett stood up straighter. "I need to go after them. I canna allow that man to harm them."

Rather unexpectedly, a smirk curled up the corners of Finn's mouth, and for a moment, he closed his eyes as though he had just heard something he could not believe. "Ye'll be needing a ship then, I take it?"

Garrett nodded, glancing from Finn to Ian. "Aye," he confirmed, wondering what his friends knew that he was not aware.

"Cormag sent a message to Clan MacKinnear," Ian said, the sound of his voice suggesting that he disagreed with their laird's decision, "and they promised to have a ship in Glasgow the day after tomorrow."

Staring at Ian, Garrett now felt inclined to doubt his hearing. Certainly, he was aware that Clan MacKinnear was an old ally and had been for centuries. As they were located mainly on the group of islands to the west of Scotland, they were in possession of a number of ships which were mainly used for trade. "They're coming here?"

Finn nodded, a serious grin on his face if ever there was one.

Feeling the air rush from his lungs, Garrett leaned forward and braced his hands on his knees, his mind spinning with what he had just heard. How was this possible?

After a couple of deep breaths, he straightened. "How?" he asked, glancing from one friend to the other. "How did ye know? I never had the chance to send a message." He shook his head. "It wouldna have reached ye in time. How could ye possibly know that I needed a ship? I didna even know it myself until two hours ago."

The two men exchanged a knowing look. However, while Finn smiled, a hint of utter joy on his face, Ian seemed to be grumbling under his breath, "Moira."

For a moment, everything came to a halt as Garrett remembered the pale beauty from Clan Brunwood whispered to have the second sight. She had been banished after betraying her own clan and conspiring to harm their laird's wife. People tended to mistrust her, wondering who would be next to feel her wrath. Would she betray them as she had betrayed her own clan? Her own people? Her kin?

And yet, Garrett could not deny that Moira had been instrumental in guiding him down his path. After all, it had been she who had urged

Cormag to send him to Gretna Green-unknown to Garrett at the time. If she had not insisted, he would never even have met his wife, and his son would never have been.

And now, here she was sending him help the moment he needed it the most. Perhaps Moira was more than she seemed to be. Perhaps she deserved a second chance.

Looking to Finn, Garrett drew in a deep breath, "Moira knew."

Finn nodded. "Aye. She went straight to Cormag, and they fought over what to do for two days." The grin on his friend's face deepened. "He never had a chance against her."

Ian's face darkened, and a disapproving growl rose from his throat as he crossed his arms in front of his chest. "He oughtna listen to that traitor when others provide loyal counsel," he grumbled, a sneer on his face that spoke of more than his disappointment with their laird's decision. "What if she had led us into a trap? We could've all been killed."

Shaking his head, Finn laughed, "I fear yer imagination is running away with ye, old friend."

Ian's countenance darkened further. "Tell me why I oughta trust her? She has never done anything to deserve it. On the contrary."

"She's been trying to redeem herself," Finn counselled, his gaze sobering as he looked at Ian. Then his gaze shifted to Garrett. "She sent ye to Gretna Green, did she not?"

Garrett nodded. "I didna know it then, but aye, she did." He looked at Ian. "I understand what ye're saying. If she's betrayed her kin once, how can we be certain she willna do so again?"

Ian nodded vigorously. "And we're not even her kin! If she didna feel loyal to them, why ought she feel loyal to us?"

Garrett shrugged. "I canna give ye an answer that will put yer mind at ease, old friend. But I can tell ye that everybody makes mistakes; everybody has regrets. Perhaps Finn is right. Perhaps she's been trying to redeem herself. Use her gift to help instead of harm."

Ian's lips thinned, and Garrett could see that his explanation was not good enough for his friend. To win Ian over, Moira would have to move the earth. Not an easy task.

"Whatever her reasons," Garrett continued, turning his gaze to

Finn, "I'm grateful for her help. I'm only wondering how she managed to convince Cormag. I mean, 'tis one thing to have me go to Gretna Green, but to send word to Clan MacKinnear and ask them to send a ship is no small favour. Why would he believe her?"

Finn laughed, rolling his eyes as though the answer should be obvious. "Why would a man believe a woman when there's no obvious reason for him to do so?" he asked, raising his brows, his eyes finding Garrett's.

Garrett frowned, remembering the moments of awkward silence he had witnessed every now and then when entering his laird's study and finding Moira there with him. Alone. "Ye mean-?"

Finn nodded. "Aye. 'Twould be easier on everyone if Cormag finally admitted that he cares for the lass."

Ian grumbled something unintelligible under his breath, his opinion clearly differing from Finn's. Still, Garrett could not help but hope that Finn was right. Cormag was an old friend of theirs, and the burden of laird had found him early in life. While he bore it well, Garrett had always thought that a loving wife by his side would ease the strain. Perhaps Moira was the one. Perhaps they could help each other.

"Do ye truly think he might offer for her?" Garrett asked Finn, ignoring the fact that Ian's face had paled at his question. "He's always been so steadfast and reasonable, not one to take a flight of fancy. 'Twould be very unlike him."

Finn nodded. "Aye, he's always been rather stuffy and ill-humoured at times, but ye canna deny that he treats her differently. He tries to hide it, but 'tis there."

Garrett nodded, knowing from personal experience how powerful love could be, how it could alter one's view of the world and rearrange one's priorities.

Since meeting Claudia, everything had changed. His world now revolved around her, and Garrett could not imagine for that to ever change. She was like the sun to him, her rays warming his soul and her steadfast position allowing him to stay the course and make his way.

He needed her back.

"Ye said the ship will be here the day after tomorrow?"

Finn nodded.

"Good. Then we shall be ready," Garrett said, knowing he would have to be patient, knowing that it would be utter torture to sit and wait, knowing equally well that Claudia was worth it.

He would find her, and then he would wring Mr. Adams' scrawny neck.

Chapter Thirty

FAITH

The first few days on board the merchant vessel, Claudia was confined to her cabin with either Mr. Adams or his sister Sophie watching her at all times. Their eyes would narrow whenever she rose to her feet to walk around the small cabin, her son in her arms as though they were one.

Claudia knew that they were suspicious of her, and, of course, they had good reason to distrust her. Still, Claudia had come to realise as she had lain awake during her first night out at sea that there was very little she could do.

As much as she wished she could simply turn the ship around, she knew not how to go about accomplishing such a task.

Since Mr. Adams had warned the captain as well as the crew, painting a rather disturbing picture of her as a woman who had lost her mind, Claudia doubted they would be willing to help. If she were to tell them that Mr. Adams had kidnapped her and her son, the captain would most likely return her to her kidnapper, offering his sympathies.

No, she could not count on their assistance.

Sabotaging the ship and thus hindering its progress had been another option Claudia had spent hours contemplating. However, she knew near to nothing about ships and what was needed to steer them through the waters. In turn, she could not even guess what to do in order to slow them down and give Garrett more time to catch up.

Where was he? She wondered. Had he managed to board a ship and was he now in pursuit? Or was her trust in him only wishful thinking? After all, they had known each other a matter of days. What did she truly know about him?

And yet, in her heart, Claudia had no doubt that Garrett was on his way, that he would come for them, that he would do whatever it took to return them home.

Sighing, Claudia looked down at her son's sleeping face, his blue eyes closed and his tiny lashes resting peacefully against his rosy skin. She could feel his fast heartbeat against her hand whenever she lay it on his small chest, ensuring he would not overheat in the stuffy cabin.

When Claudia looked up, she found Mr. Adams' gaze on her. Although he looked mostly in control, merely an underlying hint of anger on his features, there were moments of indecision or even regret. He seemed in doubt about what he had done, about what he was doing since learning of her changed circumstances. Still, she could see that there was no way for him to take a step back, to change his course without losing face, and so Claudia was certain that he would not merely allow her to go free once they reached the colonies.

No, he would not change his mind, for it would mean he had been in the wrong and that would cripple him. His whole sense of self-respect seemed to rest on the idea of him being the knight in shining armour rescuing the damsel in distress. And he clung to that conviction with an iron will, knowing what devastation awaited him if he were to consider that he had been wrong, that in this story he was in fact the villain. Sophie seemed to see her brother's indecision as well for she appeared subdued and spoke very little, her eyes filled with sadness.

If not for the situation Claudia found herself in at present, she would have felt sorry for the siblings. In fact, she was ready to accept any apology they might offer her if only they were to return her home.

However, they did not.

There was no turning back.

Claudia sighed. Garrett was her only hope. Would he come for her?

For their son? She prayed with all her heart that she would not be disappointed for placing her trust in him.

Days passed, and without a plan, Claudia simply tended to her son. She ate and slept and spoke only to the little bundle of joy she held in her arms. At night, she would hold him close, sleeping on her side on the small cot, Aiden resting safely between the cabin's wall and her body so he would not fall out. She spent hours staring down into his little face and tickling his small toes. His blue eyes would look up at her at times and come to rest on hers as though he truly knew who she was and that he meant the world to her. His smiles and soft cooing sounds were a balm to her battered soul, and whenever his little fingers wrapped around one of hers, the world seemed right.

Even if only for a moment.

Since Claudia had followed Mr. Adams' directions to the point and not tried to alert anyone to her situation, she was soon allowed out of their cabin. With her son in her arms, she walked beside Sophie across the deck, watching the sailors climb the rigging overhead as the ship cut through the waves. The wind blew strong, and the sun shone brightly. It was a beautiful day, and Claudia welcomed the fresh air, delighting in the soft rosy glow on her son's cheeks.

Knowing that any attempt to speak to the crew or even the captain would only result in a disaster - would Mr. Adams take away her son? - Claudia made no attempts to address anyone as they proceeded toward the bow of the ship. Still, she kept her ears and eyes open. After all, one never knew what small piece of knowledge might prove essential.

As time wore on, Claudia and Sophie began to walk up and down the deck twice a day while Mr. Adams kept to the cabin, his scowl darkening with each day. Although he was still unwilling to admit to any wrongdoing on his part, Claudia could see that at least a part of him deep inside had realised the truth, torturing him with what he could not accept.

One afternoon, the wind caught in Sophie's bonnet and blew it clear off her head. Shrieking, she tried to reach for it as it tumbled along the deck always moving on whenever she drew close. The sailors laughed at her attempts as well as the aghast look on her face.

Claudia, too, could not suppress a grin. "It's only a silly bonnet," she told Aiden, laughing when she saw his lips curve upward in an innocent smile, his blue eyes fixed on hers as though trying to understand what she was telling him. "Don't ever worry about such silly things."

Sinking down onto a water barrel lashed to the side of the ship, Claudia sighed, beginning to feel the strain of seeing nothing but the far ocean for days on end. What she would not give for the sight of a tree or even a bush?

Shaking her head, she laughed, but then stopped when her gaze touched something lying on the wooden boards between the back of her heels and the barrel she sat on. A frown came to her face as she squinted her eyes, shifting Aiden to the side so she could lean forward. As she did, the sun caught in its smooth, metallic surface, blinding her momentarily.

A knife!

Claudia's breath caught in her throat, and her gaze ran over the small blade. It appeared to be a carving knife as wood chips lay scattered at her feet.

Glancing around, Claudia found herself alone with no one standing nearby. Sophie was still a good distance down the deck, refastening her bonnet, the sailors' attention focused on her. However, it would not be for long.

Without another thought, Claudia reached down and picked up the small knife, hiding it in the folds of her dress. Then she moved it upward and wrapped it in the shawl slung around her shoulders. She would have to find a good place to hide it-preferably on her body-as one could never know when such a device might be of use.

"Is something wrong?"

At the sound of Sophie's voice, Claudia's head snapped up, and to her utter shock, she found the young woman standing only a few paces away, her forehead in a slight frown as she looked at Claudia.

"Are you all right?" Sophie asked when Claudia failed to answer, quick steps carrying her over. "Is something wrong with the child?" Brushing a hand over Aiden's head, she gazed down at the boy, her eyes running over him in concern.

Drawing in a steadying breath, Claudia willed a smile back onto her face, relieved that she had not been discovered. "No, he's fine. I…I was only lost in thought."

Standing back, Sophie nodded, a hint of relief in her eyes. "I'm glad."

For a moment, the two women looked at one another, and Claudia thought that under different circumstances they might have become good friends. There was kindness and regret in Sophie's gaze, and Claudia wondered how her brother had convinced her to go along with this scheme. Had he threatened her as well? Or had she simply not had anywhere else to go?

After all, Sophie's father-Claudia's uncle-was dead, and from what Claudia could remember, the siblings' mother had passed on as well. Where they alone in the world? Had they banded together in order to survive, only trusting one another?

As strange as it was-given the situation they found themselves in-they were her cousins. Part of her family.

Or they should have been.

Claudia could not deny that a world where people were disregarded simply for being born out of wedlock was a world in dire need of change, of improvement. After all, an innocent creature like her son could not be faulted for coming into the world the way he had.

Should not be faulted.

It was not right.

It was not fair.

"May I ask you a question?"

Looking up at her cousin, Claudia found the young woman watching her with utter curiosity. "You may," Claudia replied, "if I then may ask you one as well."

For a moment, Sophie hesitated before she nodded her head in agreement.

"Ask me then."

Sophie sighed, and then her mouth opened and closed a couple of times before she found the words to express what was on her mind. "You said…that man at the docks was your husband."

Claudia swallowed as the sight of Garrett on his knees, his eyes filled with despair, returned to her. "He is."

"If you had a husband," Sophie asked, a sense of unease in her eyes, "then why did you give up your son, saying he was born out of wedlock? I've never heard of such a thing. Many a young lady would marry just about anyone to prevent her ruination, to give her child a father." Consternation creasing her forehead, Sophie shook her head. "I cannot wrap my mind around why you would have done as you did."

Claudia sighed, wondering if for the rest of her life she would be telling this tale. Once she got home, her family would ask her the very same thing. "Because I didn't know," Claudia simply said, seeing Sophie's frown darken.

"You didn't know? That you had a husband? How is this possible?"

Claudia cleared her throat, her gaze drifting down to the sleeping child in her arms, wondering if one day he would hear this story as well. "I eloped to Gretna Green," Claudia told the young woman, seeing no reason to keep this a secret. Not here. Not now. "However, his brother followed us and prevented the marriage. Stubborn as I am, I refused to return to England with them and stayed behind." A small smile came to her lips as she remembered the bits and pieces of that night that had returned to her after Garrett's kiss. "Later that night, I met my husband. However, not before, I had consumed significant amounts of ale or whatever it is they serve in those parts."

Sophie's gaze widened, and a hint of horror came to her face. "Do you mean to say he took advantage of you?"

Claudia laughed, relishing the feeling as fleeting as it was. "He would never," she whispered with a conviction that surprised even her. Despite their short acquaintance, Claudia doubted she had ever known anyone as well as she knew her husband.

As Sophie listened with rapt attention, Claudia told her story and before long Sophie's eyes glowed with longing, a soft smile playing on her features. "And he came to find you?"

Claudia nodded. "He did, but he didn't know about Aiden." Her gaze sobered, and she turned her eyes to Sophie with a new intent. "He's never even seen his son. Not once."

Sophie dropped her gaze, guilt resting on her features for all to see.

"Please," Claudia whispered, reaching out and squeezing the young woman's hand. "Please. We need to get back. My son deserves to know his father. It is cruel to keep them apart. I know what you did came from a good place, but this is wrong. Can you not see that?"

A sniffle left Sophie's lips before the young woman lifted her head, tears brimming in her eyes. "I cannot betray him," she whispered, and Claudia could see that she was torn between her sense of right and wrong and the loyalty she felt for her brother. "He's always looked out for me. He's always been there." She drew in a deep breath. "It would destroy him."

Claudia exhaled, feeling hope float away. "Then help him see the error of his ways. Help him understand that what he is doing is not right. One wrong cannot be righted by another."

"I've tried," Sophie sniffled, her cheeks reddening as tears rolled down her face. "Believe me I've spoken to him again and again since we left Glasgow." She sighed, resignation in her eyes. "But he will not listen. Sometimes he says you're confused and will be glad for what he did for you later. Then he says that all this is a ruse to..."

Claudia frowned. "To what?"

"I don't know," Sophie whispered, her head bowed in shame. "Sometimes what he says doesn't make much sense."

"Is that not proof enough that what he is doing is wrong?" Claudia demanded, feeling her last chance to convince Sophie slip through her fingers.

"It's no longer about believing you or him," the young woman whispered, her eyes holding Claudia's, deep regret in them. "Whether what he did was right or wrong, I owe him my loyalty as I've always had his." Shaking her head, Sophie took a step back. "I'm sorry. I promise I shall speak to him again, but the decision is his. I cannot go against him." Then she turned and walked away, leaving Claudia behind.

Gritting her teeth, Claudia suppressed the growl of frustration that rose in her throat lest she draw unwanted attention and her behaviour be reported back to Mr. Adams. Instead, she turned and walked farther down the deck, gently rocking in her steps to ensure her son would sleep on. "Garrett, where are you?" she whispered when she had reached the bow, gazing out at the open sea. "Will you come for us?"

Despair settled on her heart, and Claudia felt tears sting her eyes.

Still, for the sake of her son, she could not allow herself to break down. She needed to be strong and not abandon hope.

Although the separation from her husband pained Claudia greatly, she knew in her heart that it would not be for good. One day, they would be together again.

If only that day was not too far off.

But Garrett had found her once. He would find her again.

Lost in her thoughts, Claudia only belatedly heard the cry from the crow's nest. "Sail ho!"

A ship?

Her heart tightened in her chest, and the air lodged in her throat. Turning to look in the direction the man in the crow's nest was indicating, Claudia spotted sails on the horizon.

"Garrett," she whispered, and all of a sudden, her heart felt a thousand times lighter.

Then a deafening shot rang through the air, and a cannon ball splashed into the water on their starboard side.

Chapter Thirty-One

DUNCAN MACKINNEAR

Cursing the swaying of the ship, Garrett made his way up the ladder and to the quarter deck, Finn and Ian following close behind. Annoyed, he noted that their feet moved with greater steadiness than his own, and for the thousandth time, he cursed the dancing waters below.

Finn chuckled, "Ye were not born a sailor, were ye?"

"Quite obviously not," Garrett retorted, gripping the rail as the ship pitched onto another wave. "My feet must think I'm drunk."

Again, Finn chuckled, his good humour unfailing as always. Ian, on the other hand, remained as taciturn and sullen as Garrett had always known him.

Upon reaching the quarterdeck, they found Duncan MacKinnear, second-in-command of Clan MacKinnear at the wheel, his bear-like hands wrapped around the spindly looking wood as he shouted orders. His deep voice bellowed down to the main deck, and his clansmen scrambled to do his bidding.

Despite his enormous size and hulking appearance, Duncan MacKinnear was a kind and considerate man and-to Garrett's great relief-a man very much in love with his wife, a wife who had only recently born him a son.

Upon hearing Garrett's tale, Duncan had been outraged, his brows had drawn down dangerously, and he had let loose a tirade about the wickedness of the English. "No offence to yer wife," he had said, welcoming Garrett and his two companions on board. "Her marrying a Scot proves her good taste." A low chuckle had sounded in his throat then, and he had slapped Garrett's shoulder good-naturedly. "Dunno worry, my friend, I give ye my word that I will do what I can to return her to ye."

Garrett had liked the bear-like man instantly, and relief had flooded his heart upon receiving such devoted support. Still, after two days at sea, his hope began to fade, replaced by dread and doubt.

Certainly, he knew that the merchant vessel had a two-day head-start, and yet, Garrett could not silence the fears that sneaked into his mind whenever he was not occupied. What if the ship had encountered a storm and sunk? What if they had changed course? What if they had been set upon by pirates? What if the earth had opened up and swallowed them whole?

Shaking his head, Garrett forced his thoughts to focus as he came to stand beside Duncan. "Anything?"

Duncan chuckled, giving him a rather indulgent look. "She's fast," he said, almost lovingly running his hands over the wheel, "but even she canna overcome a two-day head-start in such a short time. Patience, my friend. We shall find them."

Garrett nodded, crossing his arms in front of his chest so he would not do anything foolish and run them through anything essential in order to alleviate his frustration. Duncan would not look kindly on him if he were to destroy the man's beloved ship.

"What do we do when" - *when* not *if*! - "we catch up to them?" Garrett asked, feeling the need to plan, to do something that was of help instead of staggering around deck without anything to occupy his hands. "Have ye ever boarded another ship before?"

Duncan laughed, a booming sound even above the churning of the waves. "I canna say that I have," he chuckled, "but ye said the merchant vessel is English?"

Garrett nodded.

"Well, in that case, I do believe that they will surrender easily," he boasted, his eyes alight with a sense of adventure, "especially when they hear we only want to retrieve yer wife and son."

Garrett frowned. "Why do ye think so?"

"These men are no soldiers," Duncan explained. "They're tradesmen, who seek to make a profit. What do ye think they will do when faced with a savage crew of highlanders?" A dark chuckle rose from Duncan's throat, and he grinned at Garrett, a devilish twinkle in his eyes. "As strong as they pretend to be, the English still fear us, especially in these circumstances where 'tis not two armies meeting in a meadow." With conviction in his eyes, he shook his head. "I doubt they will stand and fight for a woman and child who mean nothing to them. A woman who wishes to return to her husband." Again, he shook his head. "Nay, they willna fight."

Garrett sighed in relief at hearing Duncan's assessment. Still, something nagging sat in the back of his head, and his brows drew down as he sought to give words to what had him worried.

"Ye dunno believe me," Duncan remarked, amusement in his voice as he glanced at Garrett.

"'Tis not that," Garrett assured him, running his fingers over his chin and feeling the stubble there. When was the last time he had thought to shave? Claudia had still been with him. Suddenly, it seemed like an eternity ago.

"What is it then? For there's clearly something on yer mind?"

"That man-Adams-he..." Inhaling a deep breath, Garrett remembered the few moments he had spent in his wife's cousin's presence. "I fear he is the kind of man to do something reckless when cornered."

At his words, Duncan's brows drew down and his eyes sharpened, all humour gone from his face. "Do ye think he might harm them?"

Garrett tried to swallow the lump in his throat, but it would not be moved. "I fear he might," he forced out through gritted teeth, pain radiating through his body at the thought that his wife and son might come to harm. "He struck me as a man obsessed with his perceived purpose. The moment he realised that my wife didna see him as her saviour, he turned on her." Garrett shook his head. "I saw his eyes. They spoke of madness."

For a long moment, Duncan remained silent, his watchful eyes turned inward as he contemplated Garrett's words. Then he turned to his guest, the green in his eyes once more sharp and piercing. "What else do ye know of the man? Is he a fighter? Is he skilled with a weapon? What are his instincts?"

Forcing his mind back to the moment Mr. Adams had forced Claudia on board the merchant vessel, Garrett willed himself to relive the worst moment of his life. "He's observant," he said, his gaze directed back through time. "As he walked away with my wife, I followed at a safe distance, and yet, he noticed me. He said as one trained to be invisible, he still sees more than others would think."

Duncan's lips thinned, and he nodded in acknowledgement. "He's observant then, but would ye say he's got the instincts of a fighter?"

Frowning, Garrett shook his head. "I canna be certain. When he learnt who I was, he whipped out a blade with practised ease."

Again, Duncan nodded. "What of yer wife?"

Garrett looked up. "What do ye mean?"

"What kind of woman is she?"

At Duncan's question, a smile drew up the corners of Garrett's mouth and he saw its effect in the one that lit up Duncan's face in answer. "She's fierce and daring, reckless and foolish, but passionate and devoted."

Duncan chuckled, "Ye love her dearly."

"Aye," Garrett replied, feeling his heart warm at the mere thought of her. "She set out on her own when she learnt that our son had been taken. She left in the middle of the night, following the bread crumbs Adams had left for her."

Duncan chuckle,. "Then I dunno think we need to worry about yer son as he already has a lioness by his side." He nodded knowingly. "She will protect him. Ye'll see."

Pride warred with fear in Garrett's heart. "And what of her?"

Duncan sighed, "Where her child is concerned, she willna take heed to protect her own life. Aye, if I were ye, I'd worry about her." He took a step forward, his eyes on Garrett's as he put a hand on his shoulder. "She might get hurt or she mightna. We canna know that, but," he gripped Garrett's shoulder more tightly, "ye need to trust her. Ye need to trust that ye're not alone in this. Women-especially mothers-are stronger than ye think. My own wife may look like a tiny thing, but she has a fierce nature, and I dunno dare cross her...much." A soft chuckle rose from Duncan's lips. "I promise ye that we'll approach with caution. Trust that yer wife will see to yer son, and ye see to her. Understood?"

Sighing, Garrett nodded. "Aye. Thank ye." Meeting Duncan's eyes, Garrett found that the words failed him to express his gratitude toward the bear-like man. Still, the slight nod of Duncan's head told him that the other understood him, nonetheless.

Even without knowing him, Garrett MacDrummond, Duncan MacKinnear had answered his call for aid. He had readied his ship, gathered his men and was now sailing out to sea when he ought to be home with his wife and child. It was that loyalty and devotion, the desire to protect one's kin and allies that still lived on in a highlander's blood.

"Go rest," Duncan counselled, determinedly urging Garrett toward the ladder leading down to the main deck. "Ye need yer strength. Ye have my word that I will have ye roused the moment their ship comes within sight. Go and dunno give up hope."

Nodding, Garrett did as he was bid, and yet, his heart groaned in agony. After all, he had been living on nothing but hope for the past year, searching for his wife, always hoping that he would find her. Now, his heart and mind and body were weary, and all he wanted was to return home, his family by his side and let someone else hope for a change.

Soon, Garrett promised himself. Soon, he would retrieve his wife and child and take them home.

Any other outcome was not acceptable, and Garrett did not dare dwell on it.

Chapter Thirty-Two

THE VOILE NOIRE

The moment the cannon ball cut through the sea's surface with a deafening roar, spraying the starboard side with buckets of cold and salty water, Claudia's heart stopped.

With wide eyes, she stared straight ahead, her eyes unseeing as her mind slowly pieced together what was happening. "Garrett?" she mumbled as her heart crumbled and all hope sank into a bottomless pit.

Woken by the loud racket, Aiden squirmed in her arms, his little mouth wide open and his eyes pinched shut as he wailed loudly, expressing his anger at being ripped out of his slumber so rudely. "Hush, hush, my little Aiden," Claudia said in her usual sing-song voice, and yet, to her own ears it sounded hoarse. Holding her son close, she bounced in her step as her eyes once more sought the ship approaching with daunting speed.

Darkness hung over the vessel, and Claudia gasped when she saw that one sail was pitch-black. Cannons were trained on them, and the ship's crew stood on deck. Still too far away to make out their faces, Claudia found that her mind had no trouble filling in the blanks, providing her with horrifying images of soulless savages, armed to the teeth, out for blood.

"Garrett," she whispered once again as though her plea could bring him to her side. "No, it cannot be him." Never would he risk his family's life by firing upon their ship. No, he would never be so reckless. Not with their lives. With his, certainly. But not with theirs.

The more disturbing thought was: if it was not Garrett, then who? And what did they want? Clearly, their intentions were far from friendly.

"Are you all right?"

Turning toward Sophie's voice, Claudia found her and Mr. Adams hastening toward her, their faces pale and their eyes wide as they kept glancing out to sea at the approaching ship.

Claudia nodded. "We're fine." Then her gaze followed theirs. "Who are they?"

"I don't know," Sophie whispered, her voice tinged with fear as she clasped her hands together to keep them from shaking. Then she turned to look at her brother. "Maxwell, what do we do?"

Although Mr. Adams held himself rigid, Claudia could see the same fear in his eyes that she felt in her own heart. For a long moment, he said nothing, overwhelmed by the disruption of his carefully thought-out plans. Then his gaze shifted to his sister and the look in his eyes softened as he reached for her hand. "Come, we shall speak to the captain," he said, lifting his eyes to include Claudia, "and find out what is happening."

Pulling his sister's hand through the crook of his arm, Mr. Adams escorted them across the main deck, dodging sailors left and right as they scrambled about the ship in a rather disorderly fashion. With Aiden's cries in her ear, Claudia slowly followed after the other two as they climbed the ladder to the quarter deck. One arm remained tightly wrapped around her son while the other held on to the rail to ensure she would not lose her footing.

Finally reaching the deck, Claudia settled her son more comfortably in her arms, wishing he would stop crying. Still, she could feel her own heartbeat hammering in her chest and knew without a doubt that Aiden was aware of her agitation. No doubt it was she who was the reason for his current distress. If only she could calm down.

However, that was easier thought than done under the present circumstances.

Hurrying toward Captain Ronsford, Claudia sucked in a sharp breath when she saw the man's dark red face and heard the tremble that shook his voice as he bellowed orders to his crew. Apparently, Mr. Adams saw it as well as his own face paled considerably. Still, he swallowed and with determination strode toward their captain. "Captain Ronsford, a word?"

Ignoring his guests, the captain marched around the deck, speaking to a sailor here and there before looking through his spyglass again and again as though he was still hoping that the ship gaining on them would turn out to be an illusion.

"Captain?" Mr. Adams tried again.

"What?" Captain Ronsford snapped as he spun around to glare at the unsuspecting former footman. "What do you want?"

Mr. Adams swallowed, and a part of Claudia frowned at seeing him so intimidated. "That ship," Mr. Adams said, pointing out to sea, "what does it want? Who are they?"

Closing his eyes, Captain Ronsford shook his head as though no one had ever dared ask a dumber question. Before he could answer though, the wind carried over bits and pieces of his sailors' exchange as they considered the approaching ship.

"...heard of the black sail..."

"...must be the *Voile Noire*..."

"...pirates..."

Mr. Adams' eyes flew open the moment Claudia's heart paused in shock. "Pirates?" he stammered, his arm tightening on his sister as though he was suddenly the one in need of support. "That is a pirate ship?"

Captain Ronsford rolled his eyes in annoyance. "Not pirates, you fool," he snapped. "It's most likely a privateer." Again, he lifted his spyglass and peered through. "They have yet to hoist their colours, but I'd say she looks French. Rawlings?"

Out of nowhere, a sailor appeared beside the captain. "Aye, Capt'n."

"Would you say she looks French?"

The wiry sailor nodded. "Me thinks it's the *Voile Noire*."

Captain Ronsford cursed under his breath and sent the sailor on his way.

Shocked beyond words-an utterly rare occurrence-Claudia stood beside Mr. Adams and Sophie, her son still crying in her arms, and looked at the fast-approaching ship, wishing she could wake from this nightmare. Her jaw quivered as she looked down at Aiden. She had only just found him. Would she lose him again after only so short a time?

The thought pierced her heart like a knife, and she cradled her son closer, feeling his little fingers dig into the fabric of her dress as though fearing he might lose her if he did not hold on tightly.

Swallowing down her fear, Claudia bounced her precious child in her arms, a smile coming to her face at the mere sight of him. "You need to be strong now, Aiden, do you hear me? But don't worry. Mama will look after you." After kissing his little forehead, Claudia settled him snugly into the crook of her arm, surprised that his wails had ceased, and he looked about with mild curiosity.

Encouraged by her son's trust in her, Claudia lifted her chin and straightened her shoulders. Whatever life would throw in her path she would overcome. She had made it this far, and she would not lie down and surrender now. If there was a way out of this, then she would find it. But she would need to keep her wits about her and not succumb to blind panic.

For her son's sake.

As well as her own.

"What happens now?" Mr. Adams stammered, his eyes still as wide as before.

Captain Ronsford sighed, "We're not equipped to fight. My men are not trained fighters," he stated rather matter-of-factly, resignation now coming to his eyes as his anger waned. "We were meant to leave Glasgow in a larger group of ships to provide each other with a certain measure of protection. However, repairs delayed us, and although I'd hoped to catch up to them, it seems we're not that lucky." He heaved a large sigh and then shrugged his shoulders. "All we can do now is surrender."

"Surrender?" Sophie shrieked, the whiteness of her cheeks matching her brothers. "But what will happen to us?"

Again, Captain Ronsford sighed before he nodded to a sailor nearby who immediately sprinted away. "They'll claim the ship and its cargo for themselves and take the crew and passengers prisoners."

Sophie drew in a sharp breath before they all craned their necks to see a white flag rising to the top of the merchant vessel's main mast. Surrender.

"They'll take us prisoner?" Claudia addressed the captain as she fought to maintain her composure. "And what will happen to us then? Will they take us to France?"

The captain nodded. "Mostly likely. From there, we'll be ransomed back to England. It's a practise of war, miss."

While Mr. Adams' eyes went wide with fear at this news, Claudia breathed a sigh of relief. Even if she was brought to France first, she would at least be returned to England after that. She would not have to travel to the colonies but would soon be back with her family. Then she could send a message to Scotland. To Garrett.

The smile then died on her face. But Garrett would not be in Scotland, would he? Had she not hoped all these days past that he would come after her? If he did, he would sail to the colonies for nothing, searching a vast country for his wife and son while they were already safely back in England. What was she to do?

As Captain Ronsford hurried below deck, Mr. Adams stepped toward Claudia, his eyes suddenly hard and cold as he glared at her. "Do not think this the answer to your prayers," he hissed, grabbing her arm and dragging her to the side of the ship, Sophie fluttering after them like a mindless hen. "If you believe you'll be back with your ungrateful family in a matter of days, think again, Miss Davenport."

"My name is Mrs. MacDrummond if you please," Claudia retorted, her eyes hard as she held his gaze. "You forget that I'm married."

A dark laugh rose from Mr. Adams' lips. "That is of no importance now," he hissed, leaning down until the tip of his nose almost touched hers. "We'll be taken to France, and I'm certain it'll take some time to be ransomed back...if at all." An evil grin spread over his face, and Claudia felt goose bumps rise on her arms. "I've heard awful stories about what French captives must endure. Many are not alive to be ransomed back." He glanced down at her son. "How long do you think he will survive in a French prison cell?"

Fear clawed at her heart, and yet, Claudia refused to be intimidated by this man who had already taken so much from her. Who was the very reason she found herself in this situation in the first place. Whether or not he spoke the truth, she did not know, but she knew she would not cower before him. "Remove your hand from my arm this instant," she snarled, giving her arm a jerk to free herself.

A hint of doubt came to Mr. Adams' gaze, and she was surprised to see him comply. Still, the hateful glare in his eyes remained, and he seemed to have more to say to her. "Legal pirates or not," he hissed only loud enough for her to hear, "privateers have no honour, no morals, no decency. They're barely men. They take what they want and kill those who stand in their way."

Despite his feigned bravery, Mr. Adams' mask of indifference began to crumble as he spoke of the horrors that awaited them. His own words seemed to chase away the anger that had fuelled him, replacing it with fear and dread. Red spots rose on his cheeks, and his chin quivered with each word to leave his lips. And yet, he would not stop. "I've heard they...amuse themselves with captured women," he whispered, a slight sneer coming to his face as he looked down on her. "And what do you think they'll do with wailing infants?"

Terrified despite her best efforts, Claudia forced herself to hold the man's gaze. "What happened to you?" she demanded. "Not too long ago, you saw him as an innocent." Sighing, she glanced down at her little son, his blue eyes looking up at her were full of trust. "You saw him as someone deserving of your help, your protection. What has happened to make you disregard his life as though it means nothing? He has not changed. He is still the same innocent, little boy he's always been."

Besides the dim spark of regret that briefly lit up his eyes, Mr. Adams gave no indication that he felt remorse about their current situation and how they had ended up here. He merely shrugged. "It's a harsh world. We," he drew Sophie into his arms, "learnt that long ago. It would seem that your time has finally come as well. Good luck."

Then he stepped away as though washing his hands off her and escorted his sister back to the main deck.

Overwhelmed by all that had happened in the past few moments, Claudia stood by the railing, one hand clamped around the smooth wood, and tried to breathe. Her body trembled, and she knew she needed to calm down before her son would become upset once again. She needed to keep him safe, and so she needed to keep him quiet.

But if anyone should try to harm him, she would make them regret the day they had ever set foot upon a privateer's vessel.

Swallowing the lump in her throat, Claudia felt for the small carving knife hidden in her shawl.

No matter what, she would be ready.

Chapter Thirty-Three

A CHANCE ENCOUNTER

Standing on deck with the crew and the other passengers, Claudia watched the large ship approach, its black sail billowing in the wind like a winged demon descending upon them. Two tall masts reached into the sky, and the deck of the *Voile Noire* was filled with sailors-pirates, she reminded herself! - swords drawn and pistols at the ready. As the ship drew nearer, Claudia could make out their faces, their eyes determined, and their jaws set. In truth, with the exception of their weaponry, they did not look evil, merely efficient, steadfast and committed.

Claudia's heart beat steadily in her chest as her eyes surveyed the scene. Fear chilled her limbs, and, yet, the need to sink to her knees and weep was absent. She felt strangely removed from the reality before her as though she were a mere observer and not affected by it in the least. Her mind retreated, shutting out all that lay ahead of her, and focused on her breathing, her heartbeat, keeping them steady and regular.

Hooks were flung, and Claudia heard the dull *thunk* of them grabbing onto the side of their ship, pulling it closer to the *Voile Noire*. The distance between the two vessels quickly shrunk, and Claudia barely noticed Sophie hanging in her brother's arms, sobbing fitfully. Mr.

Adams in turn seemed ash-white as though ready to faint at a moment's notice. How was it possible that he could snarl down at her one minute and then cower in a corner the next? Who was that man? And how had he become who he was?

Claudia shook her head. She would never know, and in that moment, she could not bring herself to care. All that mattered was Aiden. Somehow, she needed to find a way to negotiate with these pirates and hope they would listen. Perhaps there was a way to save her son and spare him the fate Mr. Adams had referred to with such sickening delight.

Pulling Aiden tighter into her embrace, Claudia gritted her teeth. No, she would not lose him now. Not after everything she had gone through to finally hold him in her arms.

Fortunately, her emotions still seemed to be dulled as she watched the privateer's crew board the merchant vessel, their eyes lit in triumph as they surrounded them. Her limbs felt heavy, and it took Claudia a good deal of effort to move her feet and huddle closer to the other prisoners - for that's what they were now! - as the pirates circled around them.

Their eyes were watchful, looking for resistance, ready to subdue anyone who dared speak against them at a moment's notice.

Then a shadow fell over her face, and Claudia turned her head back toward the privateer where a tall, dark-haired man now stood on the railing, his eyes narrowed as he surveyed their prize.

He was perhaps in his thirties, his dark, almost black hair cut to shoulder-length and tied in the back. He stood tall with broad shoulders and strong limbs, a sword strapped to his side and a pistol fastened to his chest. His skin looked bronzed from the sun, and his dark green eyes sparkled with mischief in the midday light, oddly reminding Claudia of her own husband. Would she ever look into Garrett's eyes again? Would she ever see them light up with wickedness?

Watching the stranger, Claudia found herself taken with the man's silent authority, and she knew without a doubt that he was the *Voile Noire*'s captain. Strength and control clung to him like a cloak, and he moved with the sure-footedness of a man who knew his place in this world. His crew was organised and well-trained, and he needed no more than a few words to put them to their tasks. "Search below deck," he ordered in French, his voice stern but not unkind.

Hope blossomed in Claudia's heart that the privateer's captain was a man who could be reasoned with. She was about to step forward and address him when one of his crew members nodded at the order issued, saying, "Aye, Captain Duret."

The breath caught in Claudia's throat at the sound of the man's name, and she found herself transported back in time to an early summer's day not long before her rash elopement to Gretna Green.

The season was slowly coming to an end, and they would soon leave London and return to Farnworth Manor. Bored yet again, Claudia had wandered through the house until she had heard her brother's voice from the drawing room. Something in the way he spoke drew her attention, and she sneaked closer on quiet feet, carefully peeking in through the small gap left by a door that had remained ajar.

"I still don't understand why Sebastian called on you," her mother said, confusion in her voice as she settled into an armchair on the edge of Claudia's view. "What did he need your help with?"

Sebastian Campbell, Earl of Weston, was a childhood friend of her brother's, who had only recently married a young woman whom he had persuaded to elope with him to Gretna Green. For their whirlwind romance alone, Claudia adored them. They were such passionate and daring people, and she envied them beyond words.

"Apparently," her brother replied, a hint of exhaustion in his voice, "he had been made aware of a rather delicate situation. A young lady, Juliet Edwards, daughter to the late Jules Edwards, Earl of Goswick, found herself unhappily betrothed and wished to end said betrothal without suffering societal censure."

From the tone in her brother's voice, Claudia could tell that her brother could not understand why a young lady should wish to be released of such a commitment. Claudia, however, could think of a number of reasons.

"Unhappy in what way?" her mother asked, and Claudia thanked her silently as she found her curiosity running away with her yet again.

If only she was not doomed to merely listen to these fantastic tales but could experience them herself!

Her brother sighed, his footsteps carrying him up and down the room. "Apparently, her betrothed was of advanced age and had been chosen by her stepfather, Lord Silcox."

Their mother chuckled.

"I fail to see how this would amuse you," Richard enquired, incomprehension as well as a hint of frustration marking his voice.

Their mother sighed, a rather indulgent look in her eyes as she looked across the room at her son, who unfortunately was hidden from Claudia's view at present. "Dear Richard, can you truly not understand why a young lady would object to being married to a man who could well be her grandfather? Young women dream of love, my dear. They want to be swept off their feet by a dashing young man and not waste their youth on one who's already in the grave with one foot."

"That's a bit harsh, Mother," Richard objected. "After all, she would gain social standing, fortune and a family of her own through such a match."

Sighing, their mother shook her head. "Well, then, let's agree to disagree. What happened then? Were you able to persuade the old man from slandering the girl?"

For a moment, silence fell over the room, and Claudia could picture her brother rolling his eyes. "Yes, we were," Richard finally said. "As Sebastian and Lord Cullingwood had called on quite a few acquaintances, Lord Dowling seemed reasonably impressed."

"Lord Cullingwood?" their mother asked, her brow slightly furrowed. "Is he not the one who recently married a young woman of unknown origin?"

"The very one."

"How is he connected to the young lady? Lady Juliet?" their mother enquired. "I do not recall her as a friend of the Campbell's, either. Why did Sebastian feel persuaded to champion her case?"

Richard sighed, "It's all very complicated. As far as I understood, Lord Cullingwood's new wife is well-acquainted or even related to the Lady Juliet. They turned to Sebastian as well as Lord Elmridge for help, who in turn approached their acquaintances, which is how I was drawn into this matter."

A gentle smile came to their mother's face. "Friends help each other. I'm glad Sebastian turned to you knowing you would help."

Richard cleared his throat. "I might have refused and suggested he do the same had I known that French privateers were involved in the matter."

Claudia's heart skipped a beat as the story began to surpass her wildest dreams. Oh, what she would not give for a knight in shining armour to come and rescue her from the dreariness that was her life!

Their mother's face paled, the smile dying on her lips. "French privateers? What on earth are you speaking about?"

Richard sighed, sinking into an armchair opposite their mother. "I cannot say with certainty," he said, disapproval strong in his voice, "as I saw no need to include myself in this matter anymore than was absolutely necessary. All I know is that Lord Cullingwood's new wife seems to have French ties. I passed a young man in the hall-dark, long hair, casual attire, a dagger strapped to his hip-and Sebastian later told me he goes by the name of Duret."

Claudia sighed. She would have given anything to have been there and met such a man!

Her mother inhaled a steadying breath. "You still have not said why that man was there. What was his purpose?"

Richard shrugged. "I did not say because I do not know. There seems to be some kind of connection, but no one elaborated, and I did not ask."

Oh, Claudia could have clubbed her brother over the head with something hard and heavy! Why on earth was he not more interested in these things? Did he find his own dreary life truly fulfilling?

"I'm only glad all is resolved," Richard continued. "As far as I know Lady Juliet is now free to choose her future husband herself, and the Duret's have left our shores, hopefully to never return." A deep sigh left his lips. "Please do not mention this to Claudia. You know how she is. I'm afraid she might see such a tale as inspiration to do something foolish."

Sighing, their mother nodded. "Perhaps that would be wise."

"Thank you."

Back on the merchant vessel, Claudia blinked as the memory slowly retreated and her eyes once more focused on the dark-haired captain of the *Voile Noire*. Was it truly him? Captain Duret? The man who had come to London last summer?

With ease, he jumped down onto the deck of their captured prize, his green eyes calmly surveying the situation as he strode forward, stepping toward the hatch that led below deck.

When he walked by her-no more than two arm's lengths away-Claudia knew that this was her only chance. If she was to speak up, it was now or never.

His boots sounded almost deafening to her ears as he strode across deck, his green eyes momentarily meeting hers before they moved on, taking account of his captives.

Swallowing the lump in her throat, Claudia took a daring step forward. "You're Captain Duret, are you not?"

Hearing his name, he stopped just as a member of his crew stepped toward Claudia, his sword raised, urging her to remain where she was.

Slowly, the captain's dark head turned until his vibrant green eyes came to rest on her, gliding over her face and lower, momentarily coming to rest on the sleeping child in her arms. "Have we met, *Madam?*"

After glancing at his captain, the pirate who had urged her back lowered his sword and stepped away.

Claudia inhaled a deep breath and then carefully took another step forward, her eyes fixed on the enigmatic captain. "We have not," she said, willing her voice not to shake as reality came suddenly rushing back at her.

All alone, with only her innocent son in her arms, she found herself on a ship that had now been boarded by a French privateer. The blood in her veins ran cold, and once again, she felt for the small carving knife still hidden in her shawl. Would she have to use it? Would this man in front of her give her reason to?

The captain's eyes narrowed, and yet, there was a hint of amusement in the way the left side of his mouth curled slightly upward.

"Then how do you come to know my name? You're English, *n'est-ce pas?*" he asked, moving closer to her as his gaze studied her face.

"I..." Claudia swallowed, then lifted her chin, reminding herself to stay strong.

Regarding her with sudden curiosity, Captain Duret smiled. "You remind me of my cousin, *Madam*." He leaned closer as though about to share a secret. "There's something fierce in your eyes. Speak your mind, and do not worry. I shall not bite." There was a devilish gleam in his eyes, and the look on his face spoke of a teasing nature.

If the situation had been different, Claudia could have come to like him.

"Very well," she said, feeling at least a little reassured. "I've heard your name mentioned by my brother. Yours," she inhaled a deep breath, her eyes fixed on his, "as well as Lady Juliet's."

Instantly, the man's smile slid off his face. His jaw tensed, and all humour vanished as though it had never been there. His body became rigid as though he fought to contain a storm that suddenly raged within him.

For a long moment, he held her gaze before he seemed to be able to regain his composure. Inhaling a deep breath, he straightened and then to her utter surprise offered her his arm. "Will you join me below deck, *Madam?* I believe you and I have much to discuss."

Glancing down at her son, Claudia hesitated, wondering if she had done the right thing drawing attention to her.

"I assure you you will be quite safe with me," Captain Duret said in a low voice so only she could hear him. It probably would not serve him to destroy the image of the ruthless privateer in front of his prisoners. "You as well as your child."

Nodding, Claudia slid her arm through the crook of his, noting out of the corner of her eye the hateful glare Mr. Adams cast at her. Unable not to, she looked over her shoulder and gave him a dazzling smile, delighting in the way his eyes almost crawled out of their sockets and his face turned red.

"Secure the ship," Captain Duret called to his crew, "and lock the prisoners below deck. I'll be in the captain's quarters." Then he turned his head back to the *Voile Noire*. "Jacques, keep a weather eye out. You know how much I hate surprises."

"Aye, Capt'n," echoed over from the crow's nest of the *Voile Noire*.

"Shall we?" Captain Duret said, casting her an amused, and yet, strangely tense smile before leading her toward the hatch and assisting her below deck.

At each and every step, Claudia wondered if she was making a monumental mistake. Was Captain Duret truly the man from her brother's narrative? And even if so, had her brother been right to be wary of him? Did an evil soul hide behind his charming face? Or was he a decent man...for a privateer?

Inhaling a deep breath, Claudia knew that no matter what the answer was there was no turning back now.

Chapter Thirty-Four

THE OTHER SIDE OF THE STORY

C linging to her son's warm body, Claudia all but staggered along the gangway toward Captain Ronsford's quarters. The privateer's captain was only two steps in front of her, holding open the door for her to step through. Then he closed it behind them, his green eyes quickly taking in their new surroundings. His long legs carried him across the small cabin, and he peeked inside a large trunk set by the back wall before examining the maps rolled out and weighed on the table. "Are you on board with your husband, *Madam*?" he asked without looking up, his fingers tracing something on the map before him.

Suppressing the quiver that rose in her throat at the mention of her husband, Claudia willed herself to remain focused. Still, she could feel a slight tremble in her knees as the turmoil of the past week caught up with her. Exhaustion washed over her, and for a moment, she felt certain she would collapse into a heap on the floor.

"Are you all right?"

Blinking, Claudia focused her gaze and found a set of dark green eyes looking into hers.

Without her noticing, Captain Duret had approached and was now lifting a hand to grasp her shoulder as she began to sway on her feet, instinctively clutching her son tighter.

Aiden whimpered in his sleep, a quiet complaint at his mother's smothering embrace.

"Sit," the captain ordered, urging her backwards until her legs bumped into something hard. Then he pushed her down, and Claudia sank onto a small cot fastened to the wall. Her limbs sighed in relief as she leaned back and momentarily closed her eyes.

"You need rest, *Madam*," she heard Captain Duret say as he urged her to lie down. "Do you wish to see your husband?"

Tears collected in the corners of Claudia's eyes. "I do," she whispered as her mind began to block out the harshness of the world. "With all my heart." Sadness filled her, and a small sob escaped her lips. "But he is not on board." Her eyes fell closed, and she felt the seductive call of slumber. "We were taken, my son and I. Forced onto the ship. We..."

Silence fell over the small cabin as Claudia's words trailed off, her mind unable to supply more. Still, she felt Captain Duret's quiet presence beside her, growing darker as the moments ticked by. "Who took you?" he all but snarled into the stillness, a fearsome threat in his voice if ever Claudia had heard one, and a part of her even pitied the man who would find himself at the other end of Captain Duret's wrath. "Is he on board?"

Claudia sighed, then rolled onto her side, gently cradling her son in her arms. "Maxwell Adams," were the last words to leave her lips before sleep claimed her.

In her dreams, Claudia found herself once again wrapped in her husband's strong arms, his gentle green eyes looking down into hers as he called her *mo chridhe*, my heart. She felt safe and loved and knew beyond the shadow of a doubt that all would be well.

Only then her dreams changed, grew darker, and she was torn out of Garrett's arms and thrown onto a ship that would see them separated for all the times to come. Panic welled up in her chest, and her heart broke as she desperately sought something to hold on to.

Aiden!

Instinctively, her arms tightened around her son, only to find him gone.

"Aiden!" Claudia called as she jerked upright, and her eyes flew open.

In the dim light of the cabin, she found herself momentarily stunned. Then she ran her hands over the small cot, searching for her precious child, her eyes wide as she looked at the spot where he had lain before.

Panic seized her.

"Calm yourself, *Madam*," a slightly amused French voice said. "Your son is here. He is well."

Stupefied, Claudia blinked, then turned her gaze toward the voice. Her breath caught in her throat when she found Captain Duret sitting by the table, her precious son in his arms and a wickedly amused smile on his lips. "You talk in your sleep," he commented, humour in his voice as he dangled a small jewel at the end of a golden necklace in front of her son.

Clearly curious, Aiden lifted his little hands, his eyes following the small gem as the light from the candle perched in the middle of the table reflected in its sides. Belatedly, Claudia realised that night had fallen.

"Nothing untoward, I assure you," Captain Duret elaborated, winking at her. "However, I was able to gather that your son's name is Aiden," he glanced down at the giggling child, "and that your husband is a fearsome Scotsman who kisses you when you talk too much." He chuckled low in his throat. "Did I miss anything, *Madam?*"

Feeling heat rise to her cheeks, Claudia pushed herself onto her feet, determined to retrieve her son from this infuriating Frenchman. However, the moment she rose, her head began to spin, and she lost all concept of up and down.

In the blink of an eye, Captain Duret stood before her, his warm hand once more settling on her shoulder, pushing her back down.

"You've slept like a rock for hours, *Madam*. I suggest you take it slow." Then he leaned down and handed her her son.

With the feel of Aiden's warm body once more in her arms, Claudia sighed, her heart calming its frantic pace. "Thank you," she whispered, lifting her eyes to meet the captain's.

A teasing grin played on his lips. "I've had many *mademoiselles* swoon at my feet," he chuckled, "but never from exhaustion." He arched his brows at her in a wicked manner. "At least not that kind of exhaustion."

Unable not to, Claudia laughed. "I have no trouble believing that you're quite popular with the ladies," she teased, feeling at least slightly refreshed after her long slumber and more like her old self. Strangely enough, when he was not keeping her son from her, Claudia found Captain Duret to be an endearing and fascinating man. Perhaps some privateers did have manners and morals after all. Still, her initial gratitude towards him could not trump her own curiosity, and so she could not refrain from adding, "However, I wonder what Lady Juliet might think of your conquests."

Instantly, his smile vanished, and his face grew dark. For a long moment, he regarded her with caution, all his earlier ease vanished. "What do you know of her?" he demanded, his voice controlled. Still, Claudia sensed raw emotions hiding beneath.

"Nothing really," she said with a shrug.

His eyes narrowed. "How do you know of me?"

"From my brother," she reminded him, gently rocking her son in her arms. "I overheard him and my mother speak of you almost a year ago. He mentioned you and Lady Juliet and how a number of peers had come together to free her from an undesirable match."

A low grumble rose from the captain's throat before he began stalking around the cabin, his green eyes thunderous and his body filled with an almost desperate need to move. His jaw clenched, and he exhaled a long, arduous breath before his fist came suddenly flying toward the wall.

Taken aback, Claudia sucked in a sharp breath. However, before his fist could collide with the wall, he uncurled his fingers and merely struck the wooden panels with his open palm, the echo of the contact reverberating in the small space.

Seeing the bewildered expression on Claudia's face, Captain Duret inhaled a deep breath and then shrugged. "There's no good reason to damage something that will fetch me a small fortune, *n'est-ce pas?*"

"None at all," Claudia mumbled, surprised by the depth of the captain's emotions. Perhaps Lady Juliet-whoever she was-had meant more to him than a simple conquest. And she quite obviously still did.

Remembering her own unfortunate situation, Claudia decided not to tease the captain further...at least not about Lady Juliet. "You're nothing like I thought you'd be," she told him, a smile on her face.

Quickly, humour returned to his eyes, and he chuckled. "Is that so? May I ask what you were expecting, *Madam?*"

Claudia shrugged, trying not to remember what Mr. Adams had told her. "Someone fearsome, no doubt. Ruthless and without conscience."

"And you're convinced I'm not that?"

Claudia shook her head. "Not after seeing you with my son."

The expression on his face softened. "My cousin is with child at present."

"So, you shall be an uncle then?" Claudia said before her brows drew down. "No, that's not right. You said she was your cousin, so..."

Captain Duret chuckled, "She's like a sister to me, so I think *uncle* would be appropriate."

Returning his smile, Claudia nodded to him. "Congratulations."

"Thank you." Sitting down on the chair he had vacated before, his green eyes sought hers in earnest. "How did you come to be on this ship? I questioned Mr. Adams. However, he seemed disinclined to share your story, and I did not think it right to torture a potentially innocent man in case I had misunderstood you."

Claudia's eyes widened. "Where is he?"

"He is being detained," Captain Duret replied. "Tell me what happened."

Sighing in relief at this rather unexpected source of assistance, Claudia told him her tale of woe; how she had run off to Scotland, discovered she was with child, given him up only to learn of his kidnapping a few days later. She told him about Garrett, how they had found each other again and then about the moment she had stepped onto the ship, following her son, forced to leave her husband behind.

Now and then, Captain Duret offered a humorous comment, but mostly he listened to her tale with a sober face, compassion darkening his eyes every once in a while.

"Will you help me get back to Scotland?" Claudia asked when she had finished. "Or will you take us as prisoners back to France?"

Captain Duret sighed, "I have a duty to my country, *Madam*." Still, the look in his eyes whispered that he would only need a small incentive in order to disregard it.

The *Voile Noire*'s captain seemed to be a truly compassionate man. A man who knew the importance of family.

"You said your brother spoke to you of me," he asked suddenly, his gaze narrowing as he leaned forward, bracing his elbows on his thighs. "Who is your brother?"

"Lord Ashwood."

"You're Lord Ashwood's sister?" he exclaimed. "*Oui*, I believe I've heard his name mentioned when I was in London." His brow furrowed. "I might even have met him. A stuck-up sort of fellow with a murderous glare who doesn't know how to smile?"

Claudia laughed, "More or less, yes, that's my brother."

"It's a small world, *n'est-ce pas?*" He leaned back in his chair. "What did he tell you about me?"

"Nothing," Claudia replied, and a grin claimed her lips as she leaned forward conspiratorially. "I was listening at the door."

This time, it was Captain Duret who laughed. "I have no trouble believing that! You strike me as one who always finds trouble no matter where she goes."

"I wouldn't say that," Claudia replied with a bit of a haughty expression. "My brother's opinion of me is too severe. He always fears that these tales might inspire me to foolishness, and so he tries his best to keep me ignorant."

Captain Duret chuckled, "After what you've just told me, can you truly fault him for it? His assessment of your character seems to be spot-on. You remind me of my cousin. In fact, it was she who insisted

going to London in order to assist...Lady Juliet." Once again, at the
mention of the ominous lady, his smile faltered, and his eyes became
thoughtful.

"Why did your cousin insist?" Claudia asked carefully.

For a long moment, Captain Duret held her gaze as though not
certain whether or not to trust her with this information. "Because
they're half-sisters. Violette, my cousin, is originally from England. It's
a rather long story."

"And she is now married to the Earl of Cullingwood?"

Captain Duret nodded.

"And they succeeded," Claudia said, watching the young captain
with rapt attention. "Lady Juliet was freed from her betrothal."

Again, he nodded, his gaze dropping to the floor.

"Have you heard from her since?"

His head rose, and his green eyes regarded her with caution.

Claudia smiled. "You do not hide your affections for her well. Any
fool would be aware that you care for her."

His jaw clenched, but he did not say anything.

"Has your cousin been in contact with her?"

Captain Duret sighed, "I do not know, but Violette has been at sea
most of the time, and now that she is expecting, she and her husband
are in France with her mother."

"As far as I know," Claudia began, remembering how she had
scoured the betrothal and marriage announcements when she had been
locked away at Crestwood House-anything to keep her mind occupied,
"Lady Juliet is still unattached."

Within a second, his eyes were back on hers, and Claudia could see
that he was holding on to his composure by a thread.

"Perhaps she is waiting for someone." Claudia sighed, "Sometimes
love finds you when you least expect it."

Rising from his chair, Captain Duret strode toward the large
windows, at present overlooking a pitch-black ocean. "That I'm aware
of," he said before he turned to look at her. "What about your
husband? What will he do now?"

Claudia swallowed, her heart growing heavy now that their conversation was shifting back to her. "He said he would come for me, for us. He promised."

Meeting her eyes, Captain Duret asked, "Do you believe him?"

"With all my heart." A long sigh escaped her. "He will come," she repeated, her voice determined as she lifted her gaze to look at the young captain. "Still, it will not be easy for him to keep his promise as he cannot simply seize another ship and pursue us."

Captain Duret chuckled, glancing at her over his shoulder. "I would think not."

Inhaling a deep breath, Claudia held his gaze. "Please, can you not take us back to Scotland?"

His shoulders tensed, and his gaze dropped from hers.

"If you take us to France," Claudia hurried on, feeling her heart growing heavier, "he will not even know. He does not know what happened here. He will still head to the colonies, believing us there." Shaking her head, she rose to her feet. "We will be apart for months, perhaps years." Stepping up to the silent man, Claudia placed a hand on his arm. When his green eyes rose to meet hers, she allowed all her emotions to show in her voice, "Please. Please help us. I believe you know what it is to be separated from someone who holds your heart."

His jaw tensed at the reminder of the woman he refused to discuss, and he turned from the window, facing her. "Our nations are at war," he stated, his eyes hard as he ignored her reference to Lady Juliet. "I cannot simply approach the Scottish coast, let alone make for a Scottish port." A hint of compassion came to his eyes as he shook his head. "I'm sorry, but it would be too dangerous. I'd be risking every life on this vessel, and I cannot do that in good conscience."

Nodding, Claudia willed herself not to crumble at his words. "I understand. But can you not perhaps wait before heading back to France? Wait until my husband finds us?"

Sighing, Captain Duret ran a hand through his black hair. "You cannot be certain that your husband is indeed following you, and even if he is, there is no way of telling when-if at all-he might stumble upon us here."

"He's always found me," Claudia replied, feeling tears streaming down her face. "He will come. He will find us. I know it."

"If only I could be as certain as you, *Madam*." Shaking his head, Captain Duret regarded her calmly. "Come," he finally said, offering her his hand.

"Where are we going?" Claudia asked as she brushed the tears from her cheeks.

"To the *Voile Noire*," the captain replied. "This vessel is to return to France as soon as possible."

Claudia's heart skipped a beat. "You're not sending me back to France?"

Glancing at her, he held open the door to allow her to step through. "Not at present," he all but grumbled, a hint of displeasure in his voice. Still, in the dim light of the moon, his eyes shone with humour. "You'll stay with me for the time being...until I've decided what to do with you."

Giving him a grateful smile, Claudia asked, "What about Mr. Adams?"

The young captain shrugged. "All prisoners will be sent to France and then ransomed back to England. It is the way things are done, *Madam*."

As he stepped toward the railing, Claudia placed a hand on his arm, holding him back. "Thank you," she whispered, seeing nothing dangerous in the green eyes that looked back into hers. "You're doing the right thing. I promise you."

For a moment, Captain Duret regarded her with a quizzical look before a teasing smile curved up his lips. "I'm not certain," he whispered, a challenge in his voice. "Trouble will find you wherever you go. It might be wise to part with you as soon as possible."

Claudia laughed, "You sound like my brother."

Feigning a shocked expression, Captain Duret shook his head. "What an utterly terrifying thought!"

Again, he turned to the railing, and again, she held him back. "If you wish," she said, seeking his eyes once more, hoping he could read her sincerity in her own, "I could get a message to the Lady Juliet." His arm under her hand tensed. "No one would ever have to know. I will not breathe a word of this."

Holding her gaze, he inhaled a deep breath. "You must be hungry,

Madam," he said, once more offering her his hand. "Allow me to escort you to the *Voile Noire.*"

Sighing, Claudia accepted his offer. Still, she could not help but wonder what had happened between the French captain and this unknown English lady. Perhaps once Claudia was back in England, she ought to seek out Lady Juliet and hope to learn from her what it was that stood between those two.

Claudia could not deny that she was utterly curious.

Chapter Thirty-Five

LOST HOPE

The days out at sea all blurred together, and Garrett felt as though it had been months since he had last seen his wife. Once again, he felt that lump settle in the pit of his stomach, filled with dread and fear and utter longing. It reminded him painfully of the time he had spent looking for her after their impromptu wedding in Gretna Green. Why was fate forcing him to be forever searching for her?

With each day that passed, Garrett's hope waned. He would not give up. Certainly not. Still, he could not deny that it felt as though the world was against them, as though their love was simply not meant to be.

"We'll find her," Finn stated resolutely as they sat in their cabin. "Her and yer son. Have faith."

Garrett snorted, running his hand through his unkempt hair. "I keep telling myself that same thing, but I canna deny that a part of me fears 'tis only wishful thinking." Glancing out the small porthole, he took in the wide expanse of the sea. "I've never been on a ship. I dinna know that..." He sighed, then turned and met his friend's gaze. "I never imagined it to be this wide. How can we find anyone out here? 'Tis like searching for a needle in a haystack."

Sighing, Finn nodded. "Aye, 'tis true." Rising to his feet, he paced the length of the room, his green eyes distant as his thoughts were drawn inward. Garrett did not know what had caught his attention, but he saw the steel that came to his friend's eyes as he stopped and lifted his gaze, his eyes seeking Garrett's. "'Tis the way of the world to put obstacles in yer way, to test yer strength, yer resilience, yer determination." He took a step closer and grabbed Garrett's shoulder, squeezing it. "It helps ye understand what ye want and how much ye want it." A knowing smile came to his face. "Do ye love her?"

"Aye," Garrett replied without a moment's hesitation.

"Do ye want her back?"

"Aye."

"Can ye imagine yer life without her? Even for a moment?"

Garrett's heart clenched painfully at the thought, and he felt his muscles tense at the pain radiating through his body.

Finn laughed, "If she is yer life, old friend, yer heart and soul and the breath of yer body, then ye will find her. Ye must believe that Fate wouldna keep two people apart who belong together, but she might test ye. Prove yerself, and she will grant ye yer greatest wish."

Touched by his friend's words, Garrett nodded, knowing beyond the shadow of a doubt that Finn had spoken about his own search for love and the one woman who was his other half. Although he had found her many years ago, he had not known then that they had been meant for each other. Doubt and fear had kept them apart until the yuletide season of the previous year.

Ever since Finn had claimed Emma as his, he had been the happiest of man.

Garrett could only hope that Fate would smile upon him as well.

"Sail ho!"

The shout echoed through the ship like the shock wave of a cannon splashing into the water right beside them. Garrett could feel it in his body, in the way his muscles jerked to a halt, in the way his heart froze, and his breath lodged in his throat.

The look on Finn's face almost mimicked his as the smile disappeared, replaced by a tense look of apprehension. "Go," he breathed, his voice faint in the stillness of the cabin.

In the next instant, Garrett bolted for the door, hearing a number of footsteps rushing here and there on deck. He flung himself down the gangway and up the ladder, emerging from the hatch with wide eyes as he scanned the horizon.

"Do ye see anything?" Finn asked behind him as they came to stand on deck, both craning their necks.

"There!" Garrett finally said, spotting a tiny dot on the far horizon, and for a moment, he simply stood and stared.

"Let's go speak to Duncan," Finn urged, pulling on his arm.

Fighting off the lead that had sunk to his feet, weighing him down, Garrett rushed to the quarter deck where Duncan and two of his men stood, a spyglass in hand, considering the other vessel.

As Garrett and Finn approached, the other two men stepped back, and Duncan turned to meet them. "'Tis one ship," he said, and the tone of his voice told Garrett everything he needed to know. "I dunno believe 'tis the merchant vessel ye described, my friend." An apologetic look rested in his eyes as he gestured Garrett forward, holding out the spyglass to him. "Have a look for yerself."

Inhaling a deep breath, Garrett stepped up to the bear-like man he had come to see as more than an ally, but a friend. Then he met Finn's gaze for a brief moment before he accepted the spyglass, feeling its smooth metal casing against his skin.

Tension clung to him as Garrett lifted the spyglass to his eye. For a long moment, he held his breath as his view cleared, and he could see the tall-masted ship on the horizon.

In an instant, Garrett knew that it was indeed not the merchant vessel that he had watched disappear with his wife and son on board. Cursing under his breath, Garrett felt his fingers clench around the small tube in his hands. "D'ye know who they are?"

Duncan sighed, "D'ye see the black sail?"

Squinting, Garrett looked through the spyglass once more. Indeed, one sail was pitch-black, and he half-expected to see a skull and cross-bones drawn upon it. "They're just sitting there," he observed, watching men like tiny ants crawl around in the rigging and walk across deck. "D'ye think they've not seen us yet? They seem to have no intention of approaching."

"At least not yet," Duncan grumbled, tension darkening his voice.

Turning to the large man, Garrett took note of the way the muscles in Duncan's jaw clenched and unclenched. "Who are they?"

Meeting his eyes, Duncan sighed, "As we rarely travel out to sea this far, I've never encountered them myself, but I've heard of the ship with a black sail. Everyone has."

Garrett swallowed as Finn stepped forward. "Who are they?"

"A French privateer," Duncan replied after a glance over his shoulder. "The *Voile Noire*. She's rumoured to be ruthless, preying on English ships like a wolf taking down sheep."

Garrett swallowed, wondering if this was another obstacle Fate had put in his way or if this was the end of his journey. "But we're not English," he objected, knowing only too well how weak his argument was.

As expected, Duncan laughed. However, it was a mirthless laughter, holding a good deal of anxiety. "I doubt her captain will make a distinction here." Holding Garrett's gaze, he heaved a deep sigh. "We ought to change course," he said, "while we still can because these men," he nodded his head toward the *Voile Noire* floating on the horizon, "will fight."

Feeling all strength leave his body, Garrett nodded, praying that his wife and son were safe...wherever they were.

Chapter Thirty-Six

FAITH REWARDED

Although simple, breakfast on the *Voile Noire* was warm and hearty, and Claudia ate with abundance. Now, that Captain Duret had all but promised to help her, her spirits had risen from the depth they had plummeted into upon seeing the Scottish coast disappear on the horizon.

"You're ravenous, *Madam*," the Frenchman observed with a chuckle as he once more dangled the small jewel in front of Aiden. Her son had taken an instant liking to the dark-haired captain and had uttered no protest when the man had snatched him from his mother's arms.

"Do you want me to take him?" Claudia asked, her voice slightly muffled as her mouth was currently otherwise occupied. "I only need one hand to eat."

Captain Duret laughed, "Finish your food, *Madam*. Your son and I understand each other."

Seeing the truth of his words, Claudia continued to eat, wondering about the man with the dangerous reputation. Although he had seemed somewhat terrifying when she had first glimpsed him on board the *Voile Noire*, he had since done nothing that would inspire fear. On the contrary, despite his claims to the contrary, Henri-information she had managed to extract after at least an hour of incessant nagging-proved to be quite the gentleman. Not only had he allowed her the use of his bed, but he seemed to be quite fond of Aiden, playing with him whenever she needed a moment to herself. "Your arms must be in need of rest, *Madam*," he had observed earlier that morning.

"He will cry if I set him down."

Rolling his eyes, Henri had snatched him from her arms then, his gaze strangely aglow and not at all annoyed as he had looked down into Aiden's little face. "Your *maman* is in need of food, *mon petit*, or she'll fall flat on her face." Aiden had giggled at that, which had drawn a large smile onto the Frenchman's face. "Yes, flat on her face, *vraiment?*"

"You'll be a wonderful uncle," Claudia observed, hoping that it would not be long before she would see Garrett play with his son in a similar fashion. "Will you return to France to see your new niece or nephew?"

Still dangling the jewel in front of Aiden, Henri looked at her, a calculating hint in his eyes. "You ask many questions, *madam*."

Claudia shrugged. "I'm curious."

"Curiosity has been many a man's downfall," he observed with raised brows.

"I'm not a man."

Laughing, Henri shook his head, "You're incorrigible."

"Again, you sound like my brother."

Rolling his eyes at her, Henri shook his head. "If your husband will not find us soon, I might have to insist you walk the plank as your influence on me seems to be most harmful."

Claudia laughed. Still, her heart skipped a beat at his words. "Does that mean you'll allow me to return to him when he comes?"

Henri's green eyes met hers. "If he comes."

"He will."

Again, he shook his head. "Your faith in-"

"Sail ho!"

At the call, they both froze, eyes locked as a moment ticked by... and then another. Then Henri sighed and rose to his feet. "We might as well go on deck to see if it is indeed your husband," he said, offering her his hand. "Or rather an English armada come to sink us to the bottom of the ocean."

"That's not funny," Claudia observed as she rose from her chair and reclaimed her son. "You should not be jesting about these things."

Opening the door for her, he met her gaze. "I wasn't jesting," he said, and a chill ran down her spine. "This is life at sea, and these are times of war, *Madam*. No more and no less."

Swallowing the fear that suddenly rose in her throat, Claudia followed the young captain on deck. As he strode toward the quarter deck, always careful to guide her steps, he exchanged a few words with his crew. "It seems it's not the English armada today," he said smirking at her. "There's only one ship."

Releasing the breath she had been holding, Claudia watched him accept a spyglass from a sailor in his crew and lift it to his face. Her heart beat frantically against her ribs as she awaited his verdict. From this distance, she could not make out more than the rough shape of a ship, which was not much to go on.

"She seems to be Scottish," Henri mumbled as he surveyed the other vessel.

"Scottish?" Claudia's heart jumped a mile high, and she had trouble keeping her voice even. "What makes you say that?"

Henri shrugged, turning to look at her. "In my line of work, one develops a certain sense for these things." Then he held out the spyglass to her. "Care to look?"

Inhaling a deep breath, Claudia nodded. Careful to balance her son in one arm, she reached for the instrument with the other.

"Do you want me to hold him?" Henri asked, doubt in his gaze as he watched her balancing act.

Claudia shook her head. "Thank you, but there's no need. It might look a bit unstable, but I found as a mother one of the first things one learns is how to continue life one-handed."

Grinning, Henri nodded. "I'll pass that along to my cousin."

"You do that." Lifting the spyglass, Claudia peered through, willing her heart to slow down so her hand would be steady.

After a moment of blurry nothingness, things finally came into focus. Her gaze ran over the ship's tall masts and down to the deck where men moved about. "They do look Scottish," she whispered almost breathless as hope surged upward. Immediately, she searched the ship, her gaze skipping from man to man until-

"It's him!"

"Are you certain?" Henri asked beside her, doubt in his voice. "We're fairly far away."

"I'm certain," Claudia replied with conviction, unable to explain that sense of recognition that she had felt upon seeing the man. Certainly, she could barely make out his face, but her heart knew him to be her husband. Somehow he had found a way to follow her, and now he was here, right there, upon the horizon, waiting to take her home.

Swallowing, Claudia tried to contain the excitement that coursed through her body. This was it. She was so close to going home, to having her family reunited. If only...

"He came for me," she whispered, meeting the young captain's eyes. "He came for us, for his family. It's what you do for someone you love."

A shadow crossed over Henri's face, and for a short moment, he closed his eyes.

Claudia wished he would finally surrender his pride and once more seek out the woman he so obviously cared for. Perhaps all this would help him see that turning his back on his heart's desire could only lead to an empty and lonely life. Perhaps if he saw love overcome obstacles, he'd reconsider.

Smiling, Claudia lifted the spyglass in her hands once more, seeking out her husband standing on the ship's quarter deck. Then she handed the device back to Henri. "He's here," she whispered and waved to the other ship, a large smile on her face.

Chapter Thirty-Seven
RISKS WORTH TAKING

S ighing, Garrett felt the last shreds of hope wither and die in his chest.

Upon hearing the call from the crow's nest, a part of him had been so certain that his search had finally come to an end. That he was only moments away from seeing his family reunited.

Now, it seemed he was as far away from fulfilling that dream as he had ever been. Where was she? Which course had the merchant vessel taken? Had they changed direction? Or were they simply too far ahead? Would he ever know?

Ignoring the pitying expressions of the men around him, Garrett ran a hand over his face, his thumb and index finger running over his brows and down to his nose, pinching its bridge. What was he to do now?

Then he heard Duncan bellow to his crew, ordering to bring the ship about and change course. Instantly, Garrett's heart tightened, and a strange sense of loss came over him as though he was making a monumental mistake. Unable not to, he lifted the spyglass to his eye once more, peering through.

Men roamed the deck of the privateer's vessel, and yet, their movements were not rushed, but spoke of leisure. A tall, dark-haired man strode onto the quarter deck, and the other sailors stepped out of his path.

"The captain," Garrett mumbled, unable to look away for a reason he could not name.

On the other side of the captain, always blocked by his body, someone moved. Someone who seemed to be wearing skirts as the wind caught in them, stretching the fabric and letting it billow in the wind.

Garrett's breath caught in his lungs as his heart ceased its normal rhythm. While his mind reasoned that the woman blocked from his view could be anyone, his heart felt a sudden pull, a small tug as though she was calling out to him.

Trying to swallow the lump in his throat, Garrett willed the captain to move, to step out of his line of sight. Instead, the man lifted a spyglass to his face, and Garrett wondered what he would see.

"Are ye all right?" Finn asked beside him. "Perhaps we should head back below deck. Ye look like ye need some rest."

"I need my wife," Garrett hissed, his attention still focused on the other ship.

"We'll find her," Finn replied, placing a comforting hand on Garrett's shoulder. "Perhaps not today, but..."

Garrett was far from listening to his friend's words as he felt his heart speed up. He held his breath as the captain lowered the spyglass and then turned to the woman behind him, offering her the device. The moment she stepped forward, Garrett's heart stopped.

"They have her!" he exclaimed all but breathless. "Her and my son." Reeling from the shock of seeing his wife's lovely face, Garrett stared, his eyes glued to the spyglass as his gaze drifted lower to rest upon the infant lying in her arm.

"What?" Finn demanded, urgency and a hint of disbelief in his voice. "What did ye say?"

Suddenly filled with the need to act, Garrett spun around to face him, reluctantly shoving the spyglass in his hands. "There, next to the captain," he said as his heart thundered in his chest. "Do ye see them?"

"I'll be damned," Finn mumbled, then turned to stare at Garrett. "A woman and child. Are ye certain 'tis them?"

Garrett nodded, then bellowed Duncan's name. Snatching the spyglass from Finn, he pressed it into the captain's hands when he stepped up to them. "My family is on that ship," he said, watching Duncan's face pale.

"What?" Squinting, Duncan peered through the eyepiece. "Are ye certain 'tis yer wife? It could be a ruse."

Without even a moment of hesitation, Garrett shook his head. "No, 'tis them. I'm certain of it." His heart skipped a beat at the mere thought of her, and he could almost feel her presence nearby. For him, that was enough. All his doubt had evaporated into thin air the moment he had laid eyes on her. But would it be enough for Duncan? And even if it was, what would they do now?

No longer were they after a merchant vessel with men who were not trained to fight. Men who only sought to make a profit. Men who felt no loyalty beyond that to their own families.

Now, they were facing a French privateer, and from what Duncan had said, one with a ruthless reputation. One who preferably preyed on English vessels. One with a crew prepared to fight. Was there any way to retrieve his wife and son without loss of life? Did he have any right to ask Duncan and his men to risk their lives in his quest to see his family reunited? What of their wives and children awaiting their return back home?

"How did she end up on a French privateer?" Finn asked, his gaze like theirs fixed on the distant ship.

Duncan shrugged, then sighed. "'Tis most likely that the merchant vessel was boarded, and they were taken prisoners to be ransomed back to England."

"Do ye think they'll be taken to France?"

Duncan nodded. "Most likely." Then he shifted his gaze to Garrett. "'Tis a most difficult situation."

Garrett nodded, torn about what to do.

"D'ye think they'll be all right?" Finn asked, his shoulders tense as his dark gaze shifted from Garrett to Duncan, understanding the dilemma they found themselves in only too well. "Will they be treated...with respect?"

Duncan shrugged. "That I canna say. Prisoners taken at sea are ransomed back home, but I canna say in what condition or what happens to them before they are freed."

Garrett felt his heart clench at the thought of what might happen to his wife and son if he were to do nothing. And yet, what could he do? He was one man.

Swallowing, Garrett looked from Finn to Ian, who was just then climbing up to the quarter deck. Both his friends were married, and Ian was a father as well. Finn might have a child soon, too. Did he have any right risking their lives? And what about Duncan and his men?

Garrett hung his head. "I willna ask ye to risk yer men," he said, knowing that there was no other way. "It wouldna be right. Ye've done more for me than I ever dared dream, and I thank ye for it."

Finn frowned. "What are ye saying?"

Garrett inhaled a deep breath. "I canna ask any of ye to risk yer lives, but neither can I abandon my family." Ignoring the impulse to argue he saw in Finn's dark gaze, Garrett turned to Duncan. "But may I ask ye to let me take one of the dinghies so that I can row over to my family."

Both Finn and Ian objected loudly, their hands grabbing his arms and trying to pull him back to face them. But Garrett stood fast, his gaze on Duncan's as the other man regarded him with a mixture of curiosity and doubt.

"What's yer plan?" Duncan asked, scratching his chin.

Garrett shrugged. "I have none. All I know is that I canna leave them on their own. Perhaps if I'm there, I can protect them until they're ransomed back home. Perhaps..."

"Ye dunno truly believe that, do ye?" Duncan asked, shaking his head. "Ye will be in no position to protect anyone. Hell, they might shoot ye on sight."

Despair descended upon Garrett as Duncan's words sank in. "There's no other way. I canna leave them."

Duncan was about to reply when a man of his crew stepped up to him and whispered something in his ear. In answer, Duncan frowned, then looked at the man with a hint of incredulity on his face before he turned to meet Garrett's eyes. "Have a look again?" he said, gesturing to the spyglass in Garrett's hand.

Feeling his heart constrict, Garrett spun around, his mind picturing all kinds of unspeakable things that might have happened to his family while he had not been looking. His hand trembled, and at first, he could make out nothing. Everything he saw was blurry and out of focus.

Forcing a deep breath down his lungs, he tried again. When his vision finally cleared, the air was promptly knocked from his lungs.

"What?" Finn asked behind him, tension gripping his voice.

"She's waving," Garrett whispered under his breath as his body trembled at the sight of her. Holding their son in her arms, she stood beside the dark-haired captain, a large smile on her face and was waving her other arm at him. If Garrett was not completely mistaken, he thought to see a bit of a smirk on the captain's face.

"Waving? Why would she wave?"

Ignoring Finn, Garrett shoved the spyglass into Duncan's hands, and before long, everyone had taken a turn, confused about what they had seen.

A slight chuckle rose from Duncan's lips as he looked at Garrett. "Of course, I canna be certain, but perhaps yer wife has found... common ground with the captain of the *Voile Noire*. Women often succeed where men fail."

Garrett frowned. "What do ye mean by that?"

"Not what ye're thinking, my friend," Duncan laughed. "But from what ye told me, yer wife is fairly difficult to silence."

Unable not to, Garrett smiled. "Aye."

"Perhaps the captain experienced a similar problem," Duncan continued, looking over his shoulder at the privateer's ship. "She didna look afraid, did she? Perhaps being a mother with a young child, she was able to gain his sympathies. Perhaps he's a father himself."

Garrett nodded. "But we canna be certain."

"We canna," Duncan agreed, his gaze gliding over his ship, lingering on his men's faces. Then he drew in a deep breath and for a brief moment closed his eyes. His teeth gritted together, and he mumbled something under his breath, which sounded as if he was asking someone's forgiveness. "Aye, we'll try. Perhaps he'll be open to ransoming them back to us. 'Twill save him the trouble of taking them back to France."

Garrett sucked in a sharp breath as he watched Duncan bellow orders to approach the privateer with caution. His heart thudded almost painfully in his chest as it was torn between relief and guilt over risking all their lives. He could only hope that all would be well. That they might manage to agree to a ransom. That they might all get out of this alive.

At least, now he knew that his wife and child were unharmed. Garrett could only hope what they were about to do would not put them at risk once more.

Chapter Thirty-Eight
UNTIL WE MEET AGAIN

"They're changing course!"

"They're heading toward us!"

"Your orders, Capt'n?"

Beside her, Henri tensed, his jaw clenching as he watched the other ship's approach. "Ready the sails!" he yelled, stepping away from the railing.

Before he could walk away though, Claudia grabbed his arm, holding him back. "Please!" she said, her eyes meeting his. "Please let us go! He came for us. He's right here. Please!"

The green in his gaze darkened as he looked at her, and she could feel the muscles in his arm tense. "I cannot allow them to approach," he said, stepping closer. "We cannot be certain with regard to their fighting strength or their intentions. You don't know this ship, *n'est-ce pas?* Or its captain?"

Gritting her teeth, Claudia shook her head. She could not lie to him.

"Then, *Madam*, my hands are tied," Henri whispered, his voice strong and full of determination. And yet, there was a hint of regret in the way he looked at her. "I have but half a crew, and I cannot risk them or my ship on such a gamble."

"My husband would never-"

"Your husband might not," Henri interrupted her attempt to reassure him, "but he is not the ship's captain, *n'est-ce pas?* Even if he wants nothing more but to retrieve you, he cannot speak for that ship's captain. I'm sorry."

Feeling all hope plummet to the ground, Claudia still could not release her hold on him.

Eyeing her hand on his arm with curiosity, Henri drew her aside. "I promise I will get you and your son back home," he whispered, the look on his face one of utter commitment, "but not here and now. Not today." His green eyes looked deep into hers. "But you have my word, *Madam.*"

"Thank you," Claudia whispered as her vision became blurry and tears spilled over, running down her cheeks. She barely saw the reassuring smile that curled up his lips, but she felt the warm hand that settled on her shoulder, giving it a gentle squeeze.

Then he stepped away once more.

And once more Claudia held him back.

"I must go, *Madam.*" There was urgency in his voice, but his tone still spoke of respect and kindness.

"I understand that you cannot wait," Claudia spoke quickly, blinking back tears as both her hands were currently occupied; one was holding on to Aiden while the other was busy preventing Henri from leaving. "Ready your ship and take your crew to safety." She took a step closer, noting the hint of confusion that came to his eyes. "But leave us behind."

His eyes widened.

"In one of those small boats," Claudia hurried on before he could object. "The sea is calm. We'll be fine."

Henri's jaw tensed. "I cannot leave you and the boy behind on the open sea."

"Henri, please!" Claudia pleaded. "We'll be fine. My husband will come and get us. Whatever you think, you must admit that Aiden and I have nothing to fear from that ship. They will not hurt us."

Watching her, Henri inhaled a slow breath. "Are you so certain you would risk your son's life?"

Claudia shook her head. "I'm not risking his life," she stated with conviction in her voice. If only she could make him understand! "I know my husband is on that ship. You yourself said that it was Scottish. Whoever these men are, they are friends of my husband's. Why else would they have agreed to pursue the merchant vessel? Why else are they out here? They are here for us. I promise you Aiden will be fine."

For a short moment, Henri looked down at her son and a bit of an exhausted smile came to his lips. Then he met her gaze once again. "Violette, my cousin," he said, "she does things her own way, and I've learnt long ago...to trust her instincts." He sighed, "It's not always easy, but I try."

Relief sneaked into Claudia's heart. "What are you saying?"

"If this is what you want, then I will not object."

Relief exploded in Claudia's heart, and she all but flung herself into his arms. "Thank you," she gasped, careful not to crush Aiden in her eagerness to show her gratitude. "Thank you so much." Stepping back, she smiled at him. "You're a good man, Henri. I know I've said so before, but I hope that you'll hear me one of these times and truly believe so yourself. I have no doubt Lady Juliet agrees with me. Please, I know how it feels to be separated from the one who holds your heart, and the thought that you might never see each other again pains me. Seek her out, Henri. For her own sake as well as yours."

The smile fell from his lips.

"Beyond the shadow of a doubt, I know that she has never forgotten you." Leaning forward, she looked into his eyes and smiled. "How could she?"

Henri scoffed, "I'm not the kind of man English ladies dream of, I assure you, *Madam*. She is better off without me."

Surprised, Claudia watched him. Never before had the man volunteered a word about the elusive Lady Juliet. "I'm certain that you're the only one who believes so," she assured him, seeing only too plainly the longing to do as she had suggested on his face. "Do not assume, Henri. Seek her out and speak to her. You will only ever know what is in her heart if you ask her." Once more, she placed a hand on his arm. "If you wish, I can deliver a message to her."

His jaw tensed, and yet, utter temptation flared to life in his eyes. "She has her life, and I have mine. I doubt we will ever cross paths again."

Sighing, Claudia shook her head. "Do as you please," she said, a chiding tone in her voice that made him roll his eyes at her. "But I must say I disagree with your decision."

"You've made that very clear, *Madam*."

"Still, if you ever change your mind," Claudia continued, her gaze serious so he would not take this lightly, "then call on me, and I will do what I can to assist you."

Holding her gaze, Henri nodded, and for once, there was no humour in his eyes. "You're a fairly unique woman," he whispered, respect shining in his green eyes. "I've never met anyone like you."

Smiling widely, Claudia blinked her eyes at him. "I completely agree with your assessment, Captain Duret. Until we meet again."

Squeezing her hand, he nodded. "Until we meet again."

Chapter Thirty-Nine

ON THE OPEN SEA

Staring at the privateer, Garrett felt his insides twist painfully when he saw men rushing to ready the sails. "They'll outrun us!" someone called, and Garrett could have throttled the man for voicing his greatest fear.

As Duncan steered their ship toward the *Voile Noire*, Garrett once more looked through the spyglass, his gaze drawn to his wife. She was still on the quarter deck with the ship's captain, their faces turned toward one another. What were they talking about? Garrett wondered, wishing he could hear what was being said.

Watching her move, the way she held herself, her chin raised, and her shoulders squared, Garrett had to agree with Duncan's assessment. There was nothing fearful in the way she stood there facing the captain. On the contrary, when the man turned away, she reached out and pulled him back.

Sucking in a sharp breath, Garrett was doomed to watch as the captain complied, stepping closer to his wife and child. More words were exchanged before the man reached out and placed a hand on Claudia's shoulder.

Garrett tensed, and although the smile on his wife's face eased his fears for her safety, he could not deny that jealousy had found a way into his heart. What had happened between his wife and the privateer's captain?

A moment later, Claudia flung herself into the man's arms, and Garrett almost lost his footing.

"Are ye all right?" Finn asked beside him.

Garrett grumbled something under his breath, unable to tear his eyes from his wife as she lay in the captain's arms. To his utter relief, she quickly pulled back, re-establishing a minimum safe distance between herself and the dark-haired captain.

"What's happening?" Finn asked, his eyes squinted as he stared at the other ship. "Can ye still see them?"

"Aye," was all Garrett could say as he watched his wife follow the captain down to the main deck. More words flew from the man's mouth, but this time they were directed at men of his crew as he pointed to one of the dinghies. Within moments, sailors scrambled to remove the cover. Ropes were fastened to its ends, which ran upward to a pulley system. "What are they doing?" Garrett mumbled, unable to make sense of these new developments.

"What's happening?" Finn asked again.

"They seem to be readying a dinghy."

"What? Why?"

"I dunno know." Keeping his attention fixed on the small boat, Garrett swallowed hard when he watched the dark-haired captain assist his wife into the dinghy. Aiden still lay in her arms, and he could see a smile on her face. What was going on? A moment ago, it seemed as though they were going to make a run for it, and now...

"They're launching a dinghy!" Duncan called as he appeared beside Garrett, another spyglass in his hands. "What's happening?"

Shaking his head, Garrett shrugged. Why did people always think he had the answers?

Stunned, they all stood on deck and watched as the dinghy was lowered to the water's surface. Then the ropes were removed, and the moment the dinghy was unattached, the *Voile Noire* raised her sails, its large black one billowing in the wind like a dark storm cloud.

Within moments, she made headway, the strong breeze carrying her farther and farther away. Looking up, Garrett found the captain standing at the stern of his ship, his gaze fixed on the small boat as though reluctant to part with it...or the woman inside.

Garrett could not help but wonder why.

"They're leaving her behind?" Finn exclaimed, a dark frown on his face as he shook his head. "Why would they do that?"

"So, we don't pursue them," Ian suggested, a scowl on his face.

Duncan shook his head. "Nah, look how fast she is. Lowering that dinghy took time and gave them no advantage. Either way we would not have been able to catch up with her."

"Then why?" Ian snapped, his eyes narrowing with suspicion as they always did when he could not make sense of something.

"I suppose only yer wife," Duncan said as he looked at Garrett, "will be able to give us an answer to that."

"Whatever the answer, it does not matter right now," Garrett replied as he hastened down to the main deck. "All that matter is that we'll get them on board. Fast." Leaning over the railing, he looked at the small boat, dancing on the soft waves like a leaf on a pond.

So close.

Garrett felt his skin itch with the need to hold them in his arms. His body strained toward them, and he felt his fingernails dig into the railing's wooden beam.

Soon, his mind whispered, urging him to remain calm.

However, his heart screamed back *Soon is not soon enough*.

Sighing, Claudia watched the privateer sail away, her gaze meeting Henri's as he stood at the stern of his ship, his face tense as though he feared for her. He had only reluctantly agreed to leave her behind, feeling a sense of duty to ensure her safety. Claudia knew she had been incredibly fortunate that it had been the *Voile Noire* to come upon them and not another privateer. What would have happened to them if they had been faced with another man? A man unlike Captain Duret? A man without respect and decency? A man without morals and compassion?

No, Claudia did not even want to contemplate such a scenario as the mere thought of it turned her stomach. Indeed, she had been fortunate, and she would never forget the dark-haired captain or the lengths he had gone to in order to assist her.

Grateful beyond words, Claudia smiled up at him, wishing to reassure him and set his mind at ease. She could see the corners of his mouth quirk and knew that he understood. Still, he remained where he was, not allowing the small dinghy out of his sight.

Shaking her head, Claudia wondered about the kind and compassionate captain with the ruthless reputation. She could only hope that one day he would come to see that love was worth fighting for, that it could overcome obstacles and lead to a happy ending.

Hopefully, one day soon.

For if there was ever a man who deserved a happy ending, it was Henri Duret.

Whispering a silent goodbye, Claudia then turned her attention to the other ship, fast approaching with billowing sails. Her eyes scanned the deck as she whispered to Aiden, who lay wide awake in her arms, his little fists waving as though he too felt the excitement of their impending reunion. "See, Aiden, your father is coming for us. I always knew he would. I-"

Her voice broke off when her gaze fell on the one man she could no longer live without.

Tall and strong, Garrett stood on deck, his hands gripping the railing as he leaned forward. The wind pulled on his dark hair, whipping it into his face as his dark green eyes burnt with intensity, their attention focused on her and her alone.

Relief stood in his gaze, and yet, his features were tense, his muscles wound tight like a spring. Even from a distance, Claudia could see the toll the last few weeks had taken on him, and she knew in that moment that he ached for her just as much as she ached for him.

His presence-suddenly so close-washed over her, and she could almost feel him. She felt his gaze meeting hers, travelling over her face, and it was like a caress against her skin. "Claudia!" he called all of a sudden, and the sound of his voice brought back all the many moments they had spent together, arguing, laughing, teasing, kissing.

"Garrett!" Claudia called back, laughter bubbling up in her throat as she waved to him. Her heart danced in her chest as it had never before, and she knew in that moment that she loved him, that she had always loved him. She belonged with him just like he belonged with her.

They were meant to be.

And then Garrett pulled himself up onto the railing and jumped into the churning waves.

Claudia's mouth dropped open, and for a heart-stopping moment, she thought he was gone. Her heart screamed out in agony, and all warmth drained from her body.

But then his head reappeared, and Claudia drew in a shaking breath, feeling her heart hammering in her chest.

Fast strokes carried him closer, his gaze fixed on hers as he swam, crossing the distance between the large vessel at his back and her small dinghy. The sails had come down, and the ship no longer cut through the waves, but was rather floating nearby, men grouped on deck, their attention focused on them.

Claudia barely noticed them.

All she could see was Garrett swimming toward her, and her heart jumped with joy the moment his fingers curled around the side of the boat. His face was dripping wet as he pulled himself out of the water, his green eyes holding hers. Claudia wanted to fling herself into his arms; however, the moment she moved toward him, the boat tilted downward on Garrett's side and a large splash of water was flung into the boat.

"Stay back!" Garrett called, alarm tensing his features once more. "Stay on the other side."

Claudia nodded, then scooted back and leaned her weight onto the other side of the boat while holding onto Aiden tightly.

Then Garrett pushed himself upward and swung a leg over. A moment later, he lay in the boat, panting and dripping with water, a large smile on his face.

As he pushed himself into a sitting position, his eyes shining as they looked into hers, Claudia could no longer hold herself back. Lunging herself across the boat, she fell into his arms, barely aware of the wetness that began to soak through her clothes. All she felt were his arms as they came around her, holding her tightly against him, as he mumbled endearments into her ear, his warm breath tickling her skin.

Claudia could have stayed like this for all eternity. However, Aiden seemed to object to being squashed between his two parents as noises of discontent rose from his lips.

Pulling back, Garrett stared down at his son, awe shining in his eyes as they travelled over Aiden's little face. For a moment, he seemed frozen, unmoving, as his chest rose and fell with each breath. Eager-ness stood on his face, and yet, there was something that seemed to hold him back. His hand rose, reaching for his son, but then paused and merely traced the air above Aiden's little face as though he did not dare touch him.

Swallowing, Garrett shook his head as air rushed from his lungs. "I've tried to picture him so often," he whispered, his gaze not veering from his son, "but he was only an idea, a thought, a dream. I couldna quite see his face." A slow smile claimed his lips, and he lowered his hand another fraction, the tips of his fingers gently brushing over Aiden's head. "I canna believe he's truly here. Right here. I can...I can touch him." His gaze rose to meet hers, and Claudia could see awe shining in his face. "He's so warm...and strong."

Smiling, Claudia nodded. "He is," she whispered, feeling tears sting her eyes. "And heavy."

Garrett chuckled, disbelief in his eyes. "He is? He looks so small."

"Carry him around all day, and we'll talk again," Claudia laughed, brushing a gentle hand over her son's cheek. "By the end of the day, my arms feel like lead, and I think I'll never be able to lift them again."

Garrett sighed, "I'd take him for ye, but..." He glanced down at his soaked clothes. "I guess I'd better change first."

Claudia nodded. "Yes, I think that'd be for the best." Still, there was one thing that she did not want to wait for any longer.

The moment Garrett turned away, looking over his shoulder at the large ship drifting nearby, Claudia reached out. Her fingers curled into the front of his shirt and pulled him back to her. She had a moment to notice a slight widening of his eyes as well as the hint of a frown drawing down his brows before her lips claimed his.

Despite his surprise, Garrett did not hesitate in his response. Cupping her face gently, he pulled her into his arms, careful not to squeeze his son. His lips moved over hers with bold familiarity, and Claudia could feel the flame between them ignite once more. "I've missed you so much," she whispered against his lips.

"I've missed ye as well, Lass." Smiling down at her, Garrett planted another deep kiss onto her lips before he pulled back, his gaze still dark with longing. "Let's go home," he whispered, a question in his eyes that conquered Claudia's heart all over again.

"Yes," she said smiling. "Let's go home."

Chapter Forty

QUESTIONS ASKED

Night was fast approaching by the time Garrett found himself in the captain's quarters of Duncan's ship. After returning to the large vessel, Garrett had led his family down to his cabin and immediately changed into dry clothes, his eyes fixed on his son. Then he had held open his arms and Claudia had gently settled his little boy into the crook of his arm.

"I dunno know what ye mean, Lass," Garrett had chuckled. "He's as light as a feather."

Claudia had rolled her eyes at him then and mumbled something about there being a difference between a moment and days on end. Garrett had barely heard her though as his son had held his full attention.

Aiden's dark blue eyes had sparkled with such curiosity and interest that Garrett had been awed by the intent way his infant son had looked up at him. His little hands had moved rather randomly and without direct focus. However, the moment Aiden's hand had touched his father's, his little fingers had curled around Garrett's thumb, holding on with a strength that had nearly taken his breath away.

"But he's strong." Trying to wriggle his finger, Garrett had found that Aiden had been far from willing to let go. Instead, he had snuggled into the crook of his arm and soon closed his eyes, his little hand still holding on tightly to his father.

In that moment, Garrett had lost his heart to his little son, knowing without thought that his life would never be the same again. The earth no longer revolved around the sun, but around this precious little boy.

And it was right that it should do so.

After a small respite, they were now all gathered in Duncan's quarters: Duncan as well as his first mate, Finn and Ian as well as Garrett and his wife and son. Aiden still slept peacefully in Garrett's arms, and his father marvelled how odd it felt to suddenly be holding his son in his arms while at the same time, it felt perfectly natural and as though it had never been any different.

"Would ye tell us what happened?" Duncan asked Claudia, a disbelieving smile on his face. "I must say I was rather taken aback when I saw ye lowered to the water in that dinghy." He laughed. "We wouldna have expected the captain to simply release ye."

Claudia sighed, and Garrett could see that she was weighing her words. "It's a rather long story," she told the small group of men assembled around her. "All I can say is that Captain Duret and I...have a mutual acquaintance."

Duncan's brows rose. "Ye do? That, I wouldna have expected. I had thought he might have been able to sympathise with ye because he was a father and husband himself."

Claudia chuckled, "No, he's not married, but he told me he'll be an uncle soon."

"What else did ye talk about?" Ian pressed, his brows drawn and his eyes dark with wariness. "How long were ye on his ship? How many days? And nights?"

Garrett was not the only one who understood Ian's questions for what they were, thinly veiled suspicions. While Finn rolled his eyes and Duncan shook his head, Claudia met Ian's gaze without flinching. Still, the look in her blue eyes betrayed her displeasure with his questions, and yet, she remained calm. "Do not hide behind politeness-if you can even call it that," she said, her chin raised as she met Ian's gaze. "Ask what you wish to know, and perhaps I will answer you."

Ian's face tensed, and he linked his hands behind his back. "Verra well. Did ye share the captain's bed? Is that why he released ye? Because ye paid him?"

If his son had not been sleeping in his arms, Garrett would have pounded his friend into the ground. Although Ian had always been a suspicious sort of man, Garrett had never before noticed the dark bitterness that clung to him.

Still, Garrett could not deny that he wanted to hear his wife answer Ian's questions as a dark part of him recalled the familiarity with which she had conversed with the dark-haired captain. Had they met before? Or-?

Claudia scoffed, crossing her arms in front of her chest. "Those are questions a husband might ask," for a brief moment, her blue eyes drifted to Garrett, "but what is it to you?" She took a step toward Ian, and his gaze narrowed. "The *Voile Noire* is gone. It no longer poses a threat to us, to you. Why would your thoughts turn to betrayal before anything else?"

Ian's face darkened, and Garrett could see that the fuse had been lit. Soon, his friend would explode, and Garrett did not think that anyone would care for such a confrontation. "Enough," he said, drawing all eyes to him. "I believe all questions have been answered. Duncan?"

Shifting his gaze from Ian to Garrett, the second-in-command of Clan MacKinnear nodded. "Aye, 'tis been a long day, and we all could do with some rest." Curiosity still lingered in his eyes, but there would be time for more questions later. Questions asked out of interest, not out of suspicion.

"Will ye talk to him?" Garrett whispered to Finn, his gaze following Ian as his friend stormed out the door.

Finn nodded. "Aye. But I doubt it'll do any good. He's grown more and more sullen these past few years. He's not a happy man, not like we are."

Garrett nodded, aware that Ian's marriage had not been a love match. Although he and his wife had come to care for one another in the beginnings of their marriage, at some point something had happened to draw them apart with each year that passed. More than once, Garrett had wondered what that had been and if there was any chance to lead them back to one another.

Unfortunately, it did not seem likely.

"I'm happy for ye," Finn said, drawing Garrett's attention back to the here and now. A large smile clung to his features as his gaze shifted to where Claudia spoke to Duncan. "Ye fit well together."

Garrett nodded. "Aye. I've thought so since the moment I first laid eyes on her."

Finn chuckled, "I know what that feels like. See ye tomorrow, old friend."

Bidding his friend a good night, Garrett walked up to his wife and Duncan. "I assume we're headed back to Glasgow."

Duncan nodded. "Ye'd assume right. Now, get some rest. There'll be time to talk again tomorrow." Smiling, Duncan looked down at Aiden, a father's pride in his eyes. "He's a braw lad. He'll make ye proud."

Garrett sighed, meeting his wife's blue eyes, "He already has."

Nodding knowingly, Duncan sent them back to their cabin before he turned to his first mate.

"He's a good man," Claudia commented as they walked along the dark gangway. "He's a father, isn't he?"

Garrett nodded, holding open the door to their cabin. "Aye. His son is only a few weeks old as well. I believe that is why he took this chance. He can imagine what it feels like to have his family stolen from him." Closing the door behind him, Garrett met his wife's gaze. "A part of me feared I'd never see ye again, Lass."

Swallowing, she nodded, and he could see the faint shimmer of tears clinging to the lashes. "As did I," she whispered before a soft smile tugged on her lips. "But then I remembered how you came looking for me, and I knew that you'd find us."

Touched by her trust in him, Garrett drew in a slow breath, reminding himself that all had turned out well. That his family was here, safe and sound. His gaze drifted lower, touching his son's sweet face as he slept peacefully, fortunately unaware of the danger he had been in. Garrett could only hope that he would remain safe from now on until the end of his days.

"Ask me."

"What?" Looking up, Garrett found a strange look on his wife's face. Her eyes were open and intent, holding his, and yet, there was a hint of a challenge in the way she stood before him. "What do ye mean?"

"Ask me about Captain Duret."

At her words, Garrett felt the room grow cold, chilling his bones.

Chapter Forty-One

ANSWERS GIVEN

The moment Ian had spoken, giving voice to his accusations, Claudia had known that at least a small part of Garrett was in doubt. Perhaps it was only natural. Perhaps it had nothing to do with who they were. Perhaps it was merely circumstantial.

Would she have wondered if Garrett had spent days on a privateer's vessel in the company of a female captain?

As much as she wanted to deny it, Claudia had to admit that despite the fact that she trusted Garrett she would have needed to hear his assurance that nothing had happened. She would have believed him, but she would have needed to hear him say the words.

Still, Claudia could not deny that Ian's accusations stung. After all, she had done nothing wrong. In fact, if she had not pleaded with Henri, she and Aiden would be on their way to France right now.

At her words, Garrett had grown still, his face pale even in the dim light from the lantern dangling from a hook in the corner of the room. Dread and even a hint of fear stood in his eyes, and a part of Claudia rejoiced at seeing it, knowing that there would be no fear without love.

Swallowing, she stepped toward her husband and gently took her son from his arms. Then she lay Aiden down on the cot in the corner, piling blankets and pillows around him so he would not roll out. Then she turned to face her husband.

While her back had been turned, Garrett had come alive again. His gaze flitted around the small cabin as he raked his hands through his hair. "Is there something ye need to tell me?" he asked, and a full second passed before his gaze rose to meet hers.

Stepping toward him, Claudia drew in a slow breath. "Ever since Ian..." Sighing, she shook her head. "You've been wondering. I can see it in your eyes."

Garrett's jaw clenched, and for a brief moment, he dropped his gaze. Then he was suddenly in front of her, his hands reaching for hers as his eyes caught her gaze. "I never meant to doubt ye, Lass. I swear it. But I canna shake that feeling that there was...something between ye." He swallowed. "I saw ye, the way ye reached for him, the way he looked at ye."

Claudia frowned. "You saw us? How?"

Garrett's teeth gritted together, and she knew every second that passed was pure agony for him. "Through the spyglass. I saw ye standing on deck, and there was something about the way ye spoke to each other as though...as though ye were in each other's confidence." His hands tightened on hers. "And so, I will ask ye. How do ye know that man?"

Squeezing his hands, Claudia looked up at him. "I never met him until a few days ago," she said, feeling at least a bit of the tension leave Garrett's body. "But I heard my brother speak of him last summer. From what I was able to gather, Henri had come to-"

"Henri?" Garrett growled out, displeasure clear on his face.

Claudia laughed, unable to help herself, "Yes, Henri. Will you let me finish?"

Inhaling a deep breath, Garrett nodded.

"Well, as I said Henri came to London to help his cousin." As best as she could, Claudia told Garrett about Lady Juliet and her unfortunate betrothal to an old man, about her half-sister's desire to liberate her from said betrothal and how she and her new husband had called upon friends and acquaintances to assist them in said pursuit. "That was how my brother and Henri crossed paths, and how

I came to know his name. And so, when his crew boarded our ship, I decided to introduce myself to him and hope that he would be willing to help."

Garrett swallowed. "'Twas dangerous drawing his attention to ye, Lass. What if he had been a different kind of man? What if he-?"

"If he had been a different kind of man," Claudia interrupted, "he would not have come to London out of fear of seeing his cousin harmed." Squeezing her husband's hands, Claudia held his gaze. "I trusted my instincts, and they have not led me astray. Henri Duret is a truly good man, and he acted more like a gentleman than those rakes in London. Besides, whether he wants to admit it or not, his heart is already taken. He had no interest in capturing mine." Biting her lower lip, Claudia smiled up at Garrett. "Not that he'd ever have had a chance."

Sighing in relief, Garrett drew her into his arms. "Aye?" he whispered, his green eyes dark, and yet, vulnerable as they looked into hers.

"Aye," Claudia responded with a smile, leaning into him. The feel of his arms around her was heavenly, and she only then realised how much she had missed him. For fear of losing faith and courage and determination, she had forced herself not to dwell on his absence, on their separation, on what it felt like to be without him. But now, all those emotions came rushing back in the form of utter relief, and she sank deeper into his arms, sighing with contentment.

Garrett's chin rested on the top of her head, and she could feel him relax as well. Tension had been on his face, in the way he had reached for her from the moment they had met again on the open sea. He, too, had lived with doubts and fears, and they had marked him. But now it was time to let them go and look toward the future.

His chest rose and fell as he inhaled a deep breath. "I love ye, Lass. Have I ever told ye that?"

Feeling a smile claim her face, Claudia lifted her head and found dark green eyes looking down into hers. Shadows danced over Garrett's face as he held her tight, speaking to the uncertainty she could see in his eyes. "I love you as well," Claudia whispered, reaching up and cupping a hand to his face.

A large smile claimed Garrett's face then, and before she had time to draw in another breath, his mouth came down on hers in a searing kiss.

For a long moment, they clung to one another, allowing past doubts and fears to fall from them, revelling in the knowledge that they had not been wrong. That they had not been deceived. That they had been right to trust their hearts.

Their instincts.

For they had led them on a winding path to the one person who was meant to walk at their side.

"All this time," Garrett began as he traced his thumb along the line of her jaw, "we've never even spoken about what we'd do once we found our son." For a moment, his gaze travelled to the peacefully-sleeping child on the cot behind her, and a blissful smile lit up his face. "I tell ye now that I've always wanted to take ye home with me, to begin a life together in Scotland." He sighed, "But I now realise that I never asked ye what ye wanted, Lass. So, I'm asking ye now."

Leaning into his caress, Claudia smiled. "I want to go back to England and see my family." Guilt claimed her heart, and she wondered what they were doing in that very moment. "I left in the middle of the night, leaving nothing but a note that in truth told them very little." She scoffed, shaking her head. "After all, I didn't want them to come after me and stop me."

Garrett nodded. "Aye, they need to know that ye're safe."

"And I want them to meet Aiden," she whispered, unable to suppress the smile that slowly stole up her face, "and you. I want them to know how happy I am and that all ended well."

Garrett chuckled, "Nothing is ending, Lass. 'Tis only the beginning."

"Only the beginning," Claudia echoed his words, realising that she had never felt so hopeful and confident about her future. All of a sudden, she knew exactly what she wanted, what would make her happy. "And then we'll go home to Scotland," she told him, not a single doubt in her heart, "and start over as a family."

Happiness shone on Garrett's face as he looked down at her. "Are ye certain, Lass? 'Tis a different way of life. 'Tis-"

"It's an adventure," Claudia interrupted as her teeth sank into her lower lip before a face-splitting grin could claim her whole. "I've always wanted that." She nodded her head. "Yes, I'm certain. I've never been more certain in my life."

That night, they spent curled up together on a single cot. Claudia's head rested on his shoulder while Garrett's arm reached around her and settled on hers. They fit together perfectly, and Aiden lay safely tucked between them, a little smile playing on his face as he slept.

Chapter Forty-Two

COMING HOME

London

A fortnight later

While Finn looked rather curiously at his surroundings, Claudia doubted that Ian would ever come to like anything English. Much less her. There seemed to be a certain animosity between them that she could not explain. However, as time passed, she came to doubt that it had anything to do with her. Who knew what demons lived in Ian's past?

"'Tis a grand city," Finn remarked as he stood with Garrett and Ian over by the pianoforte in her brother's drawing room. "I've never seen so many people in one place."

Ian grumbled something, no doubt disagreeable under his breath.

After retrieving her from the small dinghy in the middle of the open sea, it had been agreed that Finn and Ian would accompany them to London for a short visit before they would all return to the Highlands. Garrett had procured a carriage for his little family while Finn and Ian had travelled on horseback.

The way back had taken longer. However, this time they had not been in a hurry, enjoying the peaceful time they had together. Only Ian had seemed displeased with their travel arrangements. Finn, on the other hand, had been delighted. "I wish Emma was here. She'd love to see all this."

Claudia had assured him that he was more than welcome to invite his wife along the next time they travelled to London. For although she longed to see her new home in the Highlands, Claudia knew that she could never stay away from her family for too long.

Upon their arrival back in London, her mother had fallen into her arms, sobbing heartbreakingly. "I was so afraid I'd never see you again. Why did you not tell us? Of course, we would have helped you. Don't you know how much you mean to us?"

Indeed, there had been a time when Claudia had not been certain, when she had felt that she did not belong. But all that was different now.

Her family had welcomed her back with open arms, overjoyed to meet Aiden as well as Garrett. Of course, they had looked rather shocked upon first hearing that Claudia was married and had been for about a year now. However, when they all sat down in the drawing room and Claudia and Garrett had told their story, laughter had soon echoed through the room, here and there interspersed by a wistful smile or a tearful eye. In the end, all had been overjoyed to hear that Claudia had finally found a man who had conquered heart.

Claudia could not remember ever having been hugged quite this much. It seemed every time she turned around, a member of her family stood there, drawing her into their arms. Her mother and Evelyn were beside themselves with joy, and for the first time, Claudia could meet her sister-in-law's gaze without flinching. "You'll be a wonderful mother," she told her after one of those seemingly endless hugs, "and I can't wait to see my brother become a father."

Evelyn chuckled as she rocked little Aiden in her arms. "Oh, he'll do fine. He'll find his own way of showing his love."

"I know." Gazing across the room, Claudia met her brother's eye.

"I think he wants to talk to you," Evelyn whispered, her blue gaze shifting to her husband. "He missed you terribly and barely slept a wink the whole time you were gone. He would have followed you farther than the *Prancing Pony*, had he known where you'd gone."

Claudia sighed, a small smile on her face. "I'm surprised he didn't hire any Bow Street runners."

"Oh, he did," Evelyn chuckled, tickling Aiden under the chin. "But it would seem you hid your tracks well."

After hugging her sister-in-law for the thousandth time, Claudia made her way across the room to where Richard stood by the fireplace. "I heard you missed me," she addressed him without preamble, seeing the touch of embarrassment that came to his face at having his feelings revealed so openly.

Clearing his throat, her brother met her gaze, a hint of humour in his own. "The house was awfully quiet. Unusually so."

A little taken aback, Claudia smiled at him. "Are you trying to make a joke, dear brother?"

Shrugging, he grinned at her. "Perhaps. Perhaps not."

"Evelyn is wonderful," Claudia whispered, knowing that the changes in her brother were all her sister-in-law's doing. Her kind and loving touch had managed to bridge the gap between Richard and his family, reuniting them all in a way Claudia would have never believed possible.

Her brother nodded, his silver-grey eyes travelling across the room to his wife. "That she is," he whispered, a loving smile on his face.

"It is wonderful to see you so happy," Claudia told him, wondering about the man she had known all her life but never quite understood.

His grey eyes shifted back to her. "And are you happy?"

The smile that came to her face was so instantaneous that Claudia did not even have a moment to think about her answer. Not that she needed to. "Very happy," she replied, feeling her own gaze travel to the man across the room who was the source of that happiness.

As though he could feel her gaze on him, Garrett looked up in that moment and their eyes met. It was as though a spark ignited, and Claudia felt it all the way to her toes. A delicious shiver ran down her back, and for a moment, she wished they were the only two people in the room.

Garrett seemed to be thinking the same thing.

"You do smile a lot," her brother cut into her thoughts.

Clearing her throat, Claudia refocused her attention, doing her best to ignore her husband's lingering gaze. "I smile a lot?"

Richard nodded. "I know I'm not the most reliable source when it comes to interpreting another's facial expressions, but..." He shrugged. "I think you smile because you're happy."

Touched by his open words, Claudia nodded. "I do," she whispered. "I've never felt this way. Now, I finally know what you feel when you look at Evelyn."

Richard nodded, and Claudia could see that only sheer willpower kept his gaze from seeking out his wife once more. "And you are certain that accompanying your husband to Scotland is what you want?"

Claudia sighed, delighted to see her brother's concern for her. Not merely for her safety or her reputation. But for her happiness. "I am," she said, beaming at him. "As you well know I've never been able to deny myself a grand adventure."

Richard chuckled, "How could I forget?"

"Well, you won't have any chance of forgetting *me*," Claudia told him, trying her best to ignore the soft tears that stung the back of her eyes, "for I will visit you and Mother and Evelyn as often as I possibly can. We may live apart, but we'll always be a family."

Holding her gaze, Richard nodded. Then he did something he had never done before. He reached out and pulled her into his arms. "Always," he whispered into her ear, and Claudia could hear the deep emotions that clung to this one word.

The last stretch of their journey to *Seann Dachaigh Tower*, Garrett rode beside the carriage that carried his wife and son. He could feel his heart settle into a different rhythm now that he was back home in the Highlands. His lungs filled with fresh air, scented with pine, hazel and the distant aroma of the sea. The strong breeze tore at his hair, and his eyes filled with the vastness of Scotland's rolling hills.

Glancing over his shoulder, he saw Claudia peer out the window, her blue eyes wide as she gazed at the ancient fortress at the end of their path. It stood tall against a deep blue sky, its dark grey stones strong and unyielding. Situated on a small rise, *Seann Dachaigh Tower*-the old home-had seen the tides of time, its walls unbreached, protecting those inside. A thick wall ran around the inner fortress with only a large front gate to allow entrance. The main building stretched wide on two sides, more than one tower reaching higher into the sky, its windows like beacons in the dark.

More than once, Garrett had returned home after dusk, his steps guided by the glowing lights of those within beckoning him onward.

Beckoning him home.

"It's magnificent," Garrett heard his wife exclaim as she turned to Finn riding on her side of the carriage. Questions flew from her lips, and Finn did his best to answer them while Ian skulked in the saddle as he brought up the rear of their little group.

As they approached the gate, Garrett lifted his head, inhaling a deep breath. "Home," he whispered as a welcoming warmth washed over him.

Then he blinked.

Up on the wall-walk behind the parapet stood a tall figure in a billowing lavender gown, a dark cloak covering her shoulders but leaving free her wild golden hair. The wind tore at its strands, tossing them around her face, as though it wished to carry her off. Her blue eyes shone in such a pale light that they seemed otherworldly as though they truly could see things that were hidden from others. She seemed like a siren, a selkie, a spirit, and yet, the look in her eyes spoke of a very human heart.

Full of loss and longing.

Moira.

Their eyes met, and for a short moment, Garrett held his breath, his skin prickling with the knowledge of how this woman had guided him down his path and led him to his wife. If she had not insisted Cormag send him to Gretna Green, Garrett would never have met Claudia and Aiden would never have been born. And then she had interfered on his behalf yet again when it seemed that his family was all but lost to him, sending aid in the form of Duncan MacKinnear and his ship.

How had she known? Garrett could not help but wonder. *Had she truly seen what would happen? Had her dreams told her of the future?*

No matter where he had gone on his travels, Garrett had always heard whispers echo through the Highlands of people who knew more than they ought to. Whispers of those who spoke with a wisdom beyond their years. Whispers of those who could see into another's heart and read it like a book.

Still, these were only whispers full of awe, but also of distrust for people tended to fear what they could not understand. In the end, Garrett believed that it was these whispers that kept people like Moira from stepping forward and revealing their abilities to those around them...for they would undoubtedly be met with wariness and suspicion.

Garrett knew that every time Moira had interfered, she had put herself at risk, especially as an outsider. A woman banished from her own clan and forced to live among strangers.

Here, she was alone.

Unprotected without a family to stand with her, to shield her, to brave the storm with her.

Holding her gaze, Garrett inclined his head to Moira, gratitude warming his heart, and he vowed that if she ever needed him, he would stand with her and brave the storm. It was the least he could do for what she had done for him.

A small smile appeared on her lips, and for a moment, Garrett wondered if she had somehow heard his thoughts, if she had felt his vow and now knew him to be an ally. Sighing, he realised he would never know.

As he rode through the gate, Garrett wondered about what the future had in store for Moira and if she already knew. He wondered why Cormag had agreed for her to stay despite his clan's objections. And he wondered if Cormag had a more personal interest in the woman with the pale blue eyes than he was willing to admit.

Perhaps time would tell.

Epilogue

Later that day

Bundled up, Aiden rested in the crook of his father's arm as Garrett walked across the courtyard toward the outer gate. "'Tis breath-taking," he whispered to his son, a fresh summer's breeze whirling around his words. "Ye'll see."

Long ago, when Garrett had been only a boy and felt the need to be on his own, away from the crowded companionship of *Seann Dachaigh Tower*, he had found his way out of the castle walls and simply kept on walking. Eventually, he had come upon a small hill, which had all but seemed to be the centre of the world to little Garrett. Although the small rise was indeed far from majestic, rising nowhere near high enough to be called anything but a mere hill, it was uniquely situated, granting Garrett a view of the land around him.

His eyes had swept over *Seann Dachaigh Tower* a short distance away and over a large loch not far from where he stood, rolling hills and dense woods filling out the picture of peaceful tranquillity. Garrett had loved that spot from the very moment he had discovered it, and over the years, his feet had brought him back time and time again.

It was a place to be alone with his thoughts.

263

A place he wanted to share with his son.

Smiling, Garrett looked down at his little boy, picturing him running across the meadows and through the woods as he himself had as a lad. Garrett remembered his own childhood with a happy heart, and he could only hope that Aiden would feel at home here.

Straightening, Garrett glanced over his shoulder, up at the window where he knew his wife was rearranging his chamber-their chamber! With a smile on her face, she had shooed him out the door, insisting that he would only be in the way and then set to work unpacking her trunks. Garrett chuckled, wondering what he would return to.

In that moment, Claudia's face appeared at the window as though she had sensed his thoughts had strayed to her. A smile lit up her eyes, and she waved to him before disappearing from his view.

Sighing, Garrett set his feet toward the gate when he heard a familiar voice call his name. Surprised, he turned toward it and found Cormag MacDrummond, Laird of Clan MacDrummond and one of his oldest friends, striding toward him.

Dressed in plain, dark colours, Cormag stood taller than most men, his shoulders broad and his body honed by hours of training. Since their youth, Garrett and Cormag had crossed swords with each other as Cormag's late father had insisted that it sharpened the mind and humbled the heart.

Still, despite his build, Cormag often seemed to blend into the background, unnoticed by others, but watchful. His dark grey eyes missed very little, and Garrett often wondered what he was thinking as his face rarely revealed anything. As much as Cormag observed others, little did he share of himself. He spoke few words, but when he did, they were worth listening to.

Garrett wondered why his friend would seek him out.

"Welcome back," Cormag said, his voice even, and yet, it always had that authoritative tone in it that ensured his orders were obeyed without question.

Garrett nodded. "Thank ye." He sighed, glancing at his surroundings. "'Tis good to be home."

Coming to stand before him, Cormag shifted his dark eyes to

Aiden, his face immobile. "Ye have a son," he said then, and his gaze rose to meet Garrett's.

"Aye," was all Garrett said as he wondered how his friend felt about this sudden change in their circumstances. Since they had been young, they had walked side by side, but now their lives were leading them down different paths. Did Cormag long for a family of his own?

If he did so, the expression on his face did not betray any such thoughts. "Congratulations," he said, his voice as unrevealing as before. Then he shifted from one foot onto the other. "I'd expected ye to come and see me after you'd returned."

Some might have heard a hint of reproach in that statement. However, Garrett knew Cormag better than most and took note of the subtle signs of confusion that came to his friend's face. It seemed he had been truly surprised by Garrett's absence, and all he wanted was to understand.

"I meant to," Garrett explained, rocking Aiden slightly in his arms when he started to squirm. "But when I approached yer door, I heard voices." He paused, his gaze on Cormag. "I did not wish to intrude, so I decided to take my son for a walk first."

Cormag nodded in acknowledgement, his face almost completely still. And yet, Garrett noted the gentle tension that had come to his friend's posture.

After all, the one Garrett had heard Cormag speaking to had been Moira.

"Would ye mind if I accompanied ye?"

Surprised, Garrett agreed, wondering what Cormag had to say, considering that his friend generally had very little to say.

Together, they walked out the front gate in silence, the soft crunch under their boots, the only sound mixing with the gentle howling of the breeze and the bird calls nearby. The path led them away from the old tower, and before long, they found themselves on Garrett's small hill.

None of them had spoken, and yet, it was a comfortable silence that lingered in the air. The kind of silence that only existed between people who did not need words in order to converse.

"I wanted to thank ye," Garrett said after a while, his gaze drifting down to Aiden, who had succumbed to sleep, the little corners of his mouth occasionally curling upward into a smile. "Without Clan MacKinnear, I wouldna have been able to retrieve my wife and son."

Cormag remained quiet, his gaze fixed on *Seann Dachaigh Tower*.

"Finn said 'twas Moira who insisted ye send for them," Garrett said, his gaze now on his friend, curious to see how he would react at the mention of her name.

Cormag's gaze dropped to the ground before he turned to look at Garrett. "Her reasoning was sound," was all he said.

Garrett chuckled, "Ian disagreed."

"Ian always disagrees," Cormag replied before his gaze returned to the old tower.

Garrett thought to detect a hint of anger or perhaps displeasure in Cormag's tone but he could not be certain. Still, the way he inhaled a deep breath as though it was a strenuous activity made Garrett think that Ian had done more than simply disagree. In all likelihood, Ian had argued quite vehemently against Moira's interference, stating that she had no business meddling in clan affairs, that her knowledge of the future was nothing but lies.

And still, Cormag had heeded her advice and gone against Ian's counsel. Why?

"I keep thinking," Garrett said, directing his gaze back to their home, "that if I had gone to Gretna Green a day early or a day late, I would never even have met Claudia." Sighing, he shook his head, feeling his son's soft weight in his arms. "The thought sends a chill down my spine."

Cormag drew in another slow breath, his spine straightening a fraction more.

"She almost slipped through my fingers," Garrett continued, "and I would never even have known what I would have lost. Sometimes there is only a small window of opportunity, and sometimes the one person who completes us has been right there by our side for a long time. Still, no opportunity lasts forever. Eventually, it is lost."

Once more, silence fell over them as they stood side by side, their eyes directed at the old fortress. Garrett thought of his wife as she settled into her new home and wondered if Cormag's thoughts had strayed to Moira.

After a while, his friend took a step back and turned to look at him. "I have business to attend to," was all Cormag said before he took his leave and walked away.

Smiling at her husband down in the courtyard, Claudia then turned away from the window, knowing that she would never get settled in if she remained standing by the window like a love-struck girl. Still, the moment she flung open the second trunk, a knock sounded on the door, halting her progress once more.

Surprised, Claudia wondered if Garrett had already returned. However, then she reminded herself that he would not knock on his own door.

Striding forward, she reached for the handle and opened the door, curious to see who would call on her.

Out in the hall stood a young woman with auburn curls framing a smiling face. "G'day to ye," she said. "Ye're Garrett's new wife, are ye not? From England?"

Delighted with the young woman's forward manner, Claudia nodded. "Yes, I am. Would you like to come in?"

A large smile drew up the woman's lips, and she flitted across the threshold like a fairy, her movements fluid and her steps barely touching the ground. "Oh, I'm so happy ye're here. I came the moment I heard ye'd arrived." Her smile froze. "I hope I'm not interrupting ye." She glanced around and seeing Claudia had not yet unpacked trunk clasped a hand over her mouth. "Oh, I'm so sorry. I shouldna have come. I-"

"No, it's all right," Claudia interrupted, feeling an instant connection to the young woman. "Please stay. It's wonderful to have a little company,...eh?"

"Maggie," the young woman beamed when Claudia hesitated. "I'm Margaret MacDrummond, but everybody calls me Maggie. I grew up in England myself, and so, I thought I'd come here and welcome ye."

Claudia's eyes widened. "You grew up in England?" she asked, incredulity clear in her voice.

Maggie chuckled, "Aye, it doesna sound like it, does it? I came here when I came of age. My mother wanted me to marry into her old clan. Ye see, she was born a MacDrummond, but married an Englishman and left the Highlands with him." A deep sigh left Maggie's' lips, and her eyes took on a wistful look. "But her heart never quite felt at home in England."

Claudia smiled. "And neither did you?"

Maggie shrugged. "Not quite. I may have been born English, but I think of myself as Scottish now. Ye'll see. The Highlands will steal yer heart soon enough."

Laughing, Claudia gestured for Maggie to sit, "It's already been quite an adventure, exactly what I've been looking for."

Reaching for Claudia's hands, Maggie leaned toward her eagerly. "Ye must tell me everything. Is it true that Garrett saved ye from a French privateer?"

Claudia laughed, amazed with the speed of gossip in the Highlands. "I promise I will, but first tell me how you know my husband. You seem to know him well."

Maggie nodded. "Aye, I know him well. He and my husband are good friends."

"And who is your husband?" Claudia asked, momentarily thinking that Maggie with her smiles and exuberant nature would be a perfect match for Finn...before she remembered that his wife's name was Emma.

"My husband is Ian MacDrummond," Maggie said. "I believe ye've already met him."

Momentarily stunned, Claudia stared at Maggie, thinking that she had seldom seen two people more ill-fittingly matched. "Yes, I did meet him. He and Finn came to Glasgow to help Garrett."

Maggie sighed, "Oh, aye, Garrett was so miserable when he returned from Gretna Green last year. Ian was quite upset to see him thus. They tried to cheer him up, but nothing worked." Squeezing Claudia's hands, Maggie smiled at her. "I'm so glad he found ye. I only caught a glimpse of him when he rode in this morning, but he looked fairly taken with ye." A chuckle escaped Maggie's lips. "As ye do with him."

Claudia sighed, finding herself warming to the young woman with each moment that passed. "Yes, he's a wonderful man, and I'm so lucky to have found him...that he found me," she added with a chuckle.

"Will ye tell me about it?" Maggie asked with eager eyes.

"Of course," Claudia replied before she leaned closer conspiratorially, "if you tell me about a woman named Moira." During her journey north, Claudia had often asked questions about Moira, and yet, the answers had always fallen short of what she had hoped for. Moira was still an enigma...not only to her, but as it seemed to everyone else. Still, Claudia could not help but wish to know more about the woman who had sent Garrett to Gretna Green to find her.

Maggie's eyes widened, and an appreciative smile came to her lips. "Ye know to ask the right questions; I give ye that."

And thus, began a very informative afternoon as well as a friendship that would last a lifetime for as ill-fitted as Maggie was with her husband, she would prove to be the best friend Claudia had ever had.

THE END

Are you eager for more stories of Clan MacDrummond?

Dared & Kissed (book 2 of the Highland Tales) tells the story of Emma and Finn's love that grants you a glimpse into Garrett's time apart from Claudia in Scotland.

Read on for a sneak-peek!

Read a Sneak-Peek

Dared & Kissed
The Scotsman's Yuletide Bride
(#2 Highland Tales)

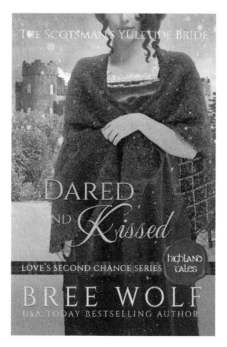

Prologue

Seann Dachaigh Tower, Scottish Highlands, December 1801

Seven Years Earlier

Drawing her cloak tighter around her to ward off the chill of the crisp winter morning, sixteen-year-old Emma Stewart of Clan MacDrummond stood on the edge of the clearing, half-hidden behind a large boulder, her deep brown eyes drawn to the young men as they crossed their swords in training.

Their faces shone rosy in the cool winter's air as they moved back and forth, the metal of their blades gleaming in the faint morning sun. Emma could feel the clash of their swords resonate in her bones as it echoed through the stillness of the small glen. A cold shiver ran down her spine, and she breathed a sigh of relief that war had come and gone long ago.

These were times of peace, and the young men of her clan were merely training to keep a sharp mind and humble heart as their laird demanded of them. He was a good and kind man and had seen their clan through many trials. Still, his health was failing, and soon his son, Cormag, would follow in his footsteps and become Laird.

Shifting her gaze to the tall dark-haired man, Emma marvelled at the stillness with which he moved. There was no exertion on his face, and here and there, it seemed as though his feet barely touched the ground. He was a strange man, the laird's son, taciturn and reticent in many ways, and yet, watchful and observant, his grey eyes sharp like those of a hawk.

Emma wondered what he saw when he looked at her, and another shiver went down her back. Quickly, she turned her gaze to the other young men, fair-haired Ian and dark-haired Garrett. However, it was the sight of Finnegan MacDrummond that made her heart leap into her throat.

At least six years her senior, Finn stood tall, his shoulders squared as he watched Ian's approach, his sparkling green eyes narrowed as he prepared for his opponent's attack. Their swords clashed, and Emma held her breath.

Laughter echoed to her ears as Finn drew back, running his hand through his dark auburn curls. "Ye fight like a wee bairn, Ian! Is this all ye've got?"

Determination and a good deal of humour rested on Ian's face as he charged toward his friend, their swords colliding once again, sending sparks flying through the soft fog still lingering this early in the morning.

Transfixed, Emma watched as the men continued their training, her eyes locked on the young man who had stolen her heart so long ago. She could not recall a time when the mere sight of him had not stolen her breath and addled her mind. He was sweet and kind, and his green eyes always sparkled with exuberance and a hint of mischief. He stood by his friends and always lent a helping hand to those who needed it. He loved this land, their home, fiercely, and yet, every now and then she could see a yearning for adventure in his eyes, to see the world and know more than the small circle of life into which he had been born.

Oh, Emma knew him well, and yet, they had never truly spoken to one another. Nothing beyond a few meaningless courtesies here and there. Emma wondered if he even knew her name.

A faint giggle drifted to her ears from the tree line in her back, jarring Emma back to the here and now. Glancing over her shoulder, she spotted Aileen and Sorcha standing half-hidden behind a large oak, their eyes glowing as they whispered to one another.

Sighing, Emma squared her shoulders, reminding herself why she was here, why she had risen so early and trudged through the woods, her hem now soaked with morning dew.

"Go," Aileen hissed from behind the tree, keeping her voice low, her eyes darting to the young men, a touch of apprehension in them as she feared that they might have taken notice.

The young men, however, were so engrossed in their training that not one of them looked up and spotted the girls standing not too far off, watching them with rapt attention.

Emma nodded, then turned back, her eyes once more drifting to Finn, her target. Instantly, her heart sped up, and panic flooded her being. Was she mad to have come here? To have agreed to their game?

Her fingers curled into her palms, and her muscles tensed as though urging her back. No, she would not turn and run. Lifting her head, Emma squared her shoulders. This was her chance-her only chance-and she would take it. After all, it was only a dare, and if Finn rejected her then at least she could laugh it off and pretend that none of it affected her in any way. All she had to do was keep a straight face and not let him see how much she cared for him.

Inhaling a deep breath, Emma stepped out from behind the boulder, momentarily grateful for the shrubbery that still hid her from their sight. Nevertheless, soon she would have to reveal herself and it was still a good distance from the edge of the clearing to where they stood with their swords crossed. Would they address her? Would they ask what she was doing here? If so, what would she say?

"Ye're a fool," Emma whispered to herself as she took another step forward. "They'll laugh at ye, and yer cheeks will turn bright red."

The moment Emma stepped around the last of the shrubbery, she froze as she found Cormag looking straight at her, his sharp, hawk-like eyes colliding with hers. The hint of a frown touched his brows, and she wondered how long he had known of her presence. Had he truly spotted her just now? Or had he somehow...known as he often seemed to know things he should not know?

"Go," Aileen hissed once more, and as though Emma's feet had a life of their own, they complied. Goose bumps rose on her arms and legs as Emma found herself walking into the clearing, her heart beating painfully in her chest as she fought down the panic that threatened to engulf her. What on earth was she doing?

The moment Cormag had stopped, turning his head to look at her, his friends had ceased their training as well. At first, confusion had come to their faces before they followed his line of sight.

Now, four sets of eyes were trained on her as Emma walked into the clearing, slowly closing the distance between them. She did her best to hold her chin high and maintain a friendly, but unaffected smile on her face. However, deep down, Emma had serious doubts that she appeared as anything else but the bundle of nerves she was. Perhaps she ought to turn and run after all!

As she drew closer, she could see their chests rising and falling with each laboured breath, the muscles in their sword arms quivering with the sudden rest. Her eyes drifted from one man to the next and then back as she willed herself not to stare at Finn lest he be able to read the intention on her face. If he did, would *he* turn and run?

Cormag's eyes narrowed in a rather unsettling way as he continued to watch her. Then he took a step back, a hint of surprise coming to his eyes as he turned to look at Finn.

Emma froze. Did *he* know?

"What are ye doing here, lass?" Garrett asked as he stepped toward her, a kind smile on his face. "Ye're not lost, are ye?"

Strangely enough, Emma managed a rather natural smile. "No, I'm not lost," she replied, a slight chuckle accompanying her words as though she truly did not have a care in the world. Surprised by this unexpected ability to mask her feelings, Emma decided to seize the moment.

Stepping around Garrett, she did her best to ignore Ian's inquisitive stare as well as Cormag's speculative gaze and kept her eyes on Finn. His green gaze narrowed slightly as he watched her approach. Still, he did not try to step away, did not address her, did not stop her in any way.

It was all the encouragement Emma needed.

Two more steps brought her to him, and she could feel the warmth that radiated off him against her skin. His green eyes held hers, and for the barest of moments, Emma thought to see something flare to life in them. Something she had never seen there before.

But Emma did not dare linger and contemplate what it was. No, she needed to move fast, or she would miss her chance.

Without a moment's hesitation, she reached up, pushing herself up onto her toes, and pulled him down into a kiss.

The moment Finn had glimpsed her standing across the clearing, his heart had slammed to a rather unexpected halt. Her mahogany curls had danced on the soft breeze, gently brushing against her rosy cheeks and giving her the appearance of a sprite risen from the earth. She stood tall and fierce, and yet, as she had approached, the dark brown of her eyes had spoken of a vulnerable heart.

Although her gaze had travelled from one of his friends to the next, somehow Finn had known that in that moment she had come for him. The moment their eyes had met, Finn had been unable to speak, to think, to do anything but stare at her.

He could not even recall her name-if indeed he had ever known it-and yet he was certain that he would never again forget who she was.

The closer she had stepped, the more his heart had felt as though it wished to jump from his chest.

And then her lips had found his.

Dimly, Finn found himself wondering if he had strayed into a dream as he felt the softness of her lips against his own and the tentative brush of her fingers against the back of his neck, uncertain and yet daring. Her body leaned into his, and for a long moment, nothing and no one else existed but them.

And then she was gone.

From one moment to the next, her touch vanished, and Finn's eyes flew open.

As her feet carried her away from him, a teasing grin rested on her face, and yet, her eyes held no humour, but something deep and vulnerable. However, before Finn could stop her, she spun on her heel and raced across the clearing.

Chuckles rose around him, and Finn blinked as Ian and Garrett approached, large grins on their faces as they looked back and forth between him and the receding figure racing toward the tree line. "I take it ye know her," Ian remarked with a teasing grin. "Ye could've introduced us. What's the lass' name?"

Inhaling a deep breath, Finn shook his head. "I dunno know."

Gawking at him, Ian laughed, "Ye dunno know? Are ye saying a lassie ye dunno even know walks up to ye and kisses ye square on the mouth? Does this happen to ye a lot?"

More laughter followed, and Finn cleared his throat, trying his best to sort through his thoughts. "No, it doesna happen a lot," he snapped, glaring at his friend. "I assure ye I'm as surprised as ye are."

"But ye like her, do ye not?" Garrett observed as he crossed his arms in front of him, a challenge lighting up his eyes. "I've never seen ye so lost for words."

Finn swallowed, shaking his head. "She's…she's something." A smile tugged on the corners of his mouth, and he chuckled. "I've seen her around, certainly, but I've never…"

"Noticed her," Cormag supplied in his usual way as though he knew precisely what the others were thinking.

Finn nodded. "Aye."

"But ye noticed her now, aye?" Ian teased some more. "I can see that she's made quite an impression. Why don't ye go after her?"

Finn's head snapped up, and for a moment, all he could do was stare at his friend.

Shaking his head, Ian laughed, then clasped a hand on Finn's shoulder. "Go and ask her name before she kisses another."

With a bit of a shove in the right direction, Finn turned toward the tree line where she had disappeared. At first his steps were measured, but before long, large strides carried him onward. His heart once more began to dance the way it had when he had felt her lips upon his own, and he wondered how he could have failed to notice her before.

Certainly, she was young, having only recently grown into a woman, but those eyes...dark and deep like a loch full of hidden treasures, and yet, warm and delicate as though a wrong word could break her heart.

Striding past the large boulder on the edge of the glen, Finn scanned the tree line, his eyes narrowing as he tried to spot any sign of her. He glimpsed her footprints in the lush, frost-covered grass a moment before soft voices drifted to his ears.

Inhaling a deep breath as his heart once again leapt into his throat, Finn stepped forward, finding his way through the dense forest, his ears guiding him, picking out more than one voice. Silently, he slipped closer until he spotted a fair-haired head bobbing up from behind a thorny thicket growing around a group of conifers.

The young woman laughed, "I thought I would faint when I saw ye kiss him," she gasped, a hand pressed to her chest. "Was it wonderful?"

Finn frowned as he edged forward, his eyes at last falling on the dark-eyed enigma who had stolen his breath. She stood with two other, equally young women-both of whom looked familiar, but whose names Finn could not recall, either. Her face looked tense as she glanced over her shoulder toward the glen. "Let us return to the tower," she whispered, a hint of apprehension in her voice as she tried to pull the fair-haired girl onward. "I'm...chilled."

"Come now, tell us of yer conquest," the other dark-haired girl urged, an eager smile on her face. "After all, ye won the dare and proved us wrong. I never would've thought that ye'd have the courage to walk up to Finnegan MacDrummond and steal a kiss."

Finn's stomach clenched as the girl's words sank in. A dare? She had kissed him because of a dare? Nothing more?

"Tell us, did it feel wonderful?" the fair-haired girl pressed, a sigh escaping her lips. "I think I would've gone weak in the knees if it had been me."

Turning her head away, Finn's brown-eyed enigma brushed a curl behind her ear. "'Twas a kiss," she all but bit out, and the harshness cut right through Finn's tentative hopes. "Nothing more, nothing less. I won. That's all that matters." Rubbing her hands together, she beckoned the other two girls onward. "Now, let's go or I swear my toes shall freeze off."

Long after they had gone, Finn still stood leaning against the conifer at his back, his eyes closed as he replayed their words in his head. It had been nothing but a dare, and he had been a fool to think more of it. To think that there had been something between them, a silent bond that had brought them to this place the way his father had often spoken of the day he had first laid eyes on Finn's mother.

As a child, Finn had often listened to his father tell this story, his words ringing with promise that one day Finn would find the same, a woman who was his other half, a woman he would recognise instantly, who would steal his breath and claim his heart.

And for a short moment, Finn had thought to have found her...and it had stunned him into speechlessness.

If only he had known from the beginning that their encounter had meant nothing to her. Nothing more but a claimed prize. A victory. A dare won.

Cursing under his breath, Finn spun on his heel and before he knew it his fists collided with the trunk of the conifer. Pain shot up his arm and into his shoulder, and blood welled up from the scrapes on his knuckles where the hard bark had cut through his skin.

Still, the pain in his heart far exceeded any physical discomfort he felt. How dare she kiss him? Before today, he had been happily oblivious to her. He had barely even noticed her. He had been content and at peace.

And now?

Now, he was achingly aware of her. He could still feel her soft touch as though she was right in front of him, and whenever he closed his eyes, he found her dark-brown ones looking into his. What had she done to him?

Would he ever be free of her? Or would he be doomed to carry her with him for the rest of his life?

Anger filled his heart, and Finn knew that he was no longer the same man he had been upon waking that morning.

Everything had changed.
He had changed.
And there was no going back.
How dare she?

Series Overview

LOVE'S SECOND CHANCE SERIES: TALES OF LORDS & LADIES

LOVE'S SECOND CHANCE SERIES: TALES OF DAMSELS & KNIGHTS

SERIES OVERVIEW

LOVE'S SECOND CHANCE SERIES: HIGHLAND TALES

FORBIDDEN LOVE NOVELLA SERIES

HAPPY EVER REGENCY SERIES

For more information visit www.breewolf.com

About Bree

USA Today bestselling and award-winning author, Bree Wolf has always been a language enthusiast (though not a grammarian!) and is rarely found without a book in her hand or her fingers glued to a keyboard. Trying to find her way, she has taught English as a second language, traveled abroad and worked at a translation agency as well as a law firm in Ireland. She also spent loooong years obtaining a BA in English and Education and an MA in Specialized Translation while wishing she could simply be a writer. Although there is nothing simple about being a writer, her dreams have finally come true.

"A big thanks to my fairy godmother!"

Currently, Bree has found her new home in the historical romance genre, writing Regency novels and novellas. Enjoying the mix of fact and fiction, she occasionally feels like a puppet master (or mistress? Although that sounds weird!), forcing her characters into ever-new situations that will put their strength, their beliefs, their love to the test, hoping that in the end they will triumph and get the happily-ever-after we are all looking for.

If you're an avid reader, sign up for Bree's newsletter on www. breewolf.com as she has the tendency to simply give books away. Find out about freebies, giveaways as well as occasional advance reader copies and read before the book is even on the shelves!

Connect with Bree and stay up-to-date on new releases: